MAMA SEES STARS

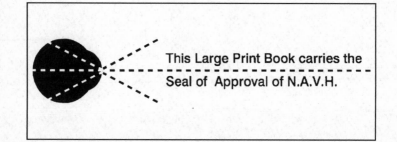

This Large Print Book carries the
Seal of Approval of N.A.V.H.

A MACE BAUER MYSTERY

MAMA SEES STARS

DEBORAH SHARP

THORNDIKE PRESS
A part of Gale, Cengage Learning

GALE
CENGAGE Learning

Detroit • New York • San Francisco • New Haven, Conn • Waterville, Maine • London

GALE
CENGAGE Learning

LIBRARY OF CONGRESS CATALOGING-IN-PUBLICATION DATA

Sharp, Deborah, 1954–
  Mama sees stars : a Mace Bauer mystery / by Deborah Sharp.
    p. cm. — (Thorndike Press large print mystery)
  ISBN-13: 978-1-4104-4292-5 (hardcover)
  ISBN-10: 1-4104-4292-6 (hardcover)
  1. Bauer, Mace (Fictitious character)—Fiction. 2. Mothers and daughters—Fiction. 3. Motion picture locations—Fiction. 4. Motion picture producers and directors—Crimes against—Fiction. 5. Florida—Fiction. 6. Large type books. I. Title.
PS3619.H35645M37 2011b
813'.6—dc23   2011032408

Published in 2011 by arrangement with Midnight Ink, an imprint of Llewellyn Publication, Woodbury, MN 55125-2989 USA.

Printed in the United States of America
1 2 3 4 5 6 7 15 14 13 12 11

To my mother-in-law,
Jeanné Sanders, who not only
embraces my books, but also
gave me a wonderful gift —
a kind and caring man
whose mama raised him right.

ACKNOWLEDGMENTS

At a signing once, a reader surprised me with a blunt question: "Why do you acknowledge all those people in your book? You're the one who wrote it." Aside from the fact my mama taught me to always say thank you, it's wrong to think an author does it all alone.

As always, I had help. The title, *Mama Sees Stars,* came from my brilliant cousin-in-law, Mark Prator. My friend and former newspaper editor, Karen Feldman McCracken, improved the manuscript, as she's done in the past. My fabulous agent, Whitney Lee, also gave it a polish, along with everything else she does. I'm grateful to all of them.

Even before I wrote the book, several people assisted in researching the movie setting. Director Brian Carroll, shooting a small independent movie in Stuart, Florida, invited me to watch. Ashlee Webster clued me in on jargon and who does what. Bet she becomes more than an intern someday! I owe a special debt to movie-set Teamster Red Bedell for behind-the-scenes schooling about large-scale Hollywood productions. As a member of Local 769 in Miami, he's worked most of the big location shoots in Florida. Jeff Rollason also helped me. Any errors, or exaggerations about murderous movie folk, are mine, not theirs. Kim Loggins invited me to the Bergeron Rodeo Grounds for a closeup with cattle.

I'm grateful to Terri Bischoff and the talented staff at Midnight Ink. Lisa Novak designs great covers; Connie Hill's editing skills save me; and Courtney Colton spreads the word about my books.

Okeechobee, Florida, the real-life prototype for fictional Himmarshee, is always in my heart. So is the world's greatest husband, Kerry Sanders, and the world's greatest mama, Marion Sharp. Both are sources of unfailing love and inspiration.

Finally, I'm indebted to those I named, to anyone I missed, and especially to YOU, for reading this book.

ONE

I waited out of camera range, holding the bridle on a saddled horse. Movie lights flooded the scene with brightness. The set was pin-drop quiet.

"Action!"

I let go of the bridle, slapped the horse on the rump, and stood back so the camera operator could capture the animal racing past. Just as the riderless horse entered a clearing, gathering speed to a gallop, a voice rang out into the silence.

"My stars and garters! Somebody's let a horse get loose. Don't just stand there, Mace! Come help me catch him."

An orange blur dashed into the animal's path, waving arms and yelling.

"Cut!" The assistant director put his fingers to his temples and massaged. I could tell him it's not so easy to rub away this kind of headache.

A short bald man in a bright red shirt

9

kicked over a chair on the sidelines. "Security!" The word exploded from his mouth. "Would somebody grab that stupid hillbilly?"

A muscled guy in a baseball cap started toward The Hillbilly, a.k.a. my mama. Cringing, I stepped forward. "She's with me."

The short man came closer and leveled a glare. "And who the hell are *you?*"

"Mace Bauer." I offered my hand. He looked at it like it was bathed, palm to pinky, in manure. "I'm the animal wrangler."

"And I am not impressed." His leathery face scrunched like he smelled a load of hogs.

As I slipped my unshaken hand into the pocket of my jeans, Mama marched to my side. She smoothed her orange-sherbet pantsuit, fluffed her platinum hair, and straightened to her full four foot, eleven inches. The jerk in the red shirt may have had her by a few inches, but she had the Mama Glare, and it was set at stun.

"Well, who the blue blazes are *you?* All we know is you're a rude little man who has no idea how to talk to a lady. By the way, Florida's as flat as a frying pan, so I can't be a hillbilly, can I?"

Whispers and a few snickers traveled around the set. His beady eyes met her glare. "I'm the boss here. The top dog. Let me put it in terms you'll understand. If this movie set was a barbecue joint, I'd own the building. I'd own the chairs and tables. I'd even own the pigs. And I'd get to say who gets to sit down for dinner, and who doesn't."

Mama, brows knit, glanced at me. "Is he saying I can't come to his rib joint?"

I shrugged.

"Well, I wouldn't want to go there anyway," she said. "I can tell you it'll never be as popular as the Pork Pit, which has been in Himmarshee forever. Not only do they have ribs to die for, they make the best peach cobbler, too. Besides, the folks at the Pork Pit know how to treat their customers. You certainly have a lot to learn about how to treat people . . ."

As Mama went on, I tried to imagine I was somewhere else. The assistant director massaged his head so hard, I thought he'd rub the hair right off his temples. Meanwhile, the old guy's face was getting purple. Jabbing his cigar, he looked mad enough to pick Mama up and toss her off the set himself.

Just then, a woman stepped up to him

with a cell phone in one hand and a sandwich in the other. She whispered in his ear. He handed her his cigar, took the cell phone, and jammed half the sandwich in his mouth. Then he began shouting into the cell.

"What kind of idiot do you think I am? I'll have your ass in the courtroom faster than you can say breach of contract . . ."

He stomped away, Mama's transgression seemingly forgotten. As he left, little missiles of what looked like roast beef launched from his mouth. I pitied the person on the other end of the call. Even though the woman was almost a head taller than him, she had to run to keep up.

The assistant director scolded Mama through tightly pursed lips: "You ruined the shot. This is your first — and last — warning."

"It's her first time on a movie," I apologized, as he stalked back to the director's tent.

Next to us, the behemoth in the ball cap still loomed. "Don't worry," I told him. "I'll make sure she understands the concept of Quiet on the Set."

The three of us watched the departing loudmouth in red. "Who is he, anyway?" I asked the security man.

"You mean besides being a First Class Asshole?"

"Language, son," Mama said, but she was smiling.

"Norman Sydney. He's the movie's executive producer, but he thinks he's God."

"How was I supposed to know you let the horse go on purpose?"

"We're shooting a movie here, Mama. The scene is supposed to look like something bad happened to one of the kids in the family. The horse is spooked, so it races off alone."

Mama's bottom lip was set in a pout. The horse, in contrast, plodded along with no whining at the end of a lead rope. He seemed happy to be heading back to the movie's corral.

The Hollywood folks were in Himmarshee doing a film about the early days of cattle-ranching in Florida. It was supposed to be based on Patrick Smith's classic book, *A Land Remembered*. But I'd peeked at a script, and cows were about the only thing it had in common with the book. Supposedly, the new working title was *Fierce Fury Past*. Hired to handle the horses, I was using up vacation time from my real job at a nature park. It was a good chance to make some extra cash. Since the film was the most exciting thing going on in our little slice of middle Florida, Mama nagged me until I got her on the set, too.

After her embarrassing interruption, we'd done five or six more takes of the galloping horse. Bored, she'd wandered off to find somewhere she wouldn't get yelled at for talking.

Now, we'd met up again, and were about to have lunch. But first I had to return the horse. Still smarting over the producer's dressing down, Mama was uncharacteristically quiet.

Saddle leather creaked as we walked through a pasture. The horse's hooves thudded on a sandy path cut through a blanket of Bahia grass. A mockingbird sang from an oak branch.

Curiosity finally triumphed over Mama's bad mood: "Have you seen any of the Hollywood stars yet? I've got my autograph book all ready. Is that Greg Tilton as good-looking in person as on the screen?"

"It's just my first day. I'm sure I will see some stars, unless one of my family members manages to get me fired from the movie."

She narrowed her eyes. "Why would any of us want to do that?"

"Just don't bug anybody. And try to stay out of trouble, would you, Mama?"

"Me? I thought *you* were in trouble. I thought you needed my help with that horse. What kind of mother would I be if I saw you in a jam and didn't step in? Besides, it was that awful man's fault for jumping all over me. He's wound up tighter than granny's girdle."

A loud whinny sounded from the horse corral. A whicker came from behind us in return.

"Rebel, what's wrong?" I made a half-turn to run a reassuring hand below his mane.

Turning back, I plowed smack into Mama, who'd stopped in her tracks. Rebel's big head hit me between my shoulders. Mama gave a sharp gasp.

"Oh, my! It's that horrible producer, Mace. I can see his bright red shirt. Your eyes are younger than mine. Isn't that him, leaning against the corral gate?"

I stepped around her to get a better view.

"I hope he hasn't come to fire you," she said.

"It's him, Mama. But he's not leaning against the corral."

I took my cell phone from my pocket and hit speed dial for Carlos Martinez, a detective with the Himmarshee police department, and my boyfriend.

Somebody had tossed Norman Sydney over the fence like drying laundry. The white, sandy ground beneath his body was stained, as red as his tomato-colored shirt.

TWO

Mama clutched at my arm. "Great Uncle Elmer's Ghost, Mace! You will not believe who is swaggering our way."

I turned. Greg Tilton strutted toward us, a bit shorter-seeming in person than on screen, but with those same broad shoulders and that devilish grin that had caused a million women to swoon.

Mama and I hurriedly shifted our positions in front of Norman's body. We stood shoulder to shoulder, staring at Tilton. He raised a hand in greeting, every bit the red-carpet Hollywood star acknowledging his fans.

As he came closer, Mama elbowed me to speak. "I'm afraid Norman Sydney's had some kind of accident, Mr. Tilton." I pointed at the body hanging over the fence about twenty-five feet behind us.

Tilton's eyes widened. Confusion and realization held a race across his features.

Then, he jumped into action. Before I could stop him, he rushed to the fence and hefted the body onto his shoulders. We ran right behind him.

"What happened?" he asked, not even out of breath.

"We were returning the horse to the corral, and saw the body as soon as we got close. I don't think you should move him, though. I already checked him over, and the cops will want to see where he was left."

He ignored me, going down to one knee and lowering the body gently to the ground. He knelt with his ear close to Norman's mouth in the classic CPR pose: looking, listening, and waiting to feel on his own cheek any evidence of breath. Within seconds, Tilton moved on to chest compressions.

"I'm experienced in medical emergencies from my job at the county nature park," I said. "I already examined him. He has no pulse. He's dead."

He kept counting, one hundred presses in a minute.

"Plus, that's a lot of blood on the ground. And, he has what looks like a gunshot wound to the back of his head."

His counting tapered off. Gingerly, he turned Norman's head to one side. His hand came away coated in gore. Finally, he seemed to absorb the fact the man was beyond his help. This wasn't a movie. Tilton wiped his hands on his jeans and got up from his knees, looking shaken.

"I'm sorry." Mama's voice was soft. "Was he a good friend of yours?"

Tilton tore his gaze away from the body. Sincerity and sadness beamed at us from those famous blue eyes. "Honestly? No," he said. "We weren't friends at all. But I respected him. With all his faults, he was a good businessman and a great producer."

All three of us regarded the mortal remains of Norman Sydney, stretched out on the ground.

"We should probably go wait for the authorities where they'll see us, on the other side of the corral. I wish you'd listened to me about moving him." I began herding them away from the body. "The cops are going to be madder than wasps with a sprayed nest."

I was thinking of one cop in particular.

"You're right. I shouldn't have touched him. It was instinct, but it was stupid."

Mama tilted her head at him. I was surprised, too. I didn't expect such a macho movie star to admit fault so easily.

As we walked away, he rubbed a hand

across his square jaw. His eyes got a far-away look. "One of my many foster fathers had a heart attack. They'd just taught us CPR in junior high, and I actually managed to save the guy. Guess I thought I could perform a miracle again."

I thought of my own father's fatal heart attack. "That must have felt good, to be able to save a man's life."

He shrugged, leaned against the fence on the opposite side of the corral from where the body had been. "It didn't win me any points, with that dad or any of the others."

I got a glimpse of the sad boy he must have been, before the movie career, before superstardom, before he was Greg Tilton, Action Hero. It almost made me forgive him for acting so rashly.

Almost.

"How come you happened to be all the way over here by the corral?" I asked.

My voice must have carried a suspicious tone, because he stopped walking and narrowed his eyes at me.

Mama piped up, "Mace is not normally rude . . . well, at least not that rude. She's just gotten awful curious about what appear to be coincidences whenever we find a body."

His eyes took in Mama — perfectly coiffed

20

hair, lips gleaming with Apricot Ice, hues of orange sherbet from the polish on her sandaled toes to the clip-on baubles on her ears.

"Find a lot of bodies, do you?" He gave us the Tilton smirk.

"It's been a bad couple of years in Himmarshee," I said.

"Well, I came out here to find the corral because I love horses. Ever since I played . . .'

". . . the young gunslinger with a good heart in that Clint Eastwood Western," Mama interrupted excitedly. "It was your breakout role."

I looked at her like she'd been replaced by an alien.

"What?" she asked. "You're not the only one who can find out things on the Wide World of the Web. Your little sister Marty helped me research the cast. *BTW,* she's a lot more patient on the computer than you are, Mace."

BTW? "Who are you?"

Tilton held up his hands. "What I was going to say, if you'd give me the chance, is that whenever I'm doing a movie that involves riding, I like to get a look at the horses as early as I can."

I might have followed that up with another

question, but Mama suddenly clutched at her chest and pointed behind me. Only a rare sight would leave her speechless. I turned to see what it was.

"I knew I'd find you out here making friends with the horses, Greg."

Even if I wasn't staring into her famous face, I'd have known that laugh anywhere. It contained the promise of fun, sex, and mystery, all rolled into one musical sound. Kelly Conover.

Tilton grabbed her by the shoulders, trying to shield her from the body. "Don't look over there, Kelly."

She frowned, deepening some tiny lines that Botox must have missed. She was still a stunning woman. But everybody knows the camera is cruel to aging actresses.

"What's wrong?" She shook off his hands and pushed past him, showing a surprising strength in her well-toned arms.

"It's our producer." Tilton followed her, and we followed him. "Looks like he was shot."

When she reached the body, Kelly stood and stared for a long moment. She didn't look shocked, or scared. In fact, her expression hardly changed at all. When she spoke, her voice was cold. The warm laugh was gone. "Now he's where he belongs, burning in the fires of hell."

Then she spit twice on the ground, once on each side of the corpse of Norman Sydney.

THREE

"Where do you suppose the police are, Mace?" Shading her eyes from the sun, Mama squinted across the pasture and into the distance.

"They're on their way. We're out in the boonies, remember? I wish they'd get here, though. I'm ready to walk away and leave this whole mess in the movie people's lap. Before this morning, we didn't know Norman Sydney from Adam's house cat."

"And what we did know of him, we didn't like." She glanced guiltily toward the body. "Not that it's my practice to speak ill of the dead."

"It's really none of my business, Mama. None of yours, either."

"Don't you worry, honey. I have no plans to get in the middle of this."

Of course, I'd heard those words before. Even so, my mama had somehow managed over the last couple of years to find herself

24

in the middle of a few spots of trouble. At the Dairy Queen, she discovered a body stuffed into the trunk of her turquoise convertible. On a trail ride across Florida's cattle country, she saw an old beau fall prey to foul play. And during her recent wedding to Husband No. 5 at the VFW hall in Himmarshee, she narrowly escaped becoming the newly dead instead of the blissfully wed.

Suffice it to say I doubted she'd stay out of this. And I suspected that once again she'd drag me in with her.

Mama took out her compact and lipstick. Making an O of her mouth, she swiped on a fresh coat of Apricot Ice. "I guess this isn't really the time to collect some of the stars' autographs." She looked at me hopefully.

"Absolutely not!" I said.

She snapped the compact shut. "That Greg Tilton is a fine-looking man though, isn't he?"

"I'm involved, Mama."

"Oh, is this Tuesday?" She widened her blue eyes at me, all innocence. "Well, you never know with you and Carlos, honey. On-again, off-again."

I'd be insulted, but she had a point. My path to love hadn't been smooth. Still, we'd managed to pave over some of the roughest patches. At least these days I could say I was dating a cop, instead of someone who'd showed up on TV as a suspect on *Cops.*

"Speaking of Tilton," I shifted the subject from Carlos and me, "seems like he would have had enough time by now to get back to the set and let everybody know about the murder."

As if waiting offstage for his cue, Tilton appeared in the distance, hurrying toward us with the assistant director and security guard right behind him. The security guard loped toward us easily, like the pro athlete he might have been. The assistant director moved awkwardly, like the last time he'd run was in high school, fleeing the bathroom bullies who wanted to dunk his head in the toilet and flush. Kelly Conover followed more slowly. A tall black man in glasses was glued to her side. I hadn't seen him before.

"Hey, y'all shouldn't get too close," I yelled as they approached. "And don't touch the body. It's a crime scene."

The guard waved his hand, but otherwise ignored me. The rest of them acted like Mama and I were invisible, which suited me fine. While the three men stood and stared at Norman, who was well beyond caring, Kelly and her friend steered clear of the scene. Now, she seemed agitated: pacing, biting a thumbnail, sneaking quick looks toward the dead man on the ground.

"What do you think that meant, when Kelly spit on the ground like that?" Mama whispered to me. "She sure seemed mad. Do you think she'd mind if I asked for her autograph?"

Autographs! I gave Mama a warning glare, and then put a finger to my lips. I didn't want her to draw attention to us, or have us get caught gossiping about the producer's murder. The farther I stayed out of this Hollywood mess, the happier I'd be. We retreated to the far side of the corral, where I could still keep an eye out for Carlos.

The man I hadn't recognized paced right beside Kelly, an arm draped protectively over her shoulders. They were at least thirty-five feet away, and spoke in whispers. I couldn't make out what they were saying. She stopped, and he faced her. It appeared he was trying to calm her down. He looked like he was practiced at it. I saw his lips moving, and then he reached over and tenderly brushed a lock of that famous golden-blond hair from her movie-star eyes.

Trim, in his early forties, he was dressed in a crisp blue polo shirt and jeans with dry-cleaner creases down the front. His skin was as dark as the Cuban coffee Carlos favors. He wore his hair in a short, natural-looking

Afro. The horn-rimmed frames on his glasses gave him a serious look.

Kelly began pacing again, wringing her hands. I wondered if she'd ever played Lady Macbeth on stage. I nudged Mama to drag her eyes away from Tilton and look at Kelly and her friend.

"What do you think? Are they a couple?"

She studied them for a moment. "Not sure. But he's definitely the ice to her fire."

"What do you mean?"

"Well, look at them," Mama said. "The more worked up she gets, the calmer he becomes. That's not a man who'd ever curse somebody's soul to eternal damnation."

As we watched, Kelly shook off his hand and stalked away. He trailed after her, and both of them headed our way. Mama and I pretended to study the ground. We needn't have bothered. They were oblivious to us. They were just on the other side of the fence, close enough that we could hear them now.

"I can't handle it, Sam. It's too much."

"You don't have to. It's over now. He can't hurt you anymore."

In the distance, a police siren wailed.

"Step back! Move outta da way. Da police are here."

I recognized the Bronx-inflected bark. Mama's new husband, Sal Provenza, bulled his way through a growing circle of movie people milling around the body. Carlos followed in the wake made by Sal's massive frame. A trio of uniformed officers fanned out, trying to shepherd the onlookers out to the perimeter.

Technically, only Carlos and the patrolmen were "da police," in Sal's Bronx-ese. But it looked like local law enforcement had the pleasure of Sal's assistance once again, whether they wanted it or not.

My stomach somersaulted at the sight of my detective beau. We were very much on-again these days, not that I wanted to go into just how much so with my mama. I hoped she wouldn't notice the blush surely rising on my face as a few choice scenes from our most recent tryst replayed in my mind. In deference to the seriousness of the situation, I clamped a lid on the X-rated thoughts. But I couldn't help the tingle I got when I looked at him: skin the color of buttered toffee; thick, dark hair; and eyes as black as bottomless caverns. Bedroom eyes. Kitchen eyes. And even in-the-back-seat-of-Carlos's-car eyes.

He raised a hand in a half-wave. I nodded in return. Both of us were maintaining our "all-business" manners.

Mama elbowed me in the side. "Why don't you go fill Carlos in on what's happened, Mace?"

"Stop poking! I told him on the phone how we found Norman. I'm going to let the man do his job. He'll come over and talk to me when he's ready."

Mama pressed her lips together. "Hmmmm."

"What's that supposed to mean?"

"Just that if I were you, I'd make sure I was close by when he questions that Kelly Conover. He probably had a poster in his bedroom of her in that white bikini from that TV show where she was a teenaged detective. Every red-blooded male in America was in love with her back then."

I snorted. "Don't be ridiculous, Mama." The words were barely out of my mouth when I glanced over at Carlos. His body posture was still *Dragnet,* but his eyes had shifted toward Kelly. And there they stayed. He actually swallowed a few times, looking like a nervous schoolboy.

And what man wouldn't be nervous? Her hair was a cascade of blond curls, reaching halfway down her back. Blue jeans, strategically torn under each cheek of her round bottom, fit like a second skin. And, of course, there were the eyes that made her famous, as green as freshly minted money.

I bit back a grin. I was more amused than threatened. Carlos's fascination with Kelly was predictable. It was just like Mama and me, forgetting poor Norman to stare open-mouthed at Greg Tilton in the flesh. These people were screen legends. Bigger than life. I understood completely.

Even so, I decided to mark my claim. I walked up behind him, placing a hand firmly on his arm. "Anything you need me to do?"

It was almost comical, the way he spun around at the sound of my voice. Guilty thoughts?

"Thanks for calling, Mace. I would appreciate it if you, Sal, and your mother would help shift these movie people back toward their base camp. A crime scene van is on the way. We don't need any more people out here tramping around than we've already had. Tell them I'll come over there when I can, and talk to whoever's in charge."

"Will do."

Who'd be in charge now that Norman was dead?

Carlos's eyes roamed the crowd. People were already beginning to disperse, moved either by the orders of the police officers or the menace in Big Sal's tone. Carlos's gaze stopped at the body on the ground.

"I thought you said somebody hung him over the fence."

I filled him in on what Tilton had done. Frowning, he took a notebook from his shirt pocket and wrote something down. "So he clearly handled the body. Anyone else?"

I told him about checking for a pulse, and how the guard and the assistant director had stood over Norman, trying to decide what to do. Then, I mentioned how Kelly had spit twice on the ground.

He raised his eyebrows at me, and then turned to look over his shoulder at the movie queen. She was crying now, collapsed on the shoulder of her comforter, Sam. Expression darkening, Carlos stared hard at Kelly, and then jotted some more words in his notebook.

Even though I said the murder was none of my business, I'd have given anything to know what he wrote.

FOUR

Greg Tilton stood ramrod straight, feet at forty-five degrees, hands clasped behind his back. He must have played a rookie cop, addressing a superior officer, in some forgotten movie.

"I established the victim was dead, beyond medical help."

Carlos's eyes were unreadable, but I saw the slightest smirk breaking through the hard set of his jaw. "At ease, Greg. We're just talking here."

Tilton seemed to relax a bit.

"You complicated things by moving the body, though."

He tensed up again. "I know. I'm so sorry. Like I told her . . ." he raised a questioning eyebrow at me.

"Mace Bauer," I said. "I'm the animal wrangler."

"Yeah. Anyway, I was moving on adrenaline and instinct. I didn't even realize what

I did until it was over. I'm sure you've been in a similar situation on the job, Officer."

"Detective," Carlos corrected him.

"Sorry. Detective."

He laid a hand, man-to-man, on Carlos's shoulder. Carlos stared at it like somebody had just dropped a rotten fish on his starched white button-down. Tilton jerked his hand back like he'd caught a hook in the palm. He checked the crowd, probably wondering who had witnessed him overstepping his boundaries.

A couple dozen members of cast and crew had gathered in the open space between the production trailers. They milled around, eating, smoking, waiting to see what would happen next. The sun was relentless, the nearing-noon temperature climbing into the nineties. Whoever scheduled the location shoot in September hadn't done their homework. "Fall" in middle Florida can still be blisteringly hot; and September holds a better chance than any other month of the year of a hurricane roaring through.

Carlos had been silent long enough to make Tilton sweat. "Who's in charge?" he finally asked.

"The director, Paul Watkins . . ." Tilton started to say.

"I'm Jonathan J. Burt, first assistant director." The officious-looking man who'd directed the morning horse scene stepped forward, interrupting Tilton. "At your service."

He looked like he was expecting a gold star. Another tiny smirk threatened to crack through Carlos's deadpan demeanor, but he banished it. I'd lay odds on what he was thinking, though: *What a weenie.*

Jonathan J. Burt was just a few inches taller than Mama. He wore a pearl-colored cardigan that looked like cashmere, gray wool slacks, and highly polished wing tips. A silk bow tie completed his ensemble. A silk tie. In Himmarshee! In September!!

"I'd like to talk to the man you have handling security," Carlos said.

"Certainly. Anything you need." The assistant director bobbed his head in time to his words. "I finished shooting the scene we'd scheduled for this morning. Can you tell us what we must do now to accommodate the police investigation?"

"You can't do any scenes by the horse corral. We'll be there all day," Carlos said. "Crime scene tape is up. Access is restricted. We may want to remove the section of fence where the victim was found. If we do, the horses might have to be relocated."

The assistant director cocked his head

toward me. "Can you do that?"

"If I need to," I said. "There's a second enclosure we're going to use for cattle."

He head-bobbed, and then turned his eyes to the crowd. It seemed like he was searching for someone. "Anything else?" he asked Carlos.

"Just carry on with your business. But keep yourselves available."

Bob-bob, head cock: "Will you need to question anyone?"

"Not yet. Let me see what I have here first." Carlos paused. "Why? Is there someone you think I should question?"

The assistant director spoke quickly. "No, not at all. No. Of course not."

The crowd was hushed, waiting for Carlos to say more. He focused those black lasers of his on Jonathan J. Burt. I could almost feel the poor man squirm under the heat. I can remember getting singed a time or two myself, when Carlos first moved up from Miami and thought my mama was a murderer.

Burt started bobbing. Just as it looked like he might open his mouth to amend his denial, a woman's shout broke the silence. "Yeeeeeeeee-haw! Let's get this party started."

Jesse Donahue, grown-up 'tween star gone

36

wrong, tossed her cowboy hat in the air, as she walked toward the assembled group. With a Rockette kick, she caught the hat on the pointy toe of her boot. Then, stumbling a bit, she plucked off the hat and returned it to her head. She looked around, probably expecting applause. She got stunned silence from the audience instead.

"Jeez, did somebody die?"

Several people gasped. Mama's hand flew to her heart. Jesse, oblivious, took off the hat again, shook out her mane of flaming red hair, and yelled over her shoulder to the trailer she'd just exited. "Toby! Get your hot little butt out here. I need somebody to party with, and there's nobody here but a bunch of dinosaurs and deadbeats."

The trailer door opened. A shirtless Toby Wyle stepped out. I recognized him from my careful reading of the National Enquirer at Hair Today, Dyed Tomorrow beauty salon, Mama's workplace. He ranked No. 7 in the tabloid's list of Hollywood's Top 10 Teen Hotties.

He stood on the trailer's wide top step as if it were a stage. And then, slowly, deliberately, he zipped up the open fly on his jeans.

I looked again at Jesse. Her face was flushed, the famous hair caked with sweat and who knows what else. As everyone

37

watched, she mounted the trailer's steps, grabbed one of Toby's bare nipples, and playfully tweaked. "C'mon, you ham. Everyone already knows you're a stud."

The tall woman I'd seen earlier handing the sandwich and cell phone to Norman hurried toward the young couple. She whispered in Jesse's ear. The troubled star clapped a hand over her own mouth, mostly hitting her cheek instead.

"Ohmigod, I'm so sorry!"

Jesse's words were a bit slurred. Apparently, the *Enquirer* had its facts straight about her and substance abuse. Eyes tearing up, she turned to her young co-star. "Toby, you won't believe it! While we were shagging all morning, somebody shot Norman Sydney."

Toby took a step backward, clutching his stomach as if he'd been punched. He was either truly shocked, or a decent actor. I couldn't remember if *Top 10 Teen Hotties* said he had real talent, or was just coasting on his stunning looks.

"Where's Paul? Does he know?" Jesse asked.

Shrugs and head-shakes moved around the crowd.

"Paul?" Carlos asked.

"Watkins. Our director." Jonathan's head

bobbed. "He's in charge of every scene in the movie."

"I thought you said you shot the horse scene this morning?" The lasers recalibrated, focusing on Jonathan again. I thought I smelled the scent of his skin, frying.

He tugged at his bow tie. Bobbed that head a couple of times.

"Well?" Carlos prodded.

Jonathan pursed his lips like the classroom tattle-tale he must have been. "Paul told me to do the scene. He said he needed some time away from the set to cool down."

"And?" Carlos waited.

"He said if Norman got into his face one more time, he was going to kill him."

His forehead glistened with a thin sheen of sweat. Now it was obvious: September really was too hot in Himmarshee to wear cashmere.

FIVE

The sandwich-and-cell-phone woman stepped out of the crowd. She smoothed the hem of a jean skirt that was far too short for a woman of her age. "I'm Barbara Sydney, Norman's ex-wife."

Her voice had a smoker's burr, and her words were missing their R's. Boston, maybe?

Carlos raised an eyebrow. I could almost see his detective's brain, fitting a jigsaw puzzle together. How "ex-" were they? Was the divorce amiable or acrimonious? Where would Barbara's piece fit?

"I'm sorry for your loss," he said.

"Thank you." For a moment, the hard features of her face softened. "I cared for Norman once, about a hundred years ago, and we did manage to stay on speaking terms after our split. But I have to be honest with you: The man was not well loved by Hollywood. If Paul Watkins *was* overheard threatening him . . ."

She paused and looked at the assistant director, contempt and skepticism written on her face. He started to explain, but Barbara raised her hand like a traffic cop. Jonathan Burt snapped his mouth shut, and stared at the ground.

She continued speaking to Carlos. "I just want you to know that on any given day, half the cast and crew might have made the same kind of threat. Hell, I've threatened to kill him, plenty of times."

A few nervous titters could be heard. But as Carlos turned his eyes on the crowd, silence descended. He missed nothing. I knew he was watching for tics, facial expressions, body language. My eyes were on Sam and Kelly. Her beauty was like a magnet, pulling my gaze in. Sam watched her, too. But Kelly's eyes seemed focused far off in the distance, or maybe in the past. What did she see?

I also noticed that her eyes were clear, with little evidence of her earlier crying jag. If I'd sobbed like she had, my lids would be swollen and puffy. My nose would be a beet. These Hollywood people must have some make-up tricks that not even Mama knows.

On the periphery of the crowd, the young star, Jesse, raised her hand. Carlos nodded at her to speak. She tossed her red hair like the head cheerleader.

"Are we gonna be here much longer?"

"Are we keeping you from something?"

"It's just that I really, really, really need some caffeine, even though the coffee here is a sorry excuse. On my last film, we had a whole coffee bar: cappuccinos, syrups, lattes, espresso — whatever we wanted."

"What's your name, Miss?"

As Carlos extracted his notebook, Jesse raised her brows at her playmate, Toby, beside her. Then she shot a disbelieving look at Carlos. She shook her hair again. "Uh-hmmm, Jesse Donahue? Maybe you've heard of me?"

He took his time writing something, and then finally looked up from the notebook. Smiled. "Sorry," he said. "I don't read the tabloids."

She waved a hand. "*Whatev.* All I'm saying is I'd love some coffee. And I'd kill to be able to find a half-skim vanilla latte in this stupid hick town."

Mama tsk-tsked beside me. Even Toby looked embarrassed. Barbara glared at Jesse. "Maybe you're too drug-addled to remember, but somebody did just kill my ex-husband. And it probably wasn't over a latte."

Jesse quickly hung her head. "Sorry, Barbara." Her mumbled voice was barely audible. "You're right."

Mama and I exchanged a glance. I put my mouth right next to her ear. "I thought that Barbara was Norman's lowly assistant this morning, the way she was running after him."

"Me, too," Mama whispered back.

Jesse's head was still down, her hair a tent over her face. Toby and the assistant director were also busy trying to avoid meeting the gaze of the producer's ex-wife.

"Looks like we had it wrong, Mama. Barbara Sydney is nobody's assistant. She's definitely the alpha dog of this Hollywood pack."

I sat next to Carlos at a long plastic table under the catering tent. Norman's murder had put a temporary hold on the morning's movie-making. Carlos, awaiting the arrival of crime scene techs from the state lab, had a few moments for a coffee break.

"I couldn't believe that little witch Jesse made such a big deal over coffee. This brew is fine." I showed my nearly empty cup to him and Mama, who sat across from us. "Almost as tasty as a latte, in fact."

"What's a latte?" Mama asked.

"It's delicious." I licked my lips.

"Wrong. It's a fancy drink with more sugar and foamy milk than coffee, Rosalee," Carlos countered. He favors the strong, black brew known as Cuban crack.

Mama had started to tell us to quit bickering, when a voice sounded above us. "Is this seat taken?"

The newcomer's melodious Southern drawl, more boarding school than backwoods, marked her as an outsider to the Hollywood crowd. One of us. Mama perked up, ready to play the down-home hostess.

"Sit right down, honey. We'd be pleased to share our table with you. I'm Rosalee Provenza, and this is my middle daughter, Mace."

The woman put down her coffee cup and nodded at me down the table. "Pleased to make your acquaintance." She offered her hand to Mama, long, tapered fingers extended gracefully. Her chestnut-colored hair was sprinkled with gray.

As the drawling woman got comfortable, Mama nodded toward Carlos. "And this handsome man is Mace's boyfriend. At least he is today."

"I'm Savannah. I'm married to Paul Watkins, the director."

Carlos slid his notebook onto the table.

She stiffened. "Are you a reporter?" The slightest edge crept into her voice.

"Nope. A detective."

She stared at him for a long moment, and then chuckled. "Well, honestly Carlos, I don't know which one is worse."

Mama leaned toward her. "Oh, I think a reporter is worse, honey. Carlos is just trying to find out the truth. All those journalists want to do is dig up dirt."

"Sometimes it's one and the same, Mama."

I leaned across the table and shook Savannah's hand. Her grip was firm, but not too firm. She looked right at me with a hint of mischief in her eyes. I liked that about her, along with the fact that she hadn't kneeled at Hollywood's shrine to youth by dyeing her hair or zapping the laugh lines around her mouth.

Carlos stood up abruptly and announced he was getting a coffee refill. Savannah's brow inched up. "He gets crazy during a case," I apologized for him.

"He's come a long way with his manners. But you have to remember, he is from Miamuh," Mama said.

When Carlos was far enough away he couldn't hear me gossiping, I asked her, "You know about what's happened, right?"

She nodded, her lips set in a grim line. "Barbara called and told me. It's awful, isn't it? I turned right around and came back to the set. I was already in Jacksonville this morning."

"Is that where you're from?"

"Only because my mama and daddy didn't make it all the way to Georgia. I was born in the back seat of an old Ford at a rest stop along US Highway 1." She grinned. "They named me Savannah anyway, since that's where we were headed when we left Eau Gallie, Florida. Could have been worse. They could have called me Eau Gallie."

"Oh Golly!" Mama laughed, hands clapped to her heart. "Honey, that's such a sweet story. Did your folks ever make it on up to Savannah?"

She sipped at her coffee. "No. Daddy took up with a stripper and ended up leaving us in a $29-a-night hotel room when I was just six months old. It was Mama and me on our own after that. She got the job in the club that the stripper ran off and left."

We were quiet. I considered Savannah's rich-looking loafers and tailored clothes, casual gray slacks and white linen blouse. Her hair was thick and glossy. Tastefully sized diamonds glittered at her ears, around her neck, and on her wedding ring finger.

She'd traveled a long way from that $29-a-night hotel room.

Mama said, "Oh, I know all about bad husbands, honey. I've had one or two myself."

"Mama's on Husband No. 5," I said. "Sal's a keeper though."

"That's not fair, Mace! You know at least one of those husbands was a good man, but a bad match. And, of course, your daddy was my life's love — until he up and died on me."

"On us, too, Mama." It always irked me when she left out the part about three young girls also losing a father.

"Speaking of husbands . . ." Savannah must have sensed the tension between us on this subject. She smoothly changed it, Southern woman that she was. "Have y'all seen mine?"

Mama pressed her lips together, stopping a stray word from issuing out. I took a quick look to make sure Carlos was still out of sight. And then I plunged in.

"After Mama and I found Norman's body, the assistant director made a big deal about your husband being missing all morning."

"What'd he say?"

Mama and I looked at each other. I hesitated, wondering how much I should reveal.

"Just tell her, Mace. Someone is bound to." Mama said to Savannah, "My daughter's an amateur detective. She's already solved a couple of murders."

"My mama exaggerates," I said, as Savannah eyed me suspiciously. "I'm staying out of this mess."

Glancing toward the serving line, I still didn't see Carlos. He probably took his coffee to go. I took a deep breath and told her how Jonathan J. Burt had as good as called her husband a killer.

"Johnny Jaybird? That little twerp!"

Savannah, imitating, bobbed her head. I immediately understood the assistant director's nickname.

"His voice is squawky, too, just like a blue jay," Mama said.

"Well, he's squawking up the wrong tree this time," Savannah said. "My husband has done just about every job there is on a movie set, from grip to script. Paul's forgotten more than that little runt will ever know about film-making!"

Savannah seemed to be working herself into a lather, defending her husband. Mama patted her hand. "Don't worry, honey. If that Johnny Jaybird is trying to cast aspersions, the truth will win out."

"Paul wasn't even scheduled to be on the set this morning. He was out scouting tomorrow's location. Today, he's shooting all afternoon, and into the evening. For all I know, that pint-sized creep took it upon himself to be Paul's stand-in. What scene did he film?"

I told her about the galloping and re-galloping horse.

"Figures. He fancies himself an action director."

"So where is your husband, then?"

I was startled to hear Carlos asking the question. We'd been so wrapped up in our conversation, none of us had noticed him hunkered over a table off to our side, his back to us. That explained the quick departure. His plan all along had probably been to sneak back and eavesdrop. How long had he listened? He turned around, regarding the three of us over the rim of his coffee cup.

Savannah coolly met his eyes. "Paul is probably off tromping through the woods right now. He loves the natural side of Florida. He wants to do it justice in the movie. I'll bet he's sitting under a cypress tree somewhere, staring up through the needles at that beautiful blue sky and imagining how things were, back in the

49

olden days."

Just as Savannah finished summing up her husband's high opinion of authentic Florida, a crash sounded in the woods behind the catering tent. A string of curses followed. A sixty-something man in a bush vest, cargo pants, and a long gray ponytail stumbled out of the palmetto scrub. His face was bright red. Skunk vine trailed from his ankles. His pant legs were stained with black mud and sopping wet up past his knees.

"Paul!" Savannah called out.

He lurched toward us, swatting at bugs with both hands. I smelled the insect repellent on him before he arrived.

"Remind me again, Savannah. Why'd I ever take on a film in this God-forsaken state? 'A Land Remembered'? It should be 'A Land Forgotten'."

Carlos stood up. "Love it or hate it, you better get used to it. Nobody leaves Himmarshee until we find out who killed Norman Sydney."

Six

"I can't believe Greg Tilton moved that poor dead man off the fence." My sister Maddie polished off one chicken drumlet and reached for another. "Maybe he thought he was doing a scene from *Rescue*."

"Which one is that now?" I asked.

Maddie snapped her fingers in front of my face, but since they were slick with pesto sauce, it was more of a *sssttt* than a *snnaap*.

"The one about paramedics. You're going to have to study up if you want to be in the film industry, Mace. People will expect you to know these things."

"I'm moving horses and critters from place to place, Maddie. I'd hardly say that makes me a Hollywood insider."

"It's an important job, Mace," Marty said.

"Do you suppose I can get Greg's autograph now?" Mama asked.

"Still not a good time, Mama," I warned.

We'd been bringing my sisters up to speed

51

on the morning's events when Mama's new cousin by marriage stopped by the table in her catering tent to talk.

"So, whaddaya think of my prosciutto and provolone panini?" C'ndee Ciancio hovered over us, beaming proudly.

"Well, honey, I'm not sure I could spell it, but I sure can eat it." Mama took a bite to demonstrate. "It's delicious, almost as good as the pulled pig on a bun at the Pork Pit."

Maddie had taken a couple of days off from her school principal's job, while her assistant principal filled in. Marty was on vacation from her job at the Himmarshee library. Both had agreed to help me with the animals, mainly so they'd get the chance to see some Hollywood stars. So far, I hadn't needed their help. But that didn't stop them from coming out to the location shoot, especially after Mama called to tell them about the murder.

Mama's new friend, the security man, only needed one look at the doll-sized Marty — big blue eyes, shiny blond hair, and a face so innocent it'd break your heart. He waved her and Maddie over to the tent to join us. My big sister didn't even need to pull out her scary school administrator routine.

Now, C'ndee glanced around the tent,

which was set up next to her catering truck. "Where's Sal?" She raked bright red finger-nails through her mane of black hair. "He loves my sandwiches."

Sal was helping the police keep looky-loos away from the corral, now a crime scene. Carlos was working out there, too.

"Wrap up a couple of those pan-ninnies in a little to-go bag, hon. I'll make sure Sal gets them when I leave," Mama said.

"Will do, Rosalee. I better run. Enjoy, girls."

Maddie waved goodbye with a drumstick. Marty toasted C'ndee with a glass of spar-kling Italian soda. "I love this raspberry flavor," she called after her. "It may replace sweet tea as my favorite."

Over the last several months my sisters and I had become friendly with C'ndee. We forgave her for bulldozing her way into Mama's wedding, not to mention for being from New Jersey. Her new business, C'ndee's Ciao, was doing well, even though no one in Himmarshee could pronounce it. The second word is Italian, and you're sup-posed to say it like "chow."

"Mace, pass me some of that *aioli*, would you?" Maddie pointed her drumlet at a little pot of sauce on the table. The Pork Pit would call it mayonnaise.

"A minute on the lips, a lifetime on the hips, Maddie."

My older sister shot Mama a glare. "I happen to be big-boned."

Marty nodded. "That's true. She is, just like the two of us are little shrimps, and Mace is tall and slender. That's genetics, Mama."

"Well, I read in the *Enquirer* that Kelly Conover triumphed over her weight issues with a cabbage soup diet. Maybe you could try that, Maddie."

"Humph!" Maddie harrumphed, a habit she must have gotten from Mama in her chromosomes.

Marty changed the subject from food to a less emotional topic. "Are you going to solve the murder, Mace?"

"I'm staying out of it. These Hollywood people are crazy."

Marty got a dreamy look on her face as she sipped her raspberry drink. "Do you suppose Toby and Jesse are really a couple?"

Mama slathered her panini with *aioli.* "Well, they were definitely coupling in her trailer. Somebody ought to call the scandal sheets and tell them about *that,* especially after Jesse sat right on Oprah's couch and told her she'd gotten treatment for her sex addiction."

"Sisters, you should have seen Jesse get all meek and scared-looking when the producer's ex-wife yelled at her," I said. "Total transformation. Something is definitely up with that Barbara Sydney."

Maddie took a sip of Marty's soda, and made a face. "Ewww, needs sugar. Wouldn't that be horrible to be Barbara, and find out your ex had been murdered?"

Mama shrugged, and swiped her knife through Maddie's pesto. Maddie pulled the plate out of her reach. "I can see you're all choked up, Mama. It's amazing you being so upset over the murder hasn't spoiled your appetite, or stopped you from stealing off my plate."

"Well, of course I mourn the passing of any one of God's creatures, girls."

"While you're mourning, you might want to wipe that dribble of pesto off your chin," Maddie said.

Mama dabbed, and then put down her sandwich. "Truth is, I can't muster up a single tear for that man. All I knew about him is he screamed at me for no good reason this morning. The great acting coach Stella Adler might say I could channel the anger I felt at him into my craft, if I can get a part."

Mama had been poring over library books

on the actor's "craft," which was vaguely troubling to my sisters and me. I was about to tell them why Norman had screamed at her, when a ruckus broke out from the serving line. Jesse's voice was raised in an angry shout.

"I won't eat that! It's not vegetarian anymore. You got blood from the roast on the serving utensil." She batted at C'ndee's spoon. "Where'd they hire you? The animal slaughterhouse?"

C'ndee jabbed back at her with the big spoon, bringing it just inches from Jesse's nose. She ratcheted up the volume on her Jersey foghorn voice. "This spoon did not touch *anything* but your precious vegetable medley. Although from what I've read about all the crap you put into your body, a little beef *jus* would be the least of your worries."

Jesse slammed her tray on the table. "Paul! You're the director. Direct yourself over here and take care of this. This woman is trying to poison me. I want her ass fired!"

I looked around the catering tent. Paul Watkins was nowhere in sight.

"Will somebody go find our has-been director, PLEASE?" Jesse's face was red, and the veins stood out on her neck. She screamed, "I want this bitch fired! Now!"

She glared at C'ndee, who backed down

56

not one inch. "Just try to get me canned." C'ndee's spoon passed so close to the young star's head, it parted her hair. "You'll find your latest Teen Diva Meltdown posted on the Internet faster than you can say 'tweet.' "

Jesse hauled back and slapped C'ndee across the face. If this were six months ago, I'd be rooting for Jesse to kick C'ndee's butt all the way back to Hackensack. But I liked Sal's cousin now, so I was pulling for her as the two women circled one another.

"Odds favor C'ndee," I said.

"If she gets Jesse on the ground, she'll have her," Maddie agreed. "She's got a sixty-pound advantage, at least."

"Yeah, but Jesse can kick like a mule," Mama said. "Remember that little show with the cowboy hat this morning, Mace? C'ndee better back out of range and keep her eye on that gal's pointy-toed boots."

We were settling in for a good catfight when Sal appeared from nowhere. He moved surprisingly fast for a man who stood six-foot-four and weighed more than three hundred pounds. He stepped in between the two warring women, separating them with his bulk.

"Break it up! Back to your corners, da two of youse."

"She started it." C'ndee rubbed at her cheek.

Sal had one massive hand on C'ndee's shoulder. He gave her a hard shake. "You oughta be ashamed of yourself. You're the adult here."

He shook Jesse with the other hand, but not as hard. "And you need to grow up and stop acting like a spoiled brat. We've got bigger things to worry about than whether you like your lunch. A man died here this morning."

"Big F'ing Deal."

Sal stared at Jesse. Maddie tsked. Even C'ndee gasped at the young woman's callousness.

"Look, I couldn't stand Norman. Neither could anyone else, though we're bound to hear all kinds of wonderful eulogies now that he's dead."

People had stopped eating in every corner of the tent. All eyes were on Jesse. She tossed her hair and continued.

"I could act like I'm all mournful and sorry, but I'm not. The man was a pig. Call me whatever you want, but I'm not a hypocrite. The only acting I do is for the cameras."

With that, Jesse gave a final shake of her curls. Then she exited, stage left.

SEVEN

"Bad news." I found Carlos stepping out of the "honey wagon," a trailer with toilets for the movie crew. "An army of paparazzi is marching our way."

He scowled at me. I raised my hands, surrender style.

"Hey, don't shoot the messenger. Plus, it gets worse: The gals from Hair Today, Dyed Tomorrow beauty parlor called Mama. They say it's all over town that your police chief is going to be interviewed on three different cable news shows tonight."

He rolled his shoulders; a vein pulsed at his temple. "We don't know squat yet. I hope he doesn't oversell."

"You mean brag about how his hotshot homicide detective from *Miamuh* is going to hunt down and catch the perpetrator of this *hay-en-ous* crime?"

Wincing, he pinched the bridge of his nose. "Something like that, yeah."

I took a quick look around the movie production's outdoor encampment, known in Hollywood lingo as base camp. Transformed from ranchland, it was a small city of semi trucks and white trailers. Some held movie-making essentials, everything from props and wardrobe, to cameras and lights. Others housed office equipment. Red stars on several trailer doors denoted actors' quarters.

Awnings had been rolled out and portable tents erected to shield cast and crew from the searing Florida sun. With the murder interrupting the shooting schedule, the movie people sat alone or in small groups. Some talked; others read. The catered lunch was over, but the craft services truck was busy, as cast and crew helped themselves to cold drinks, sweets, and afternoon snacks.

No one seemed to be paying attention to Carlos and me, standing beside a plastic picnic table behind a towering pallet of bottled water. Rolling his shoulders again, he kneaded the back of his neck.

"Have a seat," I said. "Let me see if I can get some of those kinks out."

He settled sideways, straddling the bench seat. I sat behind him, my legs on either side of his rear. The skin at the insides of my thighs felt hot where it touched his hips.

Softly, I traced a cowlick that defies the straight hairline at the back of his neck. Then I went to work, massaging out the tension and stress trapped in his neck and shoulders.

"Ahh," he moaned. "That's great. You can go harder if you want."

Harder is exactly where I wanted to go, but I restricted myself to the knots in his neck. I ratcheted up the pressure. A grunt escaped his lips, and I knew I was getting the job done.

Strong hands are a benefit of being the kind of girl who rode right alongside the boys in high school rodeo. These days, I easily heft forty-pound bags of animal chow at the makeshift wildlife shelter I established at Himmarshee Park. And I've won more than a few rounds of beer in bars, arm-wrestling tough-guy wannabes.

Like my cousin Henry always says, "It's not bragging if it's fact."

For the next several moments, I rubbed. When I quit, Carlos rolled his head. I heard a couple of soft *pops*. He leaned back against me and sighed. "You're a miracle worker, Mace."

"You don't have to leave a tip, just return the favor."

He shifted to look over his shoulder at me,

a half smile on his lips. "Oh, I intend to." His black eyes smoldered. "I have a long list of ways I plan to return the favor."

"I'll take you up on all of them, after you solve the case."

As soon as I saw the furrowing between his eyes, I realized I'd said the wrong thing. Again.

"Uhmm . . . I didn't mean it's *contingent* on you solving the case. I'd feel the same way about you even if you never solved another case."

He cocked his head at me, the frown line getting deeper.

"I mean, *of course* you'll solve the case, Carlos. You'll work it out. You always do. You're an incredible detective . . ."

He put a finger to my lips. The frown faded. "It's okay, *niña*. I know what you mean. It's just that these film people are a different breed. I feel like I did when I was nine years old and came to this country from Cuba. I need a guide, or a translator, or something."

His eyes roamed around the tented quadrangle outside the trailers. They caught, and stayed, on Kelly Conover, seated a short distance away in a camp chair in the shade.

"Maybe she's your gal," I said. "She knows everybody on the set. And she speaks

Hollywood."

Carlos rubbed his jaw, thinking. The tendon in his forearm tensed, exposed by the rolled-up sleeve of his white dress shirt. I had the urge to trace it with my tongue, traveling up along his arm, and then continuing on a steady path across his broad chest, up the other shoulder, lingering on his neck, and then onward until my mouth met the full, masculine curve of his lips.

But we were in professional mode, so I tamped down my naughty thoughts. Just to be safe, I plunged my hands into the back pockets of my jeans.

"Go ahead and talk to her," I said. "It might help the investigation. You know you want to."

Gazing at Kelly across a short expanse of well-trodden pasture, he licked his lips. I chose to interpret this is a sign of nervousness, not desire. "She does seem well connected," he said.

"Well, of course she does, Carlos. She's been around for who knows how many years."

Meow!

With my eyes following him as he strode toward Kelly, I didn't notice Maddie sidle up beside me.

"I'm surprised you let him go." Maddie

shoveled in a spoonful of chocolate chip ice cream, a craft services treat.

I turned. Marty stood watching Carlos, too. Mama wasn't with them. I hoped she was staying out of trouble.

"It's a free country, sisters. Besides, Carlos and I are past all those games." I swiped a finger through Maddie's bowl. "Mmm, good. We're in an adult relationship. I've moved on from junior high."

Marty stuck in a spoon and took a bird-sized bite of ice-cream. Maddie shot us both a look, and yanked the bowl tight against her chest.

"So, you're ready to get married, then?" Marty turned her blue eyes on me, her gaze as sweet as a baby's. But I recognized the goading tone. I backpedaled, just as she probably knew I would.

"I wouldn't go that far. I've still got time to walk down the aisle."

"Not as much time as you think," Maddie butted in. "You're not getting any younger."

I glanced toward Carlos. Kelly was standing now, with a hand on his arm. That famous body of hers was plastered against his side. He swallowed like a high school freshman asking out the homecoming queen. I could see his Adam's apple bobbing. Kelly laughed, a seductive purr.

"Better stand back, Maddie. You might get burned from the steam pouring out of Mace's ears," Marty said.

Our big sister surveyed the set of my mouth, which I knew was pretty grim. She took in the way I held my arms, one clutching the other, tight across my chest.

"Oh, yeah. You're an adult now. Maybe you can get Marty to go pass a note to Carlos during recess: *Do you still like Mace? Check yes or no.*"

I was thinking up a smart remark when a hush fell over the tented area. It was followed by the sound of breathless murmuring. "Talent on set," someone said, and I heard a snicker.

Greg Tilton paused. When nearly every eye was on him, he puffed out his chest and John-Wayne-walked to the coffee urn in the craft services truck. I swear he flexed his bicep before reaching for a cup.

"Why do these Hollywood people always look like they're making an entrance in a Broadway play?" I asked.

Neither of my sisters answered. Both stared at Tilton as if mesmerized by a cloud of golden stardust around his body. I don't think either of them was breathing.

"He's even better-looking in person," Marty finally whispered.

"The man is a Hollywood god," Maddie sighed.

I tore a few paper towels off the roll on the picnic table. "Here you go, sisters. Sop up that drool before it drops off your chins and soaks through your blouses."

"Gross!" Marty jabbed me in the ribs.

"I do *not* drool." Maddie surreptitiously ran the back of her hand under her mouth, just in case she was wrong. "Drooling is not becoming for a school principal."

We watched as Tilton, coffee in hand, strutted over to Kelly Conover. Carlos turned unreadable eyes and an impassive face toward him. Tilton's arrival gave me the excuse I needed to get closer to eavesdrop more easily on my boyfriend and the gorgeous actress. My sisters moved right along with me.

Tilton leaned toward Kelly. As he whispered something in her ear, he grabbed hold of her elbow. She tugged backwards, but he stepped with her. He looked to be hanging on even tighter. Possessive.

"Were they ever an item?" I asked under my breath.

My sisters shrugged.

"We'll have to find out what it says in *People* magazine. The shampoo girl at Hair Today will definitely know," I said.

"Mama will know. He's her favorite actor," Marty said.

Kelly inched back some more, and Tilton quickly closed the gap between them. Carlos put a heavy hand on the action star's shoulder.

"The lady isn't interested." His voice was quiet. Dangerous. "Why don't you back off?"

Wisely, Tilton did just that. He dropped his co-star's elbow and gave a good-natured shrug. "Sorry, Kel. It's been a hell of a day. I'm not myself."

His gaze returned to Carlos. "Thanks, man. I need someone to keep me in line. You're the real deal, you know that?"

Carlos raised an eyebrow. His face was still closed; hard-looking. It was his Miami face.

Tilton went on, "Being a cop and all. A detective, I mean. I just respect you guys on the force so much. I always end up acting like a complete idiot when I get around real cops. I've played so many — not to mention firefighters, paramedics, and soldiers. I try to act too familiar."

Tilton kicked self-consciously at the ground. Could that be a blush spreading up his neck?

"I forget I'm playing a role. You guys play

67

for keeps." He stuck out a hand toward Carlos. "I'm sorry, man, for being a jerk."

Carlos hesitated just a second or two, and then shook. The tense posture of his body seemed to relax, the line of his jaw softened. It wasn't exactly a smile, but it was something less than a scowl.

Just as Carlos opened his mouth to respond, a gunshot ripped through the air. In one fluid motion, he drew his own weapon, whirled toward the sound, and shouted out a command.

"Everybody, get down!"

I didn't argue, scrambling under a table for cover. My sisters followed. Most everyone followed suit, including Tilton and Kelly. I peeked out from behind a plastic tablecloth. Apart from Carlos, Toby Wyle was the only person I saw still standing. I pulled the cloth aside and pointed, so my sisters could also see the young star.

White-faced and trembling, gun still in his hand, Toby stared across the tent. My eyes followed his and found Johnny Jaybird, the assistant director. He was hanging on to the back of a folding chair, trying to stand.

"Place the weapon on the ground," Carlos shouted. "Slowly."

Toby looked at the gun he held like it was a foreign object that had magically come into his possession. He stared again at Johnny Jaybird, who had knocked over the chair. Johnny staggered, clutching his side. A dark stain seeped through his pearl-colored cashmere sweater.

"Put it down!" Gun drawn, Carlos closed in on Toby.

The teenager's eyes were enormous in his colorless face. He looked once more at Johnny, and then at the gun in his hand. He dropped to his knees, the gun dangling inches from the ground.

It landed with a thud, just as Johnny Jaybird collapsed onto the floor.

EIGHT

"Someone call 911!" Jesse Donahue pushed past stunned onlookers. "Do it now." Her voice was urgent, but calm.

She kneeled on the ground beside Johnny Jaybird. Without a wasted motion, she felt for a pulse, and then lifted his cashmere sweater and dress shirt to check the wound. Whipping off a scarf that was tied at her neck, she balled up the fabric and held it to his side.

She looked up, her gaze finding Toby. "Good thing you're such a bad shot."

Carlos stood close to Toby, unloading and checking the gun while keeping an eye on the young star. Toby's gaze was fastened on the fallen assistant director.

"It wasn't supposed to be live ammunition," he kept repeating. "It was supposed to be blanks."

The crowd pressed in: Watching. Straining to hear Toby's singsong chorus of disbelief.

It was supposed to be blanks. It was supposed to be blanks.

"Get outta the way!" A loud, raspy voice announced the arrival of Barbara Sydney. "I'm Toby's manager."

I thought he needed an attorney more than a manager at this juncture, but I held my tongue.

She pushed her way to her client, who was still dangerously pale and trembling. She put an arm around his shoulder, tenderly smoothed his hair, and whispered something into his ear. Slumping toward her, he placed his head against her chest. Then he dissolved into sobs.

She raised her eyebrows at Carlos over Toby's head. "Somebody will surely get all this as a video on their cell phone. He's just a kid. Can we take him someplace a little more private? Someplace he won't wind up on YouTube?"

Things happened quickly in the next few moments: The movie's set medic rushed in. He waved away Jesse, and conducted a professional assessment of Johnny's condition. He briefed Carlos, who then summoned Sal via his cell to help handle security in the base camp. Soon, Sal was in place, Johnny was getting emergency treatment, and a county ambulance was en route to the movie location. Carlos returned his attention to Toby and Barbara.

"He's coming with me," he said. "Is he a minor?"

"He won't be eighteen for two weeks," she said.

"Then I suggest you find his parents or get him a lawyer."

"I'm an attorney as well as a manager," she said. "I'm staying with him."

Carlos scowled at her. "Suit yourself."

Like a mother lion protecting a cub, Barbara bared her teeth at Carlos. She stalked along beside him as he took Toby by the arm and led him away.

"You're pretty good in an emergency, Jesse."

Jesse shrugged at me, popping her gum. It seemed she'd returned to her more typical demeanor: dumb, spoiled starlet.

"My father's a doctor," Jesse said. "I went with him every summer to work at a camp in upstate New York. You wouldn't believe some of the scrapes those little brats can get into."

"Seen a lot of gunshots, have you?" I asked, amused.

Another shrug. "A few," she said. "It looked to me like Toby's shot only grazed Johnny. Didn't hit anything vital."

When I raised my eyebrows, she explained. "My dad's specialty is emergency medicine. I've also shadowed him in the ER. He'd love it if I followed in his footsteps."

"Did you have the grades?"

She shrugged, implying that grades were, like, *whatev.* "I was better at acting. It's more my thing."

The young star and I sat in two camp chairs outside her trailer. The set medic had stabilized Johnny, and transported him closer to the road to wait for the ambulance. Most of the onlookers, including my sisters, followed them. I'd bet Mama had found her way there, too. I hoped she wasn't toting her autograph book with her.

Jesse chomped her gum and blew a big, pink bubble. "So, this town seems really boring. Isn't there anything to do here?"

"We've got a new library," I said. "My sister Marty works there."

Jesse crinkled her nose, probably a sign her GPA wasn't med school material.

"My mama works at Hair Today, Dyed Tomorrow beauty parlor. She does color consultations and aromatherapy."

Jesse's face brightened; the chewing motions paused. "Do they do massage, too?"

"Nope."

"Mud baths?"

I shook my head.

"Cavitosonic chambers?"

"Say what?"

"How about hot stone treatments? Does the salon have those, at least?"

"Nope. But you could go down and scoop up some of the gravel for the road project along State Road 70. It gets plenty hot sitting out in the sun."

She blew another bubble. "Are there any clubs here?"

"Not unless you count the VFW hall. We've also got a bar at the Speckled Perch restaurant. Thursday is Ladies' Night: Domestic draft beer is 2-for-1."

"Ohmigod!" Jesse rolled her eyes. "I am trapped in Hick City."

I was about to jump to the defense of my hometown when a siren sounded in the distance. It silenced me, and even seemed to affect Jesse. Her sneer faded, replaced with a sober expression. Soon, I spotted the ambulance on the highway, visible across an open, flat stretch of ranch land. I pointed it out to her as it slowed, preparing to turn down the dirt road that led to the movie set.

Within moments, Johnny would be loaded into the back. The doors would slam shut. I barely knew the man, but I still said a prayer he'd be okay.

I wondered whether Jesse did the same.

NINE

"There she is, Mace."

Marty nodded toward two people in the distance in dark blue directors' chairs. Their backs were to us. Mama sat in one; Paul Watkins was in the other. Even if his name hadn't been spelled out in blocky white letters on the back of the chair, I recognized his khaki bush jacket. His gray ponytail swung from shoulder to shoulder as he shook his head. I could only imagine the question Mama had asked him.

As we drew closer, I saw one of her library books on acting tucked beside her on the chair. I could hear the director chuckling, though, so maybe it wasn't as bad as I feared.

"Well, there you are, girls!"

"We've been looking for you for a half-hour, Mama," I said. "Is your cell phone battery dead again? The gals from Hair Today called me to find out when you'd be there. They said you're supposed to finish a color chart tonight for the woman from the Chamber of Commerce, Lori something."

"McCaskill. Lori McCaskill. Everybody knows her, Mace."

She looked at her watch, clasped a hand to her chest. "My stars and garters, where did the time go? Why didn't you girls come find me earlier?"

Marty and I exchanged a look. "We left you with Maddie. We thought it was her turn to keep track of time for our fully grown mother," I said.

"No, honey, Maddie had to go home early." Sarcasm eludes Mama. "Tonight is her date night with Kenny, and it's his turn to choose. They're going to the tractor pull."

"Poor Maddie," Marty said.

The sun was starting to sink in the sky. The energy on the set had already dropped with the exit of the ambulance carrying Johnny Jaybird. Now it seemed further diminished by the dying light. Carlos was with the other authorities, still examining the crime scene by the corral. He'd decided that moving the animals would be more disruptive than leaving them there overnight. Marty had helped me feed the half-dozen horses in the enclosure.

"Let me introduce you girls to Paul." As

Mama did the honors, it became clear why he'd been laughing.

"You see that beautiful gold cross in Paul's earlobe? Now, wouldn't you girls assume he's a man of faith?"

Considering I'd seen a drunken biker with the same gold earring toss a rival into a barroom mirror in Daytona, and then start making out with the guy's teenaged hooker girlfriend, I wouldn't assume anything. But I didn't want to get Mama off track, so I didn't say so.

"Your mother wondered whether I'd been saved," Paul said dryly.

"I quoted Romans 10:9, girls: *If you confess with your mouth, 'Jesus is Lord,' and believe in your heart that God raised him from the dead, you will be saved.*"

"And I told your mother I'd let her redeem me in a New York minute. I'm just not sure the Lord wants somebody as bad as me in his saved column."

His eyes sparkled. He aimed a purely devilish grin at Mama. He was *flirting!*

Mama didn't notice, as she was too busy offering eternal life through salvation. "Of course the Lord wants you, Paul. He may hate sin, but he loves the sinner."

"Ah, yes, but do *you* love the sinner?"

That come-on was so obvious, even Mama.

78

got it. She slapped him playfully on the wrist.

"I love the Lord," she said. "And He knows when you're being naughty."

"Okay," Paul said. "I'm being serious now. You're a beautiful woman. Have you ever thought about acting?"

Mama's eyelashes fluttered. One hand flew to her throat, while the other hid her paperback copy of "The Art of Acting" under her leg. "I'm much too modest, Paul. I hate the very thought of being in the spotlight."

Marty even rolled her eyes at that. Mama had been saying for weeks this movie could be her ticket to stardom.

"I mean it. You could be an actress. You should let me audition you."

Marty and I were transfixed. The man was a walking stereotype of a Hollywood director. Where did he keep his casting couch? We were so transfixed, in fact, we didn't hear Barbara Sydney approach. But we did hear her screech: "Oh, for God's sake, Paul. Why don't you just ask her back to your trailer to see your etchings? Can't you keep it in your pants, for a change?"

Her glare took in both the director and Mama. Mama shrank a bit, but Barbara's tirade bounced off Paul like water off a whirligig beetle.

"Is there something you need?" His tone was even.

"Yes. I need a little concern from you for your young star. Toby is still sitting in a police car, waiting for that detective to talk to him. It's inhumane."

"You're a lawyer. File a lawsuit."

"Someone had to have loaded that gun, Paul. It wasn't Toby."

I wondered how Barbara was so sure of that.

"If Norman were here," her voice was taunting, "he'd have worked things out by now."

"Yeah?" Paul stared at her. "Well, Norman's not here, may he rest in peace. And there's not a thing I can do about the fact that he's dead, or that one of my actors shot my assistant director with a gun that was supposed to be loaded with blanks. How about we let the police do their job, Barbara? Aren't they still out there, combing the scene?"

She nodded.

"So, once they finish investigating, we'll get everything sorted out."

Their eyes locked. I hoped birds and small animals stayed out of the charged space between them. Finally, Barbara blinked.

"Fine. Enjoy your floozies." She shot three withering glances, one each for Mama, Marty, and me, and then stomped away.

Paul didn't watch her go. He was staring intently at Mama, Floozy No. 1. "Barbara just gave me an idea. I see you as a beautiful dancehall girl for the scene where all the cowboys blow their money on women and liquor." He put a hand on her chin, lifted it toward what was left of the sunlight. "I'm not kidding. The camera is going to love this face."

Paul's fingers were tracing the still-smooth line of Mama's cheek when Sal blustered onto the scene. His face was as dark as a stormy sky over Lake Okeechobee. "We haven't had the pleasure," he said to Paul, "though I see you've met my wife."

Hollywood, say hello to New York City. Ego, meet Ego.

"Chill, dude," Paul caressed Mama's face before dropping his hand from her cheek. "I didn't mean any harm."

The woman who shunned the spotlight didn't give her husband time to respond before she gushed, "I'm getting a part in the movie, Sally!"

"Fuhgeddabout it, Rosie." His eyes still bored into Paul. "Everybody's heard stories about dis 'dude.' Paul Watkins is trouble

81

with a capital T, and you're a married woman. I forbid it."

Mama got out of the chair, and pulled herself up to her full height. She barely reached Sal's chest, but still she stared him down. Her eyes were narrowed, firing off sparks.

"Uh-oh," Marty whispered.

"You said it," I agreed.

We both took a few steps backward, putting ourselves out of collateral damage range.

"Meet me at my Jeep, Mama. I'll give you a ride to the salon," I shouted over my shoulder, hurrying off with Marty.

Once we were far enough away, my sister said, "That could get ugly."

"For Sal, anyway," I said. "Mama will flatten him like an armadillo on State Road 98 if he tries to come between her and that spotlight she claims to hate."

TEN

The bells on the purple door at Hair Today, Dyed Tomorrow jangled. As we came in, Betty Taylor's last customer of the day left.

"Whew." The salon owner exhaled. "This has sure been a day!"

"Honey, you have no idea!"

Mama plopped herself at the small table where she does her color charts, and launched into a long recitation of the events of her day.

As I escaped off to the side, behind the cover of a *People* magazine, she led off with Norman Sydney berating her, barely mentioning his murder in passing. She sidetracked from Paul Watkins returning to the set, to focus on what she believed was the day's headline: the casting coup for *Fierce Fury Past*.

"Oh, Rosalee," Betty clapped her hand to her cheek. "You're going to be a star! Maybe you'll get a scene with Greg Tilton."

Mama gave a modest flutter of her lashes. "Well, honey, it's not 100 percent set in stone yet."

From her nexus at Gossip Central, Betty was able to offer us a tidbit, too: "My sister-in-law's cousin's daughter works at the hospital. She says that director who got shot is going to be okay."

"Assistant director, honey. We call him the AD in the movie business."

Behind my magazine, I rolled my eyes.

Betty pointed her purple styling comb toward the pile of fabric swatches and folders, untouched on Mama's table. "So, how are you coming with that color chart, Rosalee?"

Color Me Beautiful, the folders said in purple script across the front.

"Don't fret, Betty. This won't take but a few minutes to put together. Lori from the Chamber has the same coloring as Mace. She's a pure Winter, just like Mace. I know the colors that will flatter her the most. I could pick them out in my sleep."

I lifted my face out of *People.* "It's true, Betty. She could. She's only told me a thousand times or so exactly what colors I should wear."

Mama speaks with authority on the topic. For $35, she gives a diagnosis on whether a

Hair Today customer is a Winter, Spring, Summer, or Fall. She offers counsel on wearing warm tones or cool ones, dark colors or pastels. She also throws in an aromatherapy candle, and the cardboard folder with fabric samples in colors to beautifully complement eyes, skin tone, and hair.

She leaned over and held a bubble gum-colored swatch to my face. I'd sooner be hog-tied and dunked in a pit full of gators than wear pink.

"I just want you to make the most of what God gave you, honey. Is that so wrong?"

"Your mama is one-hundred percent right, Mace." Betty approached with a gleam in her eye, wielding that comb like a weapon. "When are you going to let me go to work on that gorgeous hair of yours? It has so much potential."

I tented the *People* over my head, protecting every snarl and split end of my thick, black hair. "I was just here. How could I forget those Scarlett O'Hara ringlets you gave me for Mama's wedding?"

"That was over three months ago." Betty picked up a pair of scissors and made snip-snip noises around my ears.

"Oh, leave her alone, honey. If Mace wants to go around looking like a possum crawled in her hair and built itself a nest, that's her business."

Betty sighed, and holstered her scissors. I let out the breath I'd been holding. Inhaling, I got a nose full of the shop's warring scents: fruity shampoos and flowery conditioner, nail polish and permanent solution. I'm sure some people found a beauty parlor's signature smell pleasing, but it made me think of a fruit roll-up dipped in ammonia.

Ducking behind the magazine again, I made my way through pictures of fashion faux pas from the Hollywood red carpet, through a story about a 911-dialing dog that saved his owner, and through a profile of the movie industry's troubled young stars. Jesse was prominently featured, slouching in a booth at some New York nightclub. Her eyes were at half-mast; she clutched a drink and cigarette in her hand.

"Mace, what are you so interested in over there? Why don't you come over and tell me what you think of the chart I've put together?"

"I'm just getting to a story about a family that staged a kidnapping of one of their kids so they could get on a reality TV show."

Shaking her head, Betty stabbed a handful of combs into a sterilizing solution. "What is wrong with people today?"

"Some folks will do anything to be famous," Mama said. "Forget about the trash in that magazine, honey. We've got a better story right here in Himmarshee than anything in *People*."

Mama ran a glue stick across the top edge of some of the intense Winter colors I knew by heart: royal blue, imperial red, emerald green. She pressed them into her folder. I hoped poor Lori Whoever wouldn't mind being bossed by Color Me Beautiful.

Betty's apprentice, D'Vora, came from the back with her arms full of fresh-laundered purple smocks, still wrinkled from the dryer. "Have you got the movie set murder solved yet, Mace?"

"No interest, D'Vora. I'm staying out of this one. Plus, I may be too busy trying to keep Sal and Mama from killing each other."

D'Vora's brows went up in a question. Her purple eye shadow matched everything else in Betty's shop.

Mama waved a hand airily. "Mace is exaggerating, girls. It's nothing serious. Every once in a while, Sal has to be reminded of who's boss."

I snorted. "Keep flirting with that creepy director and we'll have another murder on our hands. Either Sal will kill him, or Barbara will kill you."

"Barbara?" All three of them turned puzzled frowns on me.

I explained to D'Vora and Betty that Barbara was the dead producer's ex-wife, and then said to Mama, "Anyone with eyes can see she has a thing going with Paul Watkins."

"But he's married." Mama frowned. "We met that sweet wife of his. She's a Southerner; name's Savannah."

D'Vora picked up a smock from the load she'd dropped on a chair and snapped it, as loud as a gunshot. "Oh, I've been there, done that. Since when has being married ever stopped a man from cheating?"

"Trouble with Darryl again, honey?" Mama looked up from her glue stick.

Betty shook her head. "That boy's name is trouble. D'Vora's too good for him, and she'll realize it someday."

"That mo-ron brought home another rottweiler puppy." She shook another wrinkled smock, crack. "Like that'll make up for him staying out all night."

"How many dogs is that now, honey? Three?"

"Four," Betty answered for D'Vora. "In a trailer."

"It's a manufactured home," D'Vora said.

"If I were you, I'd skip picking up that

12-pack for Darryl on your way home tonight," Betty said. "Drinking is a big part of that boy's problem, and all you're doing is enabling him."

D'Vora's eyes went wide. "Darryl's got me so distracted, I forgot to tell y'all the biggest news. I saw Kelly Conover yesterday in this little tiny convertible, right behind me in the drive-thru at the Booze 'n' Breeze. No make-up, her hair all knotted from the wind."

D'Vora waved her hands around her own immaculately done hair and face to demonstrate. "I was way up high in our pickup, and I could see her in the rearview. She had on a big ugly T-shirt with stains and sweat pants that looked like pajamas. She looked really upset. Not like a movie star, for sure."

The gleam returned to Betty's eye. "Maybe you could drop Kelly a hint about our services at Hair Today, Rosalee."

Mama shook her head. "No can do, Betty. On-set hair and make-up artists take care of all that for those of us in the cast. It'd be like Buck at the feed store outsourcing his cattle supplements."

"Maybe Kelly just needs a break from looking gorgeous. Did you ever think of that?" I asked.

Mama gave a thoughtful nod. "I can tell

you it's an awful pressure to be famous for your beauty, girls. People judge you all the time."

She stood, leaning close to the mirror to examine her face. Out came the Apricot Ice lipstick. She applied a fresh coat, and then popped her lips as if blowing herself a kiss. "I can understand just how that poor Kelly feels, bless her heart."

The only sound in the shop was D'Vora, snapping those purple smocks.

ELEVEN

I heard the music thumping from the Eight Seconds Bar even before I opened the door. Toby Keith was singing some song about putting America's boot in the butt of the rest of the world.

I took a deep breath of outside air, and walked in. The place smelled like man sweat and spilled beer.

The lighting was dim inside the dive just over the Himmarshee County line. But it wasn't so dark I couldn't see Jesse Donahue doing a routine out of "Coyote Ugly" on the top of the bar. Several cowboys hooted, hollered, and cheered her on as she danced back and forth. She stomped her high-heeled boots, her long legs flying in her second-skin jeans. Between the jeans' strategic rips and glittering rhinestones, and her breasts overflowing a matching rhinestone halter, she looked like she'd been shopping at the hootchie ho' outlet store.

I was surprised to see Toby in a booth off to the side. A can of Coke and a glass of ice sat beside a cowboy hat on the table. Alone, he watched Jesse's performance with a dark frown on his face.

Carlos sat at the far end of the bar. Empty seats on either side created a protective barricade, as he nursed the one beer he'd keep all night. He alternated between aiming disapproving looks at Jesse, and keeping watch over Toby. I crossed the room.

"Hey." The kiss I planted on his cheek caused a small crack in the granite of his jaw.

"Hey, yourself." He stood, smiled, and took my arm. "Let's get a booth where it's quieter."

With one last lip curl of contempt at Jesse, he steered me to a spot where he could still survey the room.

"That girl is making a spectacle of herself. It's not right." He waited for me to slide in first, and then sat beside me in the booth, both of us looking out. "She needs a Cuban *tía* for a chaperone. She'd be afraid to misbehave."

"*Tía?*"

"Auntie. Nothing gets past them."

"The real shame is that Jesse is a lot smarter and competent than she lets on." I told him about how in-charge she'd been when Toby shot Johnny Jaybird.

Then I nodded toward Toby. "He doesn't look like he's enjoying Jesse's showy side much. I thought you'd have him in jail by now, enjoying bread and water and doing hard labor."

"Well, he's a minor. And I'm not sure about intent. Toby swears he thought the gun was loaded with blanks. The reason he thought that is because it's a replica of the prop gun. The one with the blanks is still in the possession of the prop master. They're really careful about that on movie sets, ever since Brandon Lee was fatally shot on the set of *The Crow*."

"So the copy was loaded?"

He nodded.

"Where'd it come from?"

"Good question. Toby says he found it right outside his trailer before lunch. He decided to pick it up and rehearse with it, thinking it was the gun with blanks."

"So it was planted?"

He picked at the paper label on his beer bottle. "Looks like it."

"By whom?"

He shrugged. "Are you going to investigate, as usual?"

"You can wipe the smirk off your face.

93

This one is all yours. I hate to say it, but I don't really care who murdered that jerk of a producer."

He winked at me. "So you say now. We'll see. Anyway, I still have a lot of questions to answer about how that gun came into Toby's hands. Prosecutors like their i's dotted and t's crossed when it comes to filing formal charges of attempted murder, or even assault."

We both glanced toward Toby, who still hadn't poured his soda. He stared morosely into the glass of ice.

"He's not going anywhere," Carlos said. "Besides, Barbara's protecting him, and she can be pretty persuasive."

I raised my brows. Where was the hard-case Miami detective of a year or so ago? Carlos had tossed my mama into jail on less evidence than he had here. Of course, there were extenuating circumstances with Mama. There always are.

"The kid has had it pretty rough." He sipped his beer. "His parents see him as an investment. The way Barbara tells it, she's the only person in the world who really cares about him."

"Yeah. Earning fifteen percent off him really brings out the maternal instinct."

He leaned back in the booth and frowned.

"What?"

"It's a rare day when you're more cynical than I am. Who's Miami here and who's Himmarshee?"

"Can't help it. I don't trust these Hollywood people. I can't tell their real emotions from their fake."

Across the room, Jesse was trying to pull one of the biggest cowboys up on the bar to dance with her. Instead, he lifted her into the air like she was a fluff of dust. He had one hand on her butt, and the other on a breast as he spun her onto the dance floor. Jesse made no effort to remove either hand.

"My daddy would have whipped me like a mule if I ever acted like that."

"Toby looks like he's considering doing just that," Carlos said.

The young star's eyes were slits. His fists were clenched. Before we could react, he sprang out of the booth, raced across the floor and jumped onto the big cowboy. He looked like a Yorkie going after a Great Dane.

"Get your hands off her!" Toby hung on, pounding one wimpy fist against the cowpoke's broad back.

Jesse wriggled free of the fight, just as Carlos and I rushed the dance floor. We weren't fast enough to stop the cowboy from plucking Toby off his back like an annoying bug. He dangled him two feet off the floor, with Toby squirming like a puppy held by the scruff.

"Don't hit him in the face," Jesse yelled, backing away. "Not in the face!"

Carlos pulled out his detective's gold badge just as the bartender rushed in, hoisting a baseball bat. The cowboy wasn't too drunk to weigh the consequences of going up against either the badge or the bat. He swung Toby a couple of times, then tossed him to the floor. Raising his hands in the air, he stepped away backwards. His friends tightened into a knot around him. I saw Carlos wade in, holding his badge high and shuffling the cowboy toward the door like a calf cut from the herd.

Toby, stunned, was flat on his back like a plopped-over turtle. I offered him my hand. He gathered his breath, and then moaned as I helped him off the dirty floor.

"You're lucky that bulldogger didn't pound you into dirt," I said. "He's a big ol' boy."

"What's a bulldogger?"

"A rodeo cowboy who specializes in wrestling 500-pound steers to the ground."

His mouth dropped open as he stared after the departing cowpoke.

"The Eight Seconds Bar is a rodeo hang-out," I said. "Eight seconds is how long a rider has to stay on a bull or a bronc to qualify."

"That doesn't seem like very long."

"Try it sometime. It feels like an eternity." I supported him as he limped to a seat. "Speaking of getting hurt, how are you?"

He rubbed gingerly at his right elbow, and then leaned down to touch his knee.

I signaled the bartender. "Can we get some ice?"

Toby slowly raised his right arm. "I must have hit the floor on this side of my body."

"What were you thinking?"

His eyes darted toward Jesse. My gaze followed his to find her in the crowd, flirting with a new cowboy. Seemingly forgotten: the fight and Toby's close call with the bull-dogger.

"She's not worth it."

I immediately regretted my words, as Toby's head snapped back toward me. His face reddened. "You don't even know her!"

"I know what I see. She's playing you, Toby."

His eyes got round. "She is not! She cares about me. We're in love."

No wonder Carlos went easy on him. He was like a lamb, gamboling innocently to slaughter. Just as I was wishing I had my sister Marty here to help me find some sensitive, soothing words, the bartender delivered a beer bucket of ice. I divided it into three bar towels, and gave them to Toby.

"Rest those where it hurts."

His beautiful lips curved into half a smile. "I don't think the bar has enough ice for that. I wonder if this is how the bulldogged steer feels?"

I laughed, and felt the tension between us fade. We sat for a few moments. Toby shifted the icy towels to their best advantage, while I checked out the bar scene. I was watching for Carlos to return when the door swung open. Barbara stepped through. Toby saw her, too. His face brightened, and he sat up straighter. He yelled to her and waved. She didn't notice. Paul Watkins was right behind her, and she turned, crooking a finger into his collar to pull him inside.

Paul threw an arm around Barbara's shoulders. She turned to press every inch of her body to his: breast to chest, groin to groin, thigh to thigh. They broke apart, and then beelined to a corner booth.

At our table, a few moments passed in awkward silence. "She must not have seen you," I finally said to Toby. "And the music's really loud in here."

He shrugged. "Barbara's laydar is up."

"Laydar?"

"Yeah, like radar, except it detects the prospects of her getting laid."

I turned my head. Barbara straddled Paul's lap; his hands were under her blouse. Their shared kiss was hot enough to singe the red leather seats in their corner booth.

"It looks to me like her prospects are pretty good," I said.

TWELVE

I tossed the keys to my Jeep into the gaping mouth of Al, my combination coffee table art and conversation piece.

"Nice dunk," Carlos said.

"Thanks."

"That still kills me."

"What? That I'm such an incredible shot?"

He grinned. "No, that you keep a dead alligator's head in your living room like a sculpture. Who does that?"

Before Al was a taxidermy exhibit, he was a nuisance gator, which basically means too many people moved into what used to be Al's Florida domain. My state-trapper cousin and I wrestled the ten-footer out of the swimming pool of a newcomer — who loved the notion of living in a natural setting, until nature came to call.

"Hey, don't they say art is in the eye of the beholder?" I asked.

"I think that's 'beauty' that's in the eye,

niña."

"Well, Al was beautiful, in his way. It's not his fault he crashed some guy's pool party."

Carlos shuddered. "*¡Dios mío!* Lucky no one was killed."

I looked over at Al, in profile. As always, I imagined that beady glass eye of his judging me. *Murderer,* it said.

A plaintive yowl issued from the bedroom. It was followed by another, even louder.

"Hush, Wila!" I made the *Shhhh* sound, to no avail.

Carlos nodded toward the room, where my foster cat was pouting under a pile of dirty clothes. "Is she going to speak to me tonight?"

"Oh, she'll speak, but more likely she'll speak *about* you rather than *to* you."

Wila's Siamese nose was out of joint because the two of us normally had my little cottage to ourselves. Tonight we had company. Carlos and I usually used his apartment in town when we got together. But he was renovating, and his one bathroom was out of commission. I didn't think his landlord would appreciate me peeing in the backyard.

I still couldn't believe I shared my living space with a noisy cat. I'm a dog person. Wila came my way the summer Mama discovered a dead man in her turquoise convertible. With everything else going on back then, it seemed too complicated to try to find the cat a real home. She turned out to be smart and funny, with a personality all her own. Truth is, Wila's grown on me. She's pretty cool, for a cat.

Meowrrrrr.

Well, except for that. Siamese love to hear the sound of their own voices. Kind of like Mama, come to think of it.

Carlos covered his ears.

"She'll settle down after I feed her," I said. "Then she'll get used to you being here. Just don't try to approach her before she's ready."

MEOWRRRRR.

"You don't have to worry about that." Wincing from the sound, he took a seat on the couch.

After I set out the cat's food, I puttered about the kitchen. I grabbed a couple of beers, a can of peanuts, and a roll of paper towels for Carlos and me.

"Don't go to any trouble," he called from the living room.

I looked at the meager offering. Martha Stewart I'm not. "You don't have to worry about that."

The cat waited long enough so she

wouldn't seem desperate. Then, streaking past Carlos like she believed speed made her invisible, she tore into the kitchen to eat. A blessed quiet reigned in my cottage. Nights were getting cool enough to open the windows. Nature sounds filtered in through the screens. A bullfrog croaked from a distant creek. An owl hooted. The breeze ruffled leaves on the oak trees that shade my property.

When I joined Carlos, his head was leaned back on the couch, his eyes closed.

"You asleep?" I whispered.

"Just resting my eyes." He took the bottle of beer I offered, and gave me a weak smile. "Long day."

"Probably be another one tomorrow."

He took a swallow of beer. Closed his eyes again. I waited what I thought was an appropriate time, and then asked, "So, who do you think killed Norman Sydney?"

His eyes slowly opened. He shook his head. "You're kidding me, right?"

"What?"

"Not tonight, Mace. I just want to kick back and unwind. I don't want to be interrogated."

I got a little huffy. "It's hardly an interrogation. It's just one little question."

"I thought you weren't interested in trying to solve this case. You said, and I quote: *Those weird Hollywood people can kill each other off for all I care.*"

"Right. And I'm not getting involved. That doesn't mean I'm not curious, though."

"Curiosity killed the dog."

"Cat," I said. Sometimes Carlos confuses his English-language aphorisms.

"Okay, cat." He rested his head on the back of the couch again.

I looked at his face and saw stress and fatigue written there. Carlos was right. I had vowed to steer clear. And it wasn't worth us arguing over. I clinked my bottle softly against the one he held in his hand.

"Bottom's up," I said. "Let the stress release begin."

By the time we polished off our beers and half the can of peanuts, we were both feeling mellow.

"How about dessert?" Carlos said.

I remembered finishing off a bag of Oreos in front of the TV.

"Sorry, I don't have anything sweet in the house." I picked a stray peanut off his chest.

"I think you do." He looked at me, desire suddenly sparking in those bottomless-pool eyes.

"Oh."

I fed him the peanut. He bit gently at my

fingertip, and then ran his tongue around the nail. With his finger, he traced a trail across my lips, down my chin, and then slowly, slowly along the outside of my throat. I swallowed. When his lips followed the path his finger had made, I shivered, even though my body was the opposite of cold.

"Yeah," he said. "Oh."

He brought his face back to mine. Our lips met. His tasted like peanuts. That wasn't a problem. I could eat peanuts all day.

I stood, held out my hand, and pulled him to his feet. "On second thought," I said, "I might have a sweet treat or two hidden in my bedroom."

"*¡Qué bueno!* I love a treasure hunt."

Afterward, I lay in my bed behind Carlos as he slept. With my thumb, I followed the curlicue of a cowlick at the back of his neck. I straightened it, and then watched it spring right back to its original position.

It struck me that our relationship was a little like that stubborn curl. I could try to force it into something it wasn't, or I could just let it grow the way it wanted to. I listened to the even rhythm of his breathing. Heat from his body warmed me as I pressed my naked body against his. I felt well loved. It seemed like more than just the physical afterglow of sex. Was it real happiness?

I wanted to shower, but I could feel myself dropping off to sleep. I felt the familiar heaviness, the letting-go of muscle tension in my limbs. I was beyond relaxed. Why fight it? My body had just begun floating downward into the mattress's soft embrace when the shrilling of the telephone jarred me back to consciousness.

Beside me, Carlos grumbled and buried his head in a pillow.

The nightstand clock said 10:37 — late for idle chit-chat. I hoped nothing had happened to Mama, or to one of my sisters. The number displayed on the phone was local, but not one I recognized. My hand shook a bit as I picked up the phone and said hello.

"Hey, darlin', long time no see."

I gasped, and felt Carlos's body go rigid beside me. He was wide awake now.

"Well, say something, why don't you?" The caller's tone was light, joshing. "Sorry it's late. I just wanted to call to let you know it looks like we're going to be working together out there on that movie set."

I tried to get my tongue and lips to form

some words. All I managed was a little squeak.

A low, sexy chuckle came over the line, hitting me hard in the memory bank. "I expected a little more of a response to the news than that."

Instinctively, I turned my back to Carlos, hunching my shoulders and tucking the phone close to my mouth. Even in the dim moonlight that shone through the bedroom window, I knew Carlos would be able to read the emotions on my face. If he did, what would he see?

A tapping issued from the phone, like the caller was knocking the mouthpiece against something to make sure it was working.

"Is this thing on? Are you there, Mace?" He paused. "It's me. Jeb Ennis."

THIRTEEN

The Bar J Ranch crew arrived with its own soundtrack. A stock trailer squeaked and rattled as it rolled over rough pasture toward the movie set's cow pen. About two dozen head of Brangus cattle lowed from inside. Hauling the trailer was a big Ford dually, a pickup with four wheels on the rear axle. George Strait's *River of Love* floated out through the open windows of the battered truck. Three cowboys crowded onto the front seat. I recognized the driver of the white truck by his black hat.

"I've got a bad feeling about this, Mace." Maddie squinted at the truck, shading her eyes from the mid-morning sun. "Besides, I thought Jeb lost his ranch. How'd he even get this job?"

I shrugged. I didn't trust my voice. The fact my stomach was in my throat would surely make the words come out funny. Plus, I didn't want to get into a big discussion with my sister about Jeb, the first male to pluck out my heart and stomp on it. Even after all these years, I always ended up making excuses for him, which made me feel like a sap.

Marty smoothed her blond hair behind her ears. "I heard he's been working hard to rebuild Bar J. He'll probably do whatever he can to earn a few extra bucks."

"Humph!" Maddie snorted. "So he can squander them again, no doubt. What a loser."

"Remember Maddie, *'Blessed are the merciful, for they shall obtain mercy.'* "

Mama was capable of chastising Maddie with a verse from Matthew, even as she reached over and rearranged my hair. Then she licked her finger and rubbed at my cheek. "I can't tell if that's dirt or manure, Mace. Either way, it's not a good look."

I jerked away. "Like I care, Mama. This isn't a fashion shoot. I'm working here."

"Humph!" Maddie glared in Jeb's direction, and crossed her arms over her chest. "Oh, you care, sister. That's the problem."

I shrugged again, in what I hoped was a carefree manner.

We were gathered at the corral. The crime scene investigators had finished, even removing the section of fence where we'd found Norman. The movie set's carpenters hurriedly patched it with similarly weathered wood. Mama and my sisters came to help me feed and water the horses. We also worked on preparing saddles and other tack for an upcoming scene.

Mama hadn't done much actual work, unless you count sitting on the fence and telling the rest of us how we were doing everything wrong.

At the corral, I'd filled them in on the details of Jeb's late-night call, omitting the specifics of what I'd been doing in my bedroom just before the phone rang.

"What'd Carlos say?" Marty asked.

"Not a thing," I said. "I ended up walking the phone out to my porch, but you know how small my cottage is. Jeb and I only talked for a few minutes, but I know Carlos heard every word on my end. When we rang off, I remember I called Jeb by name."

"You can be sure Carlos heard you. That man doesn't miss a thing." Clucking her tongue, Mama shook her head. "Too bad, too. It finally seemed like Carlos and you were becoming a real couple."

"Nothing happened, except Mace got a call from an old boyfriend," Marty said. "Carlos won't treat that like it's the end of the world."

Maddie raised her eyebrows at our little sister. "Really? There's already bad blood between Jeb and Carlos. Don't you remember how they went round and round over Mace, the summer Mama found her corpse?"

"That poor man in my convertible trunk had a name, girls. Please don't call him my corpse."

When I told Mama and my sisters about the phone call, I didn't add that when I finished talking to Jeb, Carlos was asleep. Or pretending he was. I tiptoed into the bathroom for a quick shower. When I finished, he was gone. He hadn't even said goodbye.

Now, here was Jeb, climbing from the driver's seat of his truck. We watched as he swung out a long, lean leg. One foot, in a worn Ariat boot, hit the ground. The other soon followed. When he stood up and adjusted those tight jeans over the long lines of his body, my traitorous heart skipped a beat. Dammit.

I heard a low whistle beside me. "Say what you will about the man. He still looks like sex on a stick."

"Mama!" The three of us gasped at once.

"I can't help it, girls. I'm only stating the obvious."

A frown creased Maddie's brow. "Just how close did he say the two of you would be working?"

"Not that close. Once he delivers the cattle, I bet Jeb leaves his ranch hands behind to see to what the movie people need."

"*Riiight,*" Maddie said. "With Kelly Conover and Jesse Donahue here on the set . . ."

"Not to mention the beautiful Mace Bauer . . ." Marty added.

". . . still mooning over her long-ago affair with Jeb; star-crossed lovers since they were teenagers." Maddie clasped a hand over her heart, or at least where her heart would be if she had one.

I didn't want to give Maddie the satisfaction of looking, but my eyes defied my brain. A teenager no more, Jeb was all man as he unloaded his cows. Brangus, a mixture between Angus cattle and the heat-tolerant Brahman, were big and beefy. They looked nothing like the rangy half-wild creatures known as Florida Cracker cattle, which would have been true to the period of Patrick Smith's book. Then again, not much about the movie seemed true to the book.

I could feel Maddie's eyes on me as I watched Jeb. She took her hand from her heart to wag a finger. "Mark my words: That man will stick around, and that'll mean trouble for you."

Greg Tilton was on horseback out in the pasture, rehearsing for his scene. He hadn't lied when he said he was experienced. His hand was easy on the reins, and he had a good seat on the Quarter horse we'd saddled for him.

He was cast as Toby's father. The scene would have him racing at a gallop to the corral, where Toby would be waiting. Tilton was costumed in frontier garb, Florida cow-man style: lace-up boots to keep out the snakes, a slouchy hat to repel the rain, and a braided leather cow whip coiled on his saddle.

Of course, he should have been riding a little Cracker horse, like in the book. But Tilton was a big, muscular guy. He'd dwarf such a small horse. Plus, the horse's gait is like a pogo stick. Bouncing around the saddle like a little kid's jack-in-the-box wouldn't befit a movie hero.

Pulling up at the corral, he swung easily out of the saddle. Mama and my sisters were a distance away at the supply trailer, supposedly measuring out horse feed for the evening. But I saw them whispering and pointing. I hoped none of them asked Til-ton for an autograph.

As everyone stood around waiting for lights, camera, and director to be ready, Til-ton leaned against the rustic fence with the horse's reins in one hand, his hat in the other. He looked posed: The Florida Cow-hunter on the Open Range.

Suddenly, a warm breath of air on the back of my neck distracted me from stargaz-ing. I caught the faintest scent of sweat and hay, with just a hint of cow manure. I knew exactly who was there.

"Boo!"

My heart pitter-patted, dammit.

"Your cattle all settled?" I asked.

"Easy breezy," Jeb answered. "How'd you know it was me?"

"I'm psychic."

He came around to face me. "How about the horses? Any trouble?"

"Not unless you count the body we found draped over their corral yesterday."

"Yeah, I heard about that. Guess some-body wanted to make sure he'd be seen."

"I wish they'd have done it someplace else. People are starting to think Mama and I are some kind of Grim Reapers."

"This is the second murder y'all have been mixed up in, right?"

"I wouldn't say we're 'mixed up' in this one. We were just unlucky enough to stumble on the body. And it's the fourth."

Jeb took a step backward and whistled. "Four? Now, you know I love being around you, Mace. But maybe you shouldn't stand so close."

I'd have been offended, but his smile took any meanness out of the jibe. And what a smile it was: white teeth in a face tanned by hard work in the Florida outdoors; sunlight dancing in the golden flecks of his eyes. There went my heart again. It had a mind of its own, dammit.

"Hey, you're the one who came over here to me." I put my hand in the center of his chest and gave a gentle push. "I don't recall issuing you an invitation to stand close."

He grasped my wrist, and pulled my hand tighter against his chest. I couldn't help but notice the heat of his body, and how lean and hard the muscles felt beneath the snap buttons of his cowboy shirt. I remembered how easily those buttons popped open.

Jeb leaned toward me. His lips were inches from my ear, his breath hot against my cheek. "Since when do old friends like us need an invitation?"

Over his shoulder, I caught a glimpse of Mama and my sisters. The three of them

115

scowled at me like Puritans preparing to pin on a scarlet letter. I turned, but not before I saw Maddie mouth *You're crazy.* Mama shook her head at me. Marty bit her lip and looked worried.

As soon as I got the chance, I was going to tell them there was nothing to worry about. Yes, I was still physically attracted to Jeb. He was my first lover, and he was still flat-out gorgeous. But he was also more trouble than he was worth. And I was in love with Carlos. I'd never risk what I had with him for a quick roll in the hay.

"Back off, cowpoke." I pushed him, hard enough to show I meant it this time.

Surprise played across his face. I was a little hurt I didn't see disappointment there, too. I wanted him to give up on me, but not *that* easily.

"I thought we were friends." His mouth drooped down at the corners.

" 'Friends' being the operative word. I'm involved with someone, Jeb."

"That Spanish cop from Miamuh. Still?"

"Yeah. His name's Carlos. And he's Cuban, though he speaks Spanish."

"It's serious?"

I thought that over for a moment. An image from last night came into my mind, of us spooned together in my bed. A warm feeling washed over me. Desire, yes, but contentment, too.

"Yeah," I said, "we're serious."

"Lucky guy."

"Lucky me. Which is why I'm trying hard not to screw things up," I said. "I'll ask you to respect that."

Jeb put up his hands. "I surrender. You're the boss, and your wish is my command."

"Yeah, right." We both laughed, falling into an easy familiarity. "So how come you're still here? I thought for sure you'd deliver the stock and head back to the ranch. You still have that former prom queen at home, waiting on you to marry her?"

He took off his hat; ran a hand through his dusty blond hair. "Yeah, but I don't think I'm the marrying kind, Mace."

"No duh."

Avoiding my eyes, he glanced around at the assembled actors and extras, the camera operators and grips. My gaze followed his. Paul Watkins was deep in conversation with Toby, and Barbara was right beside the two of them. Tilton's horse, still saddled, was inside the corral, though I didn't see the action star. Jeb's eyes continued roaming the set.

"Looking for somebody?"

He grinned, a bit sheepish. The cowboy

117

hat went back on his head. "I thought maybe Kelly Conover might be around."

"You're a hound, you know that?"

"I never claimed to be anything but," he said.

Finally, a call went out across the set. "Settle, everybody!"

High above us, a huge light on a crane powered on, washing the scene with brightness. A clipboard-carrying production assistant rushed toward me, speaking into the radio headset she wore. She stopped, and said to me, "They're shooting Toby's scene, where he's waiting for his father at the corral. That horse with the saddle has to be moved out of there."

"No problem," I said. "I'm on it."

As I started toward the corral, Jeb brushed my cheek with his lips. "For old time's sake," he whispered.

I kept walking. Maddie glared. Marty gnawed her lip. Mama crooked a finger and beckoned me toward them. I shook my head and continued toward the horse, grateful that at least Mama wasn't yelling this time.

My fingers rose to my cheek. The spot Jeb kissed felt warm. Dammit.

I was almost to the gate of the corral when a loud boom sounded from above. In an instant, all hell broke loose. The horses spooked, racing in a panic around the small enclosure. People started screaming. Shadows seemed to be falling toward me from the sky. I heard Mama's voice rise above the others: "Watch out, Mace!"

I didn't know whether to run or duck. The space around me suddenly got hot. Involuntarily, my eyes squeezed shut. An explosive force struck from one side, propelling me off my feet and into the air.

FOURTEEN

I coughed, gasping for breath. A suffocating weight crushed my body. When I opened my eyes, all I saw was dirt. My mouth was full of it. Had I already died and been buried in the earth? But then slowly, the smell of hay and sweat and a trace of manure reached my nose.

"Are you all right?"

Jeb's voice floated toward me from somewhere above. Maybe I wasn't dead after all, since I suspected Jeb was unlikely to be upstairs with the angels. It took a moment to orient myself. The weight I felt holding me down was Jeb's body on mine. The rodeo champion buckle on his belt dug into my right hip. I shifted slightly to look out over the ground. My head moved, which was a good sign. I saw three familiar pairs of shoes leading a pack of feet running toward me. Marty's boots looked like doll shoes. Maddie's were the same style, but bulldozer-sized. Mama sported sling-back sandals in raspberry patent leather.

Unless there was a shoe store in heaven peddling sherbet-colored footwear, I was still alive. Jeb rolled off me.

"Mace?" Jeb asked again.

"Yeah, I guess I'm okay," I answered slowly. "What happened?"

He sat up. Shaky, I stayed where I was, stretched out on the ground.

"That big light up there blew up." He pointed skyward, to the crane above our heads.

I'd barely begun to comprehend what he said when the crowd of feet arrived. Marty led the way. "Oh, sister, I was so scared!"

Mama was next. "Jeb, tell me my baby's not hurt."

Maddie, panting, brought up the rear: "I predicted trouble for Mace the moment I saw *him* on this movie set."

"Hush!" Mama scolded her. "Jeb probably saved your sister's life."

"I wouldn't say that, ma'am." Modestly, he ducked his chin and reached across the ground for his cowboy hat.

"Oh, yes you did," Marty said. "You were just like the action hero in a movie, shielding Mace from harm."

"Hello?" I gave a weak wave. "Remember

me?" I heard a murmur of voices in a growing crowd. Someone said, "The wrangler's alive. Radio Barbara, and tell her there'll be another delay."

Marty crouched beside me. "Of course we remember you! Look at these shards of glass all around you, Mace."

Pieces of the light, heat-blackened and jagged, littered the ground. The largest had fallen exactly where I'd been standing. I raised myself up to my elbows to get a better look. When I turned my head to the left, pain stabbed at my neck and right shoulder. I grabbed at it. "Ow!"

Jeb put his hand on the ache, gently massaging. "I hit you like an offensive lineman. You're really gonna hurt in the morning."

From my vantage point on the ground, I saw a highly polished pair of men's loafers working their way through the crowd. I recognized them from last night, when they'd been lined up under my bed.

Just then, Jeb put an arm around my waist, pulling me to a standing position. My eyes traveled up from those loafers to dark gray dress slacks, to the badge buckled on the belt at Carlos's waist. Still a little weak at the knees, I swayed. Jeb clutched at me, pressing me close against his side.

Carlos got to us just as Jeb tenderly picked

122

a clod of dirt from my hair.

"You should have seen it, Carlos! Jeb was so brave."

As Mama's words rushed out, a scowl worked its way across my boyfriend's face.

"That light blew up and nearly killed her," Maddie added. "Jeb knocked her clean out of the way. Good thing he's used to mugging cattle."

Jeb tightened his embrace. Carlos's frown deepened.

"You okay, Mace?" he asked.

Jeb spoke before I could answer. "She's fine. I was in the right place at the right time."

"So it seems."

I tried to wriggle out of Jeb's hold, but I didn't have all my strength back. And, as Maddie had pointed out so flatteringly, Jeb is accomplished at roping and restraining reluctant heifers. He held on tight. The two men locked eyes. Carlos was the first to look away.

"I need to go find out what happened with that light."

"Wait . . ." I started to say.

"Your cowboy friend seems to have everything here under control."

"Carlos, stop . . ." My words bounced off his back as he turned and stalked away.

123

We stood silent until Mama spoke: "Well, he sure didn't stay long."

Jeb shifted, but kept me in his hold. "Who put the burr under his saddle?"

"You did, Jeb." Maddie assumed her lecturing posture. "Have y'all ever heard of something called the savior complex? Well, Carlos has got it."

"He thinks he's our Lord Jesus?" Mama gasped.

"No, because of events that happened in his past, he thinks he should be able to save everybody. Psychologically, he needs to feel like a protector. But he wasn't here when Mace needed protection."

"Paging Sigmund Freud," I said. "We've got an amateur trying to practice psycho-analysis."

"Glad to see you haven't lost your knack for sarcasm," Maddie said. "Criticize me all you want, but let me remind you: I studied psychology and human behavior in college while you were off communing in the forest with the plants and animals. Carlos may be mad at himself, but you're the one he'll end up punishing, Mace."

As Maddie's words hung in the air, I glanced at Marty. Eyes glued to Carlos as he pushed his way through the crowd, she was working on her bottom lip like it was a hunk of taffy.

Jeb was back with his cows; I was back to myself. And now I was angry. Had someone deliberately tried to hurt me? Was it personal? Or, was the light blowing up over the corral at just that moment a coincidence in a string of convenient coincidences? I intended to find out.

"Barbara, do you have a minute?"

Norman Sydney's ex-wife was stalking across the set, a can of Coke in one hand and an ice-pack in the other. She rolled her eyes and checked her wristwatch. "I'm on my way to see Toby. I have thirty seconds. What can I do for you?"

Learn some manners, I thought. But I said, "You heard about the light this morning?"

She nodded. "I wasn't far away when it exploded. I saw for myself you weren't seriously injured, as did many other witnesses."

"I'm not interested in suing you, Barbara. I want to know, do you think the light was sabotaged?"

"What's your name again?"

I told her.

"Ah, yes. Somebody told me about you. You're some kind of hillbilly detective, right?"

"Guess so." I didn't bother correcting her about our dearth of hills.

"Well, Mace, the more salient question is whether this latest incident is linked to Norman's murder. If so, it means someone wants to impact the movie, maybe even shut it down. Frankly, you're not important enough to the film to be a target."

Was that supposed to make me feel better? "Well, who is?"

"Lots of people. The actors, the director, me."

"You?"

She shrugged. "I was Norman's business partner. I control the money. And in Hollywood, like everywhere else on earth, everything comes down to money." She looked at her watch. "Your thirty seconds are up, Marsha."

"Mace."

"Whatever."

As she started away, I said, "Just one more thing. If it was deliberate, who has a motive? Who'd want to shut you down?"

She stopped, and slowly turned. Her eyes avoided mine. "I really don't want to say."

"Look, this is important."

She glanced around, like she was checking for eavesdroppers. We were alone outside, about fifty feet from the production office trailer. After I'd convinced my sisters I was okay, they returned to town. Mama had disappeared somewhere. Sal was out on the road to the ranch with the cops and movie security people, fending off reporters and curious townsfolk. Carlos was talking to the electrical chief who supervises lighting and powering for the set.

"I'm the last person to gossip," Barbara leaned toward me and whispered, "but Greg Tilton is unhappy with some of the cuts that have been made to his role. He made his feelings quite clear to Norman, and now to me. More importantly, I saw him skulking around this morning by the lighting equipment. What business did he have there?"

She positioned her wristwatch under my nose. "Now, I've got to run. Time is money, Marsha."

Mace.

Perks reflect an actor's place on Hollywood's totem pole. Lesser stars share trailers. Big ones relax in spacious luxury. Finding which trailer at base camp was Tilton's didn't take long, given my great powers of deduction. That, plus his name was above the red star on his door.

I climbed three metal steps to the door, and knocked.

127

"I'm rehearsing," came a muffled voice from inside.

"It's Mace, the animal wrangler." I yelled through the door. "I'm the one who was nearly killed by that light this morning. This won't take but a minute."

Footsteps echoed from inside. The door opened. Tilton was still in his period costume. I guess the wardrobe people figured the rougher and more rumpled his clothes looked, the more believable he was as a Florida frontiersman. Those famous blue eyes assessed me. It was surreal. I still struggled to get my mind around the fact I was standing face to face with the most famous action hero on the planet.

"I heard about the accident," he said. "You okay?"

I rolled my neck, lifted my shoulders. Winced. "I'll live."

"Good to hear." He stood back, motioning me inside.

The place looked like a high-end man cave. Black-out shades covered most of the windows. A glossy leather recliner was positioned in front of a big-screen TV. The black granite top of a coffee table gleamed. A fat script, a heavy rocks glass, and an expensive-looking bottle of Scotch, *Glen*-something, sat atop the table.

He nodded at the bottle. "Want a drink?"

"I'll pass on the Scotch, but some water would be great."

As he went to fetch a bottled water for me from the fridge, I checked out the living area. The room was neat, nearly devoid of human touches. No jacket was tossed over a chair. No open book rested on an arm of the sofa. The only thing out of place was a white coffee cup, which had been washed and set to dry on a dish drainer in a double sink.

Maybe all those years rotating through foster families had taught Tilton to never become too much at home.

My eyes were drawn to the one thing in the room that seemed personal: a display rack over a door that led to a small bedroom showed off a mounted, kid's-style rifle. I pointed at it when Tilton returned.

"Is that little .22 rifle from a role?"

"Nah, I've had that since I was a boy. It's about the only link to my childhood that has good memories attached."

"How so?"

He set a coaster on the black granite, placed the glass of iced water on that. Looking at the rifle, he smiled. "One of my first families, the foster dad was a good guy. Rural. Salt of the earth. He taught me to

129

hunt, and he taught me about firearms."

My surprise must have shown on my face. He chuckled.

"Remember Charlton Heston? He was a president of the National Rifle Association. Our director, Paul Watkins, collects guns from all the movies he's done. Not everyone in Hollywood is a Second Amendment-hating liberal."

"I didn't think they were," I lied.

"Right. Anyway, they gave me that old Winchester for Christmas. It was a hand-me-down from one of their 'real' kids, but it meant a lot to me." He reached up, brushed a speck of dust from the barrel. "It still does."

I wasn't sure what to say. I thought of Mama and my sisters, and the father I'd loved so much. I couldn't imagine not having kin, a close family to call your own. Silence hung between us. He hadn't taken a seat, so I didn't either. Both of us were still standing.

My eyes shifted from the rifle to a series of promotional posters from his most famous roles. They filled the walls where family photos or paintings might be displayed.

I stepped closer to the wall to check out the Greg Tilton filmography.

"Pretty lame, huh?"

"Hey, you've had a great career. I can see how you'd be proud."

He sat in his leather recliner. "Just so you know, someone in my publicist's office had already hung them when I got to the set. It makes me feel like some kind of museum piece. Nothing like having a pictorial record of growing old, in 27x40-inch frames."

Funny about perception: When Tilton looked at the posters, he saw himself aging. I saw him saving the world. I had to shake off that good-guy image if I was going to question him about what I'd come to find out. I circled back to stand in front of his chair.

"Look, don't take this the wrong way, but did you have anything to do with that light blowing up this morning?"

He cocked an eyebrow. "Man, you don't waste any time, do you?"

"Life's short."

"What makes you think I'd have anything to do with that?"

I weighed revealing what Barbara had told me. Why was I worried about protecting a woman who never asked how I was, who couldn't even be bothered to get my name right?

"Barbara said she saw you hanging around the lighting gear." I filled him in on what she claimed was a possible motive that he'd want the picture shut down.

When I'd finished, he smirked at me. "A highly reliable source, Barbara."

"What do you mean?"

He poured himself a glass of whiskey, pointed the bottle toward the sofa next to his recliner. "Have a seat. You're making me nervous."

I sat, stiffly. I was sure to have a bruise where Jeb knocked me down. Not taking my eyes off Tilton's, I waited for him to answer.

"Listen, I've been in Hollywood a long time. I'm used to people lying about me, spreading gossip. I'm not surprised the same bullshit is happening here. But that's all it is." He took a swallow of the Scotch. "I'm completely happy with my role in this film. I wanted the part, and I wanted to work with the other actors they've hired."

"Even Toby?"

"Especially Toby. He's the next Leo Di-Caprio."

I searched his face for evidence he was lying, or being sarcastic. I didn't see it.

"Maybe you should ask Barbara what she was doing when she claimed she saw me."

"Barbara? What would she have to gain?"

"She wanted out of this production almost

from the start. It's bleeding money, and she never believed there'd be an audience for the film once it's finished. You know she and Norman were still in business together, right?"

I nodded.

"Well, they fought like crazy about even taking on this project. Barbara would have had a good reason to see her ex-husband dead. Now that he is, she'd be a lot better off financially if this movie would just go away."

He drank again, his blue eyes beaming sincerity at me from above the rim of his glass.

FIFTEEN

Leaving Tilton's trailer, I looked up to see clouds massing and a helicopter circling. Stymied on the ground, the media was taking to the air to try to get pictures of the private ranch where *Fierce Fury Past* was filming.

When the sun peeked out, I caught a quick flash from the corner of my eye of a sparkling diamond earring and chestnut-colored hair.

"Hey, you!"

As Savannah Watkins turned toward me, a wide smile lit her face. "Girl, I am so happy to see you standing on two feet. I heard about your close call. You must feel as lucky as a cat on a cream truck."

"Yeah, I should buy a lottery ticket," I said. "Listen, you knew Norman pretty well, didn't you?"

She nodded, thick hair swinging against her cheek.

"How about his ex-wife?"

"Oh, I know Barbara. Everybody in Hollywood knows Barbara. Why do you ask?"

I'd only met Savannah the day before, but for some reason I felt I could trust her. Maybe it was the Southern accent. Maybe it was her friendly, down-to-earth manner. She didn't seem like the rest of the Hollywood crowd.

"You want to grab a quick cup of coffee?" I asked.

As the chopper made another loud pass, Savannah glanced upward. I did, too. It was flying low enough that I spotted a cameraman. He'd slid the door open on the passenger's side, and was aiming a long lens our way.

"Vultures!" Savannah spit out the word.

"Don't worry," I said. "The cattleman who owns this ranch is politically connected. There's also a colony of endangered wood storks in a swamp on his land. It won't be long before he pulls the right strings to shut down the air space up there."

"Really?" Savannah looked impressed.

I nodded. "Environmental concerns."

We made our way to the craft services truck, and helped ourselves to a couple of coffees. Once we were seated comfortably in two chairs in the shade, I detailed my suspicions about sabotage. I told her how Norman's ex-wife had pointed me toward Tilton, who in turn had aimed me right back toward Barbara.

"What do you think?" I asked. "Is somebody trying to derail this movie?"

Savannah blew on her coffee and took a sip. Balancing the cup gingerly between her knees, she poured in another packet of sugar. "Girl, your mama wasn't kidding when she said you're a detective. Didn't you say you were going to stay out of it?"

It wasn't clear from her voice if she was being critical or just curious. When I looked at her, though, she grinned.

"I don't always do what I say I'm going to do," I shrugged.

Her tone got serious. "Well, Barbara was right when she said money is king in Hollywood. And Greg hit the mark about this picture being Norman's baby, not hers. She didn't want to do it, and she didn't want Paul as the director, either. With Norman dead, I'm sure she'd love to pull the plug, but she can't. Contractual obligations."

"Would a murder and a string of accidents make it easier for her to shut it down?"

"Maybe. But plenty of productions have gone on after horrible accidents, or the deaths of their stars. In the '80s, a helicopter crashed and killed Vic Morrow and two young kids on the set of *Twilight Zone.* They finished that film. When Heath Ledger died from drugs, he'd just completed his part on *The Dark Knight;* but he was only halfway through a Terry Gilliam film. Both of those projects went on to be released."

A dim memory surfaced. "Didn't that helicopter decapitate somebody?"

She shuddered. "Yeah, Vic Morrow, the star; and one of the child actors, too."

Thinking about that gruesome scene, suddenly the shock of finding Norman's body hanging on the fence didn't seem so horrible after all.

Sipping her coffee, Savannah stared into the distance. "It might be different with a murder, though," she said thoughtfully. "The fear of who might be next could be debilitating to the production. More importantly for Barbara, it could also raise an issue of liability."

"How so?"

"Well, what if it turns out someone *is* stalking victims? Suppose nothing is done to ensure the safety of the crew and the actors. If anyone else were to die or get injured, their family would certainly have grounds to sue the production company for negligence."

I remembered how quickly Barbara assumed I was going to sue over the light.

"Barbara told me any number of people could be possible targets. I've been wondering more about who might be a suspect," I said. "Who hated Norman Sydney that much?"

Savannah pursed her lips. "That's a long line, honey."

"Yeah, but hated him enough to commit murder?"

Her expression became wary. She glanced over each shoulder. We were alone, sitting off by ourselves in the shade of a big oak tree. Unless someone was perched among the leaves — I quickly scanned the branches above, just to be sure — we couldn't be overheard.

"Norman had issues with women," she finally said.

"Like he cheated? He was a player?"

"Worse. Let's just say he had some dark tastes when it came to sex. Very young women. Multiple partners." She cupped a hand to her mouth, whispering the last words. "Not all the girls were willing."

The disgust must have registered on my face. She nodded. "Awful, right? But it's true; the Hollywood casting couch at its worst. Many a starlet got her first big break in a Norman Sydney production. He made sure they paid for the opportunity."

"Kelly Conover?"

"I don't know for sure. Probably."

"Jesse Donahue?"

Savannah nodded decisively. "And it wasn't just girls. Norman had many wealthy, powerful friends with a taste for young men. He threw parties, stocked with hopeful young actors."

I thought of Greg Tilton. Was that possible? Then, Toby's smooth-cheeked face popped into my mind. My stomach clenched in revulsion and anger. If what Savannah said was true, Norman Sydney was a sexual predator. His murder suddenly seemed like deserving punishment.

"He wasn't a nice man, Mace. Lots of people on this set could have wanted to kill him."

"It's weird, Savannah. When I try to think about which of these stars might have done it, it's hard for me to see them as real people. I keep getting them mixed up with their public images."

Those larger-than-life movie posters in Tilton's trailer ran like a slideshow behind my eyes. I blinked them away.

"I know what you mean," Savannah said. "I've been part of the industry for a long time; now mostly by marriage. But when I look at Toby, for example, I see him the way he's usually cast: a troubled boy turning into a man, who always ends up doing the right thing."

"Right," I said. "I saw him just like that, playing a part in a TV show where he was in a juvenile detention center. He ended up saving a younger kid from a brutal guard."

"*Locked Up,*" Savannah said. "What's Kelly Conover's image?"

"Fragile, but with deep reserves of inner strength," I supplied.

"Exactly. Like the beaten single mother who had to track down the molester who kidnapped her daughter."

"*The Screwbox,*" I easily filled in the title, even though I'm not as big a movie buff as Mama and my sisters. "How about Jesse?" I asked her.

Savannah's pretty face darkened. "Jesse's got a big problem. No one even remembers she was a talented young actress once. All the public sees is her climbing out of a car without undies, or shoving drunkenly at the paparazzi as she stumbles out of some night-club."

"You know, Jesse's a lot smarter than she lets on." I told Savannah about Jesse's father, the emergency room doctor, and the

140

girl's own medical expertise.

"You'd never know it. Jesse better figure out whether she wants to be Jodie Foster or Lindsay Lohan." A brief flash of anguish crossed Savannah's face. "Jesse told Paul she wanted this role to help her get back to practicing her 'craft.' I hope she can do that, become a respected actress again."

I wondered about that flicker of pain. Had Savannah once had her own Hollywood dreams?

"Did you ever want to be an actress?" I asked.

"Hell no!" She chuckled. "I'd rather die than drag my ass down a red carpet."

"What about Tilton? Did he want this movie for the same reason as Jesse? Did he want to stretch as an actor?"

"No, it's simpler for him. He needs a hit."

"Barbara doesn't think it will be a hit," I said. "She also said Tilton's not happy that Toby's getting more and more screen time."

Savannah shrugged, raked her fingers through that glossy hair. "That's the business, Mace. Movie stars age in dog years. And there's always another young pup barking at the old dog's heels."

"But Tilton is a legend. He's saved the world in about a million different ways. The guy is *always* the hero."

Savannah clucked her tongue, just like Mama does. "C'mon, honey, you aren't that naïve, are you? You do know that real life is nothing like the movies, right?"

Sixteen

A ring of masked bandits surrounded Kelly Conover and Greg Tilton. The thieves were insistent, demanding the two stars hand over the good stuff.

Tilton tossed an apple slice at one of them.

Kelly squealed. "Ohmigod, how cute is that?"

"That little guy should go out for the Yankees," Tilton said.

Sitting back on its hind legs, a raccoon had snagged the snack in a front paw, like Cal Ripken Jr. at shortstop. He'd already polished off that slice, and was angling for another one. I'd seen enough.

"Those are wild animals, not pets." I could hear the lecturing tone in my own voice, but I didn't care. "You two are turning them into beggars."

"Oh, but look how sweet they are! See their little black masks?" Kelly asked.

"Yeah. They're wearing them because

they're embarrassed. Raccoons are only a step up from rats. Keep giving them food, and they'll have all their buddies swarming the place before you can say 'suckers.' "

"You're nothing like a rat, are you, buddy?" Tilton threw another piece of apple.

With a threat of rain in the air, I'd been taking a wooded shortcut to check on the horses in the corral. I came upon the two stars and their pack of raccoons in a clearing. Like everyone I ever caught at Himmarshee Park trying to feed the alligators or any other animal, Kelly and Tilton wanted to convince me they weren't doing any harm.

"It's just a few pieces of fruit," she said. "No big deal."

"It is a big deal," I said. "Wild animals are meant to forage for natural sources of food, not depend on humans for hand-outs. You're making them dependent, and also taking away their fear of humans. That's not good for people, or for the animals."

"Who made you boss of the forest?" Tilton asked, crossing his arms. Kelly giggled.

I was going to scare them with a story about a seventy-four-year-old woman in Lakeland, Fla., who'd been mauled by a gang of wild raccoons. All she'd tried to do was shoo them from begging for food at her front door. I was distracted, though, by a quick flash of pink and a blur of movement through the woods.

Peering into the trees, I saw the tall, good-looking guy who had tried to calm Kelly after Mama and I discovered Norman's body.

He crouched, and watched us from the shadows. Apparently he didn't realize his bright pink shirt made him easier to spot than a city slicker at the rodeo. When he saw me staring, he stood up and emerged from the trees into the clearing.

"I heard arguing," he said. "Is everything all right, Kelly?"

Tilton's mouth tightened. "Everything's under control, Sam."

"I'm fine, sweetie." Kelly gave him a warm smile. "We're just getting yelled at about how we're destroying all of the outdoors by feeding a couple of pieces of fruit to a few raccoons."

"Just watch," I said. "This handful here will turn into a crowd by tomorrow. By the next day, it'll be a mob. You'll wish you'd never seen their little masked faces."

Sam didn't say anything. His eyes bored into Tilton. The star took an uneasy step away from Kelly, putting some space between them.

Brushing some dirt off a fallen pine tree, Kelly sat. "What are you working on?" she asked Sam.

"Not much, yet. Between the weather and . . . well, what happened . . . Paul's only been able to shoot a few scenes. There'll be some good stuff from that scene Johnny Jaybird shot, though."

"How is Johnny?" I asked.

All three of them turned to me, blank looks on their faces.

"As a director?" Tilton asked.

"*Noooo,* as the victim of a gunshot." These Hollywood people were too much. Unless something directly involved them, they weren't interested.

"Oh, yeah. Of course," Kelly said. "He's doing well, thank God. They say he'll only be out a couple of days."

"So Jesse was right when she said it was just a flesh wound. He's lucky," I said.

She shrugged, and tossed one of the raccoons a slice of the orange she was eating. Tilton laughed, and gave her arm a playful jab. "You'd better watch out. Mace is going to take you to the woodshed."

I glanced at Sam. Brow furrowed, body tense, he looked like he'd like to launch Tilton to that same woodshed from the end of one of his clenched fists. Kelly's gaze followed mine.

"Sam, I missed lunch. Would you be a sweetheart and go back to my trailer and make us something? I'll meet you there in a little while."

Sam smiled at her. "You're hungry?"

"Starving!"

"That's a good sign. I'll grab some stuff from craft services. How about one of my famous cheese and veggie wraps?"

"Yum, yum, yum." Kelly licked her lips. Both men stared at her tongue.

As Sam went off down the trail, she called after him. "Don't forget to use low-fat cheese. And put the sugar-free salad dressing on the veggies, okay?"

Why bother eating?

Sam signaled with a thumb up. "I know, Kelly. I remember."

"He remembers a lot of things," Tilton muttered under his breath. "What's he even doing here, besides shadowing you? That guy's totally in love with you, Kelly."

Watching Sam disappear into the trees, she shook her golden curls. "I doubt that, Greg. Even if he is, what am I supposed to do about it?"

"You could try telling him the truth."

I was hoping they'd forgotten I was there,

and would reveal something interesting. But Kelly whispered, making a joke. "Please, Greg, not in front of the children." Her gesture took in the raccoons and me.

He laughed, and the secret confessions mood was broken. I was still racking my brain for the scoop on these two. Had they ever been a couple? Mama had nothing stored in her vast reservoir of Greg Tilton trivia, which made me think they hadn't. Or, at least not publicly. I decided to find out if maybe all those *People* magazines stashed at Hair Today might have missed something.

"How long have you two worked together?" Starting innocently, I'd inch my way to more personal questions.

"Don't Go in the Water." Tilton mimicked a deep-voiced movie announcer.

"Say what?"

"That was the title of our first film together. What was it, Kelly? Fifteen, sixteen years ago?"

"Twenty-one."

"Man, we're old!"

"Speak for yourself," she said. "I'm ten years younger than you."

He gave her a long look.

"Well, almost." She smiled slyly. "Anyway, all I remember from that shoot is I nearly

148

froze my ass off, and I screamed a lot."

"You were a great screamer. Not bad in a bikini, either." He waggled his eyebrows at her.

"How'd you have time to notice? You got killed in the first reel."

"Yeah, my character didn't even have a name. I was Surfer No. 2."

As they went deeper into memory mode, I studied their body language, searching for outward signs of their relationship. Were they friends? Foes? Lovers? Tilton had joined Kelly on the fallen log. Their knees weren't touching, but they were close. The two of them seemed more chummy today than they had the first time I saw them together.

"So, you've been friends a long time?"

"Long enough," Kelly said.

"Long enough to know where each other's skeletons are buried," Tilton added.

Before I could start to unearth some of those skeletons, Kelly looked at her wristwatch. "Gotta shove off," she said. "I don't want to keep Sam waiting."

"You've kept him waiting for years. What's another few minutes?"

She punched her co-star in the arm. Judging from his grimace, it wasn't a playful punch. "You must not have heard me ask you nicely to stop discussing private matters." Her voice was cold; no trace of the famous laugh.

"Don't mind me." I made the lock sign over my lips. "I'm a vault."

"Yeah, we've heard that before, haven't we, Kelly?"

She ignored him, turned to me. "Look, I'm sure you're a nice woman. But people like us don't spill our guts to people like you."

People like me?

"People like you," I drew out the words, "who don't know enough to stay away from wild animals, shouldn't be allowed out into the woods. By the way, those adorable little critters you love so much can also carry rabies. Be careful."

"Are you taking notes, Greg?" Kelly asked sweetly. "Wouldn't it be embarrassing if the world's most famous action hero was done in by a raccoon?"

Seventeen

I'd almost reached the corral when a snippet of conversation floated toward me through the trees.

"I'm not saying you should be a nun. Just don't make a fool out of me."

The voice was Toby's, striking a note between defiance and desperation. I ducked behind a myrtle bush, scaring a redbird into flight. Peeking through a branch, I saw the young star, still wearing his cowboy hat from the night before at the Eight Seconds Bar. A waterfall of red hair revealed his partner.

Looking nothing like a nun, Jesse wore a spaghetti-strap T-shirt, braless, and a pair of skinny jeans. A snake tattoo curved up around her belly button above the jeans' hip-hugger waist. She leaned against the fence of the corral, right next to Toby. They held hands, fingers entwined.

"I'd never make a fool of you, Toby. I

made a promise."

Whatever her vow had been, Jesse sounded like she sincerely meant to keep it. Then again, she was a professional actress. And I'd seen her performing last night at the bar.

They stood for a few moments without talking. The clouds in the sky were darkening. I noticed a fire ant mound on the ground just a foot or two away from my hiding spot. If these two weren't going to reveal anything more compelling, staking them out wasn't worth getting soaked by rain or feasted on by ants.

"Hey," Toby's face lit up with excitement. "Wouldn't it be cool to take a couple of these horses out for a ride?"

Jesse turned to survey the animals inside the corral. She shook her head. "No way. We'll get into trouble."

The surprise I felt showed on Toby's face, too. "Since when has getting in trouble ever stopped you? C'mon, Jess!"

When he started to clamber up the fence, I knew I needed to put a stop to his plan. Stepping onto the path, I called out, like I'd just happened upon them. "Can I help you with something, Toby?"

He quickly jumped off the fence. Sticking his hands into the pockets of his jeans, he shot me a guilty look. Now I knew how my sister, the principal, felt when she busted kids for sneaking cigarettes in the bathroom.

"I just wanted to pet some of the horses," he lied.

"That's fine. But I need to be at the corral if you want to get close to them. I'm responsible for making sure none of the horses — or the humans — get hurt out here."

He tugged at Jesse's hand. "Let's go inside and check them out. Okay if we do that, Mace?"

"It's okay with me." I looked at Jesse. It didn't seem okay with her. She held on to Toby's hand, but dug in her high-heeled boots when he tried to lead her to the corral's gate.

"You know, we should really get going." She shot a nervous glance at the biggest horse, a Percheron that had been cast to pull a plow in a farm scene.

"You can stay on this side of the fence," I said to Jesse. "I'll lead him over to you, if you want."

"Nah, I'm not in the mood." She waved her hand like she couldn't be bothered with the big draft horse. I've been around enough horse-shy people to recognize the signs, though. Jesse was afraid of horses.

"No problem," I said. "Maybe another time."

"Whatev." She tugged Toby away from the fence, and then turned to me.

"Besides, I'd rather talk to you than to some stupid horse. I've been wanting to ask you something since this morning."

"Ask away," I said.

"How did it feel when that light almost killed you?" Her eyes gleamed with curiosity.

"Well, I'm not sure I had the time to really 'feel' anything at that moment. I can tell you I'm feeling a little stiff right now, from taking that tumble onto the hard ground."

"But what were you *thinking?* Did you think you were about to die?"

"That's a weird question."

"Well, did you?" she insisted. "Did you think about all the things you wouldn't ever get to do? Did you feel sad? Were you frightened?"

I glanced at Toby. He shrugged, seemingly embarrassed by her burning intensity.

"How the hell do I know?" I snapped at her. "Listen, even on my best days, I'm not big on talking about how things 'feel.' Plus, it happened so fast, I didn't have time to get all emotional."

"Oh." Her face fell.

She looked so dejected, I threw her a bone. "I guess if I had to pick a feeling, it'd probably be afterward, when I felt really grateful to be alive."

She nodded, as if that satisfied her.

"Why so many questions?" I asked, leaving out the adjective "weird."

"I'm an actor." She ran a hand through her russet curls. "I use feelings for motivation: How would someone feel in a certain situation; how would they react? What does someone do when they think they might die?"

"You mean besides trying to avoid dying?" She smiled.

"I get it," I said. "I guess."

She switched gears. "Good thing about that gorgeous cowboy, huh?"

"What do you mean?"

"The one who saved you. He looked like the real deal."

She ran a tongue around her lips, a she-wolf drooling over raw meat. Toby dropped her hand.

"What's the story with him?" Jesse asked. "Is he single?"

I felt my face get hot and a rush of some type of emotion. What was it? Jealousy? Aggravation? Pity for poor Toby, who seemed so taken with this tramp?

"You planning on putting another cow-boy's spurs on your charm bracelet, Jesse? It must be getting pretty crowded after your little exhibition at the bar last night."

Toby rubbed at the knee that got bashed in the bar fight. He cast his eyes to the ground; his mouth was grim. He had no trouble getting in touch with *his* feelings, it seemed. Was that why he was such a good actor? A young DiCaprio, Tilton had said.

I consulted his face, like a road map to his emotional state: disappointment. Jealousy. Embarrassment. Toby would make a terrible poker player.

After the two of them left, no longer holding hands, I finally got the chance to check on the horses. No problems there, thank goodness. I filled their water trough, and then tossed enough hay for all the horses in the corral.

I was inside the trailer, stowing tack and grooming gear, when I heard a familiar voice. The tone was angry, though I couldn't make out the words. Even so, I knew it was Mama. I hurried outside, but didn't see her. Maybe she was around the back of the trailer.

As I followed the sound, her voice went low, dangerous: "I know what you did to my daughter."

I hugged the metal of the trailer, inching my way closer. Then I heard Mama utter these words: "Hurt her again, and I'll kill you."

I leapt away from the horse trailer. I looked to the left of Mama. I looked to the right. I looked in front of her and behind her. I was certain of it: There wasn't another soul around. Apparently, she was leveling threats at a vacant field.

"Mama?"

She turned, a bright smile on her face. "Hi, honey!" She glanced at a sheaf of paper in her hand. "Which way sounds better, Mace? *I know what you did to my daughter . . .* or, *I know what YOU did to my daughter . . .* Did you notice I added that finger-point there, on the word *you?* I improvised."

I just stared at her. What the hell?

"Honey, I can hardly believe it! Paul's made my dancehall girl a speaking part. What do you think about that?"

That was a question that would require some additional thought. In the meantime, I noticed Maddie coming toward the corral, carrying a take-out box with three cold drinks.

"We're in back of the trailer," I called.

I waited for my big sister, knowing she'd want to hear all about Mama's venture into the movie business, too.

"Sweet tea, from Gladys' restaurant." Maddie held out the container for us to help ourselves. "C'ndee Ciancio might be a catering whiz with *tiramisu* and *pasta fagioli,* but the woman cannot make iced tea to save her life. The sugar's got to go in when the water's boiling hot."

Thanking Maddie, we took our plastic cups.

"Well, I'm glad the tea's not hot now. I hope it's not too cold, either," Mama said. "I have to protect my throat. The voice is a tool, you know."

"Well, *something* is a tool," I said.

My sister raised her eyebrows.

"Go ahead and tell her, Mama," I said.

"Which of these do you think sounds better, Maddie?"

Mama gave her line reading again — twice — and then filled both of us in on how the movie's director decided her star quality was simply too luminous to hide in the background of a scene.

"Does Sal know about this?" Maddie asked.

"Sal is my husband, girls. He's not my master. Besides, if he really loves me, he'll want me to do what I love. I just know he's going to be so proud of me!"

158

I heard a crack of thunder. A storm was headed our way.

EIGHTEEN

Paul Watkins held his lips inches from Mama's. He stroked her arm suggestively, and then whispered into her ear. Suddenly, she hauled back to slap him across the face.

"I know what you did to my daughter!"

Beside me, Marty flinched and let out a small gasp. Maddie and I just chuckled. Paul grabbed Mama's wrist to stop the slap seconds before it connected. Then the two of them turned away from the dancehall, a replica in every detail, except it had no walls. The director and the newest star in the Hollywood firmament were all smiles.

"Don't worry. She's just acting," Paul said to Marty. "Your mother barely needs me to rehearse her. She's a natural."

"Well, she's a natural something all right," Maddie muttered.

"I heard that!" Mama frowned at my sister. "You are not going to spoil my big moment with your negativity."

Lightning and thunder had postponed any outdoor scenes involving the horses. When the first drops fell, Mama had left Maddie and me at the corral without a second thought. "Girls, I can't stand out here in the rain," she said. "Suppose I'm needed on the set? My hair and face would be a wreck."

She'd tented a nylon tarp over her platinum locks and made a dash for it. "Meet you at the dancehall!"

"Humph." Maddie donned the rain poncho she'd brought. "That's a new excuse."

"Mama will never run out of reasons to get out of work," I said.

While Maddie and I finished with the horses, Marty called to say she was on her way back to the movie set. We had told her where to meet us, but had revealed nothing else.

Now, Mama turned her attention, and a 100-watt smile, back to Paul. "So, what would you say Ruby's motivation is? What kind of life has she had? I want to know *everything* about her."

Her hand rested on Paul's arm. Her eyelashes fluttered like butterflies circling an overripe piece of fruit.

"Well," the director leaned back and stroked his chin, "Ruby has always been a beautiful woman."

"Uh-huh, uh-huh, I can relate to that." As Mama nodded like a bobble-headed doll, we rolled our eyes.

"She's always been able to get exactly what she wants from men."

"Goes without saying."

"But she's had some tough breaks," Paul said. "Some difficult times."

"Been there, done that, too."

"So she becomes a prostitute out of desperation."

"A Protestant?" Mama cupped a hand to her ear.

"A prostitute," Paul repeated.

Mama's mouth dropped open. Maddie gulped. Marty giggled.

"Didn't you tell me Ruby was a dancehall gal?" Mama's question came out in a squeak.

"A euphemism," Paul said. "That's what Ruby tells her mother in letters home to Georgia."

A parade of emotions marched across Mama's face: Disgust. Ambition. Indecision.

"I don't suppose she can get saved, can she, Paul? Have her come to our lord Jesus?"

He shook his head, ponytail bouncing against his back. "No time. There's just the one scene, Rosalee. But it's an important one."

Mama chewed at her lip.

"It's crucial, in fact."

She tapped her cheek, considering. "Well . . . if it's crucial. Essential to the story?"

"Absolutely."

Mama squared her shoulders and smoothed her hair. I knew she'd made up her mind.

"Now, what does my costume look like?" she asked. "I have some ideas for the kind of dress Ruby might wear."

As the two of them put their heads together, Paul took Mama's arm and walked her through the empty set. In one dim corner a player piano sat on wheels. Barbara Sydney stood to one side of the piano. Her eyes shot daggers at the departing director and his newly minted actress.

A sharp elbow jabbed me in my left side. From the right, a hand darted across the table to pinch me on my hand.

"I see him," I hissed at my sisters from behind the rim of a coffee cup. "There's no need to leave me battered and bruised."

I watched Carlos from the lunch table where I sat with my sisters. He stood at the entryway to the catering tent, checking out the hungry crowd inside. The downpour had momentarily quit; he carried his raincoat over his arm.

"I'll bet he's looking for you, Mace," Marty said.

"Doubt it." Maddie shook her head. "He's not carrying the weapon he'd need to beat some sense into her."

"Oh, that's nice, poking fun at domestic abuse," I said.

"I'm simply using exaggeration for effect. Though if someone would hand me a switch off a tree, I'd give you a few cracks across the rear myself. When are you going to grow up, Mace?"

"Maddie's right."

"About beating me with a switch? I never thought you'd condone violence, Marty."

"Stop joking around," Marty said. "It wouldn't kill you to go offer to get him a cup of coffee or a soda."

"What is this, 1950? I shouldn't have to stroke his fragile male ego all the time. I love the man. He knows that."

Maddie folded her arms over her chest. "Oh, does he now? Have you told him?"

I avoided her stern look. "Not exactly."

"What's that mean?"

"Yeah," Marty ganged up on me, too.

"Explain."

"Well, one time Carlos said, 'I love you,' and I said, 'Right back at ya.' "

Maddie choked, sputtering out the soda she'd just sipped. Marty, across the table, shook her head. "Get up and go over there, you simple fool."

When Maddie, beside me, added a hard poke in the rib to Marty's scolding, I knew I better take their advice.

Carlos looked relieved when he spotted me weaving through a maze of tables toward him. That was a good sign. But then his expression turned guarded, which wasn't as encouraging. By the time I reached him, he was wearing his closed-off, detective's face. I plowed ahead anyway.

"Hey sailor, can a girl buy you a drink?"

I saw the tiniest crack in that granite jaw. Could it be the embryo of a smile?

"I'm on duty, ma'am. But I wouldn't say no to a cup of coffee."

"Coming right up," I said. "Sorry they're not serving *café Cubano.*"

"Anything with caffeine will do." He reached out a hand to my chin, then gently turned my face this way and that. "You don't look too bad."

"Flatterer."

"No, seriously. I've been worried. How

are you, Mace?"

I didn't want to mention how my body ached where Jeb had sacked me.

"I'm fine. Did you find out how that light blew up?"

"Nobody knows anything," he shrugged. "The lighting guy says it happens sometimes. He says there's always somebody watching the equipment. He doesn't believe it was tampered with."

I told Carlos how Barbara had tried to cast suspicion about sabotage onto Tilton, and how he then did the same concerning her possible dark motives. Carlos slid his little book from his top pocket and made a couple of quick notes. When he put it away again, an awkward moment passed in silence.

"Listen . . ." I began.

"Mace, I . . ." Carlos said at the same time. He motioned for me to speak first.

"I just wanted to tell you there really is nothing between Jeb Ennis and me. That was high school, Carlos — a long time ago."

He put up a hand to stop me. "I wanted to apologize for acting like such an idiot. I went a little crazy when I saw you lying there on the ground."

The worried look on his face gave me a warm feeling. I offered him my hand to

166

shake. "Friends again?"

He took it, pulled me close, and brushed my hair with his lips. "Much more than friends, *niña*."

His breath was hot against my ear. An electric charge spread from my ear past my heart and all the way down south.

"Much more than friends," I agreed.

I got a coffee for Carlos while he picked out his lunch. As we returned to where my sisters sat, each of them signaled me silently, hiding their thumbs-up below the tabletop. No doubt, they'd done a play-by-play of Carlos and me making up. I was sure to get the highlights later, complete with their game analysis. We sat, Carlos draping his raincoat over the back of a chair.

"Any leads on the murder?" Maddie asked, just as he took his first bite of eggplant parmigiana.

"Let the poor man eat in peace," Marty said.

He swallowed. "You know I can't talk about the investigation, Maddie. We're still collecting and analyzing evidence."

"How are you keeping the press at bay?" Marty asked. "I thought the paparazzi would be swarming the set like ants at a picnic by now."

"Well, this ranch is private property, and

the production company is paying dearly for the right to use it. They've beefed up security to keep out looky-loos and the media. Those security guys aren't afraid to rough somebody up to get their point across."

As he ate, my sisters fired questions that he couldn't — or wouldn't — answer. From who had the best motive for murdering Norman, to whether the light could have been sabotaged, he offered a series of shrugs, head shakes, and can't-says. Finally, he pushed back his empty plate.

"I hear that dessert table calling my name."

"Bring me a little serving of that eggplant, would you, Carlos?" Maddie called after him.

Marty and I exchanged a look.

"What?"

"Didn't you already have the barbecued ribs?" I asked Maddie.

"So?"

Carlos had barely left the table when I felt Marty pinch my hand again. "Uh-oh." She nodded toward the entrance.

The rain had started again. Jeb Ennis shook the wet off his cowboy hat, brushed it against his thigh, and peered around the dimly lit tent. As soon as he spotted me, he waved and hurried over.

"The seat's taken," Maddie said to him.

"I won't stay long." He sat beside me, in the seat Carlos had just vacated. "I just came by to check on you, Mace."

I glanced over my shoulder. Carlos had his back to us, caught up in a bottleneck at the serving line for lunch. He was probably waiting to get Maddie's second helping. For once, I was grateful for her hearty appetite.

"I'm-just-great-Jeb-thanks-again." The words tumbled out of my mouth, as if they too wanted to speed him on his way. "Didn't you say you needed to get back to the ranch? Lots-to-do-back-home-right?"

"Yeah, but I'm dying for a cup of coffee." He looked around the tent again. "I don't suppose you've seen Kelly Conover eating lunch, have you?"

As Jeb's eyes roamed the crowd, I searched out Carlos's location. He'd left the lunch line, and was perusing the pastries.

Maddie said, "I just saw Kelly at the production trailer, Jeb. Why don't you head over and see if she's still there?"

"Was she still outfitted in that skimpy bikini top and short-shorts? I didn't think it was *that* warm out," Marty added.

I thought the picture my sisters conjured of Kelly Conover wearing Daisy Maes would propel Jeb from Carlos's seat, but he stayed put.

"Now that is something I'd like to see, but first I need my coffee. I also want to make sure my special gal is okay."

Maddie groaned. Marty looked nervously across the tent in Carlos's direction. Sure enough, he was threading his way through the tables on his way back to us. He balanced Maddie's plate in one hand, and his dessert and a fresh cup of coffee in the other. As I caught his eye, he grinned . . . until he noticed who was sitting next to me. Jeb had just draped a protective arm around my shoulder.

Carlos spun and detoured, hurrying away from us. At the door, he tossed the plate with Maddie's eggplant as well as his dessert into a large garbage can. Now, the storm was pounding a drumbeat on the roof of the tent. I thought for a moment he'd stop by our table to get his coat.

But he never even glanced back as he walked outside into a driving rain.

NINETEEN

A tiny forkful of lemon meringue pie stalled on its way to Marty's mouth. She stared over my shoulder. Maddie kicked me under the table. I leaned over to rub my shin.

"Is it Carlos? Did he come back?"

Speechless for once, Maddie shook her head. Marty's blue eyes were enormous. She lowered her fork and whispered a name like a prayer.

"Kelly Conover."

I'd rather it was Carlos. But he hadn't returned to the tent. Moments after he stalked out, Jeb left, seemingly unaware of the trouble he'd caused with that casual arm around my shoulder. The irony was that Jeb's Hollywood fantasy woman was now showing up at the dining area just after he'd managed to doom my relationship, and then disappear.

I turned in my seat. Sam had come in, too, glued to Kelly's side. I waved. She smiled at me, and signaled with a *Wait-a-minute* finger. The two of them exchanged a few words, Sam's dark head bent toward her golden one. Then he walked to the dessert table, while Kelly headed our way.

"Okay if Sam and I share your table?"

Her demeanor was 100 percent movie star: breathy voice; twinkling eyes; dazzling smile. My sisters were still staring. I gestured for her to have a seat, as we scooted our chairs around to make room. Kelly was gracious as I made introductions. She struck me as a bit fake, the head cheerleader being sweet to the unpopular girls in the cafeteria. My sisters either didn't notice, or they didn't care.

"I'm a big fan," Maddie finally managed to choke out.

Kelly gushed her thanks, like it was the first time she'd ever heard such an original compliment.

My little sister simply sat there with a goofy grin on her face. When Kelly said, "You have such beautiful eyes, Marty," she blushed like the captain of the football team had just asked her to go steady.

Then the star then turned to me. "I owe you an apology."

"Don't worry about it."

"No, Greg and I acted like spoiled children with those raccoons today. That man always manages to bring out the worst in me. I'm sorry. Will you forgive me?"

You could have tumbled me over with a tickseed flower. As she searched my face with those big green eyes, I managed to sputter out something like, "S'fine." I felt my mouth shifting into a smile, probably just as goofy-looking as Marty's.

Sam's arrival at the table, bearing a brownie cut in half, saved me from saying or doing anything more embarrassing. I hadn't technically met him, so Kelly performed introductions all around. I took the time to try to regain my composure. I had to forget she was a Hollywood movie queen, and treat her like I'd treat anyone else. Anyone else, I'd flat-out ask what I wanted to know.

"Something has been bothering me since the day Mama and I found Norman's body," I said. "Sam told you, 'It's over now. He can't hurt you anymore.' What did that mean? How had Norman hurt you?"

The two of them exchanged a long look. Finally, Kelly seemed to come to a decision. She touched her friend's shoulder. "It's all right, Sam. I want to talk about this. Now that Norman's dead, everyone's saying how he wasn't that bad. I can't stand to hear such a lie. He was a lowdown bastard."

She looked at my sisters and me. "You want to hear how low?"

Kelly confirmed what Savannah had hinted, pouring out her heart about how Norman raped her when she was starting out in the movie business.

"He said I should come to a dinner party at his house so we could talk about a part he had for me. I should have known something was off when I got there. All the other guests were men."

Tears pooled in her green eyes.

"How old were you?" Marty's voice was soft.

"I'd just turned sixteen."

Beside me, Maddie inhaled sharply. Sam held tight to one of Kelly's hands; Marty patted the other. Kelly went on, sketching out the details — how she'd taken such care with what to wear; how her dress was ripped and stained afterward; how her own mother had forbidden her to go to the police.

"She said we wanted to keep Norman on our side. He could make my career."

We were transfixed. It was like watching a movie, only Kelly was right here and real. Sam's face was etched in reflected pain. Finally, Kelly's torrent of words slowed, and then stopped. She sniffled. Sam whipped a tissue from his shirt pocket and handed it to her.

"So, Mace, that's how he hurt me, and that's why I hated him." She delicately blew her nose. "I consider his murder a blessing from God, but I didn't have anything to do with it. That's what you suspected, isn't it?"

I studied my hands, folded on the tabletop in front of me.

"Of course she didn't," Marty quickly said.

Kelly was staring at me when I raised my eyes. Sam was, too.

"I'm sorry," I said. "I didn't know the whole story. All I saw was you spitting on the ground and damning his soul."

She shrugged. "What can I say? I'm part Roma . . . gypsy, you'd call it. Plus, I'm an actress. So I'm a drama queen *and* I'm hot-blooded."

Everybody chuckled. Even if the laughter was more forced than genuine, it let me off the hook. I felt sorry for Kelly. Her story was heartrending. But that didn't mean I didn't still suspect her. If anything, what she'd just revealed gave her a compelling motive for murder.

Breaking off a tiny nibble of the half-brownie Sam brought, Kelly announced they needed to leave. Maddie at least waited until they were halfway to the door before she helped herself to the leftover sweet.

"Normally I don't approve of cursing, but Kelly was right when she called that awful man a bastard. Sam seems nice, though." She popped the brownie into her mouth.

"I wonder if my boss, Rhonda, would like him?" I looked across the table at Marty. "What do you think, sister? Ohmigod, don't tell me I'm becoming a matchmaker, like Mama!"

Marty's gaze followed the movie star and her friend, making their way to the exit. "Your boss might be smart and beautiful, Mace, but that wouldn't matter to Sam. He's already in love, with Kelly."

"Well, it's not reciprocated," I said, recalling the conversation between Kelly and Tilton.

"Doesn't matter," Maddie said. "There's no passion like unrequited love. Sam would go to any lengths to make Kelly care for him like he cares for her."

As Maddie's words echoed in my head, I remembered how Kelly's pain showed on Sam's face. How he worried when she was hungry. How he was ready with a shoulder or a tissue when she cried.

How far *would* he go to make all Kelly's problems go away?

■ ■ ■ ■

"Maddie, please get your fork out of my dessert plate. I'm still eating." Marty pulled her pie closer to her body, shielding it like a prison inmate with the crook of her left elbow.

We'd extended lunch, waiting for the storm to play itself out. I listened to the last drops of rain drizzling down on the roof of the tent. Suddenly, Sal stomped in through a side entry. It looked like all the day's dark clouds had found their way onto his face.

Mama ran to keep up, trailing him in full costume as Ruby. She wore a towering red wig. Her red satin dress featured a big skirt and a breathtakingly tight bodice. A cameo pendant was cradled in the deep crevice of her cleavage.

"Don't you want me to be happy, Sally?" Catching up, she tugged at his wrist. He didn't answer, just shook her off like an elephant evicting a gnat.

Mama's voice cracked. "Sally, please don't be mad at me. I can't take it." Her eyes glistened with tears.

Sal stopped. He turned toward his trembling bride. At our table, Maddie made the sign of a fishing pole, reeling him in.

"Snagged like a speckled perch," I agreed.

"Hush, they'll hear you," Marty warned.

"Look at that," Maddie said. "Mama even looks pretty when she cries. If that was me, my eyes would be all puffy and as red as her dress."

"Ruby's dress," I said. "But I know what you mean. My nose would be dripping like a snot faucet by now. And I'd look like Rudolph, lighting the way for Santa's sleigh."

I pushed back my chair. "I'm getting some more coffee. Anyone want anything?"

Marty shook her head. Maddie said, "Bring me one of those big muffins with the cinnamon crust on top, would you?"

She caught the glance I stole at her plate. A single smear of meringue and just one crumb from Kelly's brownie remained.

"Don't worry. I'll take the muffin home and save it for breakfast."

"Sure you will."

"No bickering, you two," Marty said. "I'm trying to eavesdrop on Sal and Mama."

I had less interest in that endeavor than Marty did. I'd seen the Sal and Rosalee Show, and this was yet another rerun. I made my way to the serving area.

I loaded Maddie's muffin on a tray, and was at the condiment table, adding sugar and cream to my coffee, when I glanced to the side of the tent. The show was still in progress. Sal had enfolded Mama in a big bear hug. He was now comforting *her*. Sniffling, she snuggled into his protective embrace. I imagined a critic's summation of this familiar, two-character play.

Outcome: predictable. Ending: clichéd. Plot: visible from a mile away.

As my gaze lingered on Sal and Mama, I became aware of the sound of someone beside me, breathing. I jumped. It was Barbara.

"You scared me," I said. "Where'd you come from?"

Her eyes didn't leave Sal and Mama. "I want you to deliver a message," she said. "Tell your floozy of a mother that Paul Watkins is my man, and I'm not fond of sharing."

"Really?" I said. "I wonder what Paul's wife, Savannah, would say about that?"

"Why don't you ask her? She'll tell you somebody could get hurt crossing Barbara Sydney."

With that, Barbara grabbed a long, serrated knife from the dessert table. She poked at the muffin I'd chosen for Maddie, flipping it onto its side. Then she cleanly sliced off the cinnamon crumb top, and dropped the decapitated pastry on the floor at my feet.

TWENTY

I had a gentle Quarter horse saddled and ready. The horse stomped a foot, shivered, and shook all over. Jesse backpedaled so fast her boots kicked up splatters of mud in the corral.

"Is it angry?"

"Only at that horsefly." I waved a hand to shoo the insect. "That's what horses do when they're trying to stop it from stinging."

"Does it mind if I get on?"

"His name's Zeke; and honestly, he'll pay less mind to you climbing on his back than he does to that horsefly."

She took a few tentative steps in Zeke's direction. Her eyes traveled from the ground up to the saddle. "I'm not sure I can do it."

"All that working out you do at the gym? You should be able to haul yourself up onto his back with no problem." I demonstrated. "See? You always mount from the left. Foot in the stirrup. Hand on the horn. Then swing your right leg over his rump. It's kind of like getting on a motorcycle."

"Motorcycles don't bite."

"Neither will Zeke. He's very well trained." I swung down out of the saddle again, and stood on the ground. "Your turn."

She backed up. "I have to confess something, Mace. This is the closest I've ever been to a real, live horse."

Her voice was small, scared. All her swagger was gone. It was the first time Jesse had seemed vulnerable. Human.

"I really needed this role, so I lied about being a good rider to get it. I should have been practicing, but every time I got near a horse, I chickened out. They're so big."

Her voice shook, like she might start crying. I actually felt sorry for her. "Don't worry," I told her. "I'm right here, and we'll take it slow."

"I really appreciate you agreeing to do this, Mace. I know you don't approve of me."

"Don't mention it." I waved a hand, purposely ignoring the approval part. "I just want to make sure nobody gets hurt around the horses."

I clutched Zeke's reins, extending my

other hand to Jesse. She inched toward me, and I gently took her wrist. "You put your hand out flat, palm down, and let him sniff at the back." I turned her hand over. "That's how he gets to know you."

After she let Zeke get her smell, I guided her hand all along the horse's neck, down to the chest. "Don't pat. Stroke. And give him a good scratch there, in the middle of his chest. He can't reach that spot, so he'll appreciate it."

By the time we'd worked our way all the way back to his rump, under his belly, and up his neck again, Zeke was totally relaxed. Jesse was getting there. I had her ball her fist and gently stroke his muzzle. "See how soft that nose is? Like velvet," I said. "Now, feel those stubbly whiskers."

A smile spread across her face. The horse rubbed his head against her chest. "See? He likes you," I said. "Which figures, since Zeke is a male."

Jesse's face went pink. "I know my reputation. It's not fair. Guys who hook up with a lot of girls are studs. If a girl does the exact same thing, everyone calls her a slut."

"Yeah, well welcome to the world, Jesse. Life's not fair."

"You can say that again."

When she was ready, I helped her into the

saddle. "You're going to do great. We won't go far; and you and Zeke are already old friends."

I adjusted her stirrups, and then handed her the reins. "Don't hold them too tight, but don't let them drop, either. We'll ride out together, and I'll show you what I mean."

I mounted one of the other horses, and we set off at a slow walk. Jesse watched closely, mimicking everything I did. Now that she was more comfortable with the horse, she was a fast learner.

"You can talk to him, you know. Lean over and give him a scratch now and then."

She ran a hand along his neck, under the mane. "You're a good horse, Zeke." At just that moment, he bobbed his head up and down. Jesse's laugh was pure girlish delight. "Look, he agrees with me!"

We rode for a short distance on a rutted path through open pasture, until we came to a fork that led to a hardwood hammock. "Those big trees are so pretty," Jesse said. "Is it safe to ride through there?"

"Sure, that bit of woods runs between the base camp and the parking lot." I turned my horse toward the fork, and Jesse followed. The tree-shaded path was wide enough for us to ride two abreast. "That's a live oak," I pointed toward an ancient specimen, weeping with Spanish moss. "See how its branches grow almost sideways like that? It's like they're reaching out to touch all of nature around them."

"Cool," she said. "I can see that. The limbs are spread out almost as wide as the tree is tall."

I pointed out a couple more things — ground the wild hogs had torn up, digging for roots and bugs with their snouts; a hawk soaring on an air current in a now-clear sky. Mostly, we kept a companionable silence, with me offering words of encouragement or gentle correction. Jesse's horseback scene was scheduled to be filmed in two more days. That wasn't much time to bring her skill level to where it needed to be. But I decided not to mention my misgivings to her.

"Is Toby a good rider?" I asked.

She shrugged. "Not as good as Greg Tilton, but I think he's okay."

After all the rain, the sky was a washed out blue. Afternoon sun filtered through the trees that grew close to the path, warming my back. Leather creaked. The horses snuffled. A woodpecker drummed against the bark of a slash pine. It was as good a time as any to bring up the subject I wanted to raise with Jesse.

"You know, Toby really seems to like you."

She stared at the horn of her saddle, tracing a circle on the top with her thumb.

"Do you like him?" I asked.

She nodded, but didn't raise her eyes to meet mine. "I'm not ready to settle down, though. I just turned twenty-one. Toby's even younger. I don't even know who I am yet. I don't want to be half of some ridiculous Hollywood couple: Jesby. Tobee. J-To. I'm my own person, you know."

I watched her, hoping she'd raise her head so I could read her expression. That's when I noticed Zeke's ears prick forward. Seconds later, I heard the sound, too. Something loud crashed toward us through the woods. Zeke startled, sidestepping quickly away from the noise. Jesse, clutching the saddle's horn like a life preserver, shrieked in fear.

"Stay calm," I said quietly. "Just hold on to Zeke's reins and run your hand along his neck. He just hears something, is all. You reassure him. You're both okay."

Jesse did as I told her, and the horse was fine. But the noise kept coming our way. We both peered into the trees. "What is it, Mace? Are there grizzly bears here?"

A moment later, Toby stumbled onto the sandy path ahead of us. Blood covered his face. His clothes were dirty and torn. Silently, he reached a hand in our direction, and then collapsed in a heap on the ground.

TWENTY-ONE

Toby struggled to stand. He staggered, and fell again.

I swung down from my saddle. Jesse leapt straight off Zeke, leaving the horse's reins hanging. She'd barely hit the ground before she started running to Toby. I grabbed the reins of both horses and followed.

Toby had managed to hoist himself to a sitting position. He watched, looking dazed, as we approached. He was filthy. Leaves clung to his hair, normally so flawless. Scratches crisscrossed his face. Dirt streaked the back of his torn shirt. Both knees of his jeans were stained.

"Someone tried to run me down in the parking lot." He put a hand to his head, and it came away red with blood. "I think I'm hurt."

Jesse performed a quick check, peering into his hair to see the source of the oozing blood. She looked up at me. "Scalp wound . . ."

"It hurts, Jess . . ."

". . . bloody, but not deep."

She studied his pupils, checking for brain injury or shock. Lifting the torn shirt gently off his body, she surveyed his bare chest and back for evidence of other wounds. Toby's voice was weak, but he kept talking:

"I was running away, but I tripped and fell. When I felt the asphalt, I kept rolling. I came to a stop in a muddy ditch." He gingerly fingered his bloodied hair. "I think I smacked my head on a rock."

"So the car didn't hit you?" she asked.

He shook his head, wincing in pain.

"Can you stand up?" I asked him. "We'll get you up on one of the horses and take you to the medical trailer."

Still holding both sets of reins in one hand, I extended the other to Toby. Jesse did the same. Together, we pulled him to his feet.

"Can you walk?" she asked.

He tested his weight on one leg, and then the other. He grimaced. "I must have hurt the same knee that got smacked at the bar."

She leaned down to feel for swelling. "How bad's the pain, scale of one to five?"

"Two, maybe," he said.

"You'll probably live." Jesse grinned at

him. "But I think we should get you to the medic, just to be safe."

"I don't want to live if I can't have you."

Her forehead wrinkled. "Very funny, Toby. What film is that line from?"

"It's not from a movie. I mean it. You realize what's important when you're hiding in a ditch, wondering if somebody's going to make a U-turn and come back to try and kill you." He stroked her cheek. "I love you, Jess. I want us to be a couple, for real."

Jesse cut her eyes toward me. I pretended to be studying the ground.

"No response?" Toby searched her face, looking for an answer he didn't seem to find.

It was so quiet, I could hear the horses swishing their tails. Still, he stared at her. I coughed quietly, and then cleared my throat. I wanted to ask another question. "Did you see what kind of car it was?"

He couldn't tear his eyes from Jesse, even though she gazed indifferently into the trees.

"The car?" I prodded.

Finally, he looked at me. "It was white, or at least light in color." His voice was thick with hurt. I was pretty sure it wasn't from the physical injuries. "I'm not sure what kind. It might even have been a truck, or a van. It happened so fast."

"What about the driver?"

"Big hat. Sun was glinting off the windshield. I couldn't tell who was behind the wheel. Sorry."

So the vehicle was possibly white, like half the movie company's rental fleet. And the driver might have been a man; or maybe a woman. He, or possibly she, was young . . . or maybe old. Carlos was going to love getting this report.

We were about to help Toby onto my horse to take him to the medical trailer when we heard another crash in the brush. It was followed by a string of curses. Barbara emerged, yanking spider webs from her face.

"There you are, Toby!" Her tone was scolding, until she seemed to register that her star client was bruised and bloodied and leaning on Jesse.

"Ohmigod, what happened?" She rushed to push Jesse out of the way.

"I've got him, Barbara," Jesse said. "He had an accident. It doesn't look serious."

"An accident?" She cupped Toby's face, looking into his eyes. She touched the blood staining his brow. "My poor baby!"

He tried to jerk his head away. "Somebody tried to run over me in the parking lot. Don't worry. I survived. Your fifteen percent is safe."

Barbara dropped her hand from his face like she'd touched a hot stove. She looked stunned, crushed by his cruel words. Then again, she had been an actress way back when.

"You didn't happen to see anything, did you?" I asked her.

She narrowed her eyes. "What's that supposed to mean?"

I shrugged. "Nothing. Just that Toby didn't see who almost hit him. Maybe you noticed somebody burning rubber out of the parking lot."

"I was nowhere near there. I was in Toby's trailer, waiting for him, until one of the production assistants told me Toby was headed into town. I was on my way to check to see if his car was gone, when I got lost trying to take the shortcut to the parking lot."

I was going to follow up, try to find out how Barbara came to be around each of the locations where someone had been hurt, when a shout sounded from the trail: "Hey, is Sam with you guys? We were supposed to go to dinner, but he stood me up. I can't find him anywhere."

Kelly Conover stood in the path, shading her eyes and looking in our direction. When I answered that we hadn't seen Sam, she hurried on her way toward the parking area. Not even a backward glance. How typical. She didn't notice Toby's disheveled state; it didn't directly concern her.

I helped Jesse onto Zeke, and then got on my horse, so Toby could ride double behind me. Helping to pull him up, it occurred to me Toby moved pretty well for someone who'd just taken a bad tumble into a ditch.

"I'll meet you at the trailer, Toby," Barbara called out as we left.

"Don't bother." He didn't even look at his manager. He hooked his hands around my waist. "Okay if I hang on like this, Mace? I'm not hitting on you or anything."

"If you were, cowboy, it'd be the most exciting thing to happen to me all year."

Toby chuckled, which I took as an encouraging sign that his injuries weren't too bad. As we rode off toward the trailer, Toby bouncing a bit behind the saddle, two questions ran through my head.

What would make Sam miss the chance to take Kelly to dinner? And why did Barbara emerge from the woods near the parking area, if she'd been in Toby's trailer on the opposite side of the set?

Twenty-Two

"Look, everybody! There she is . . . Hollywood's newest star."

My cousin Henry rose from our table at Gladys' Diner and lifted his voice over the breakfast din. Mama paused at the door to make a proper entrance. Preening, she fluffed her hair, smoothed her lemon yellow pantsuit, and took the measure of the room.

Once she was sure all eyes were on her, she made the rounds, bestowing cheek kisses and beauty-queen waves to the customers. Henry whistled as she did a red-carpet amble along the counter.

Sitting with my sisters, I muttered, "Don't encourage her, Henry. She's just one air kiss away from Hollywood Diva as it is."

"Amen," Maddie said.

"Oh, let your mama have her fifteen minutes, girls. It won't kill you."

Sitting back down, Henry stole a biscuit from Maddie's plate. Despite the poke she gave his hand with her fork, Henry polished off the biscuit in two bites. Then he grabbed another one from Marty's plate. She glared. "Just because you came in late doesn't mean you get to eat our food, Henry."

"Jeez, Marty!" he said. "Since when did you start suffering from PMS?"

When Henry zeroed in on my plate, I raised my steak knife at him: "Don't even think about it."

Gladys' restaurant had done a makeover, replacing the wagon-wheel hanging lamps and gingham tablecloths with soft lighting and tasteful landscapes. There was some grumbling at first, as Himmarshee doesn't take well to change. But the grub was still good, and people were getting used to the new look.

Mama sidled up to the table just as Charlene, the waitress, got there with a coffee pot and Henry's breakfast order, the Hungry Hog. "I guess I'll have to get your autograph, Rosalee. I hear you're going to be in the movie."

"It's just a small part, Charlene." Mama lowered her eyes, signaling modesty. "But it's absolutely crucial to the plot. Or so my director tells me. That's Paul Watkins. He's the one who noticed I had a certain star quality."

I mentally amended that to *false* modesty.

She said, "Let me just borrow your pen and pad, honey, and I'll give you my John Hancock."

Charlene refilled our cups, then put her coffee carafe on the table and handed Mama a blank sheet from her pad. As Mama worked out her new movie star signature — "Do you girls think I should put a star right here, between Rosalee and Provenza?" — Charlene pulled up a seat.

"I hear you're teaching Jesse Donahue how to ride, Mace."

"How'd you hear that, Charlene?" I glared at Mama, the teller of secrets.

Shrugging off my question, the waitress babbled on excitedly, "I've been watching her ever since she was a little girl. Why, I've seen her grow up on screen. What's Jesse really like? Has she slept with as many men as they say? Is it true she's on heroin?"

Mama started to give her version of the real Jesse, but I cut her off. "She's not a drug addict so far as I can tell. I think people have the wrong idea about Jesse."

Maddie snorted.

"What does that mean?" I asked.

"I don't like her," Maddie said. "Making a spectacle of herself the way she does? If she was my daughter, her hide would be double-tanned by now."

Henry slathered butter on a biscuit from his own plate, finally. "Forget about Jesse," he said. "What's the story with Kelly Conover? Now, there's a woman! Is she nice? Is she as pretty in person as in the movies?"

Marty sighed. "She's beautiful, even more so than she looks on screen. Tiny, too. She's hardly any bigger than me."

"I wonder if that's what people will say about me, once my movie comes out." Pausing mid-autograph, Mama's face took on a dreamy look.

"Well, Kelly's not tiny everywhere," Maddie sipped her coffee, "thanks to the miracle of silicone and a skilled plastic surgeon."

Marty looked over each shoulder, a guilty look on her face. "Keep it down, Maddie. That's mean, and people may hear you."

"Kelly's fake bosom isn't exactly a secret." Maddie said. "The scandal sheets have even run before and after pictures. Besides, her boobies look like two jumbo honeydews balanced on a plank of plywood. You are such an innocent, Marty."

Charlene took Marty's scowl as her exit cue. Mama stood up and called after her, "You forgot to take my autograph, honey . . . Well, okay, I'll leave it with your tip."

Marty said, "You know, I get really tired of y'all treating me like a child . . ."

"Don't blame me! I didn't say a word," I said.

Maddie snickered. "C'mon, Marty . . . only a moron would think those 'girls' of Kelly's are real."

"Well, they look real enough to me," Henry said.

"See my point?" Maddie sat back, arms folded.

Marty pressed her lips together and glared at our big sister.

Mama examined her profile in the mirror behind the counter. "I wonder if I should think about plastic surgery, girls. It's quite common in Hollywood. And speaking of Hollywood, I see some folks in the corner I didn't get the chance to talk to about my movie."

Waving, she traipsed off to another round of *My Life on the D List,* Himmarshee style.

Henry smacked his lips and closed his eyes. "I had a poster of Kelly in a crocheted bikini taped to my bedroom ceiling. I spent many happy hours dreaming of the day she'd be my bride."

"Dreaming, right," I said.

"Bride, right," Maddie added.

We both looked at Marty, but she didn't

chime in to rag on our cousin.

"Maybe y'all will think I'm a *moron* for saying this, but all you ever do is pick fights," Marty said. "As for you, Henry, while you're so busy drooling over Kelly, you might not have heard a crazed murderer is loose on the movie set. Mace already had a close call. And now someone tried to run over Toby Wyle. Anyone could be next. Y'all seem like you don't even care."

"Calm down, Marty. You're not acting like yourself," I said.

"Don't tell me how to act, Mace. Maddie always criticizes, and you always tell people what to do. Maybe all three of you should be spending more time thinking about who's responsible and how to stop them."

With that, Marty grabbed Henry's second biscuit right out of his hand. She took two big bites, tossed it back on his plate, and stalked out of the diner.

TWENTY-THREE

All of us stared as the door of Gladys' slammed shut. Even Henry stopped eating long enough to watch, open-mouthed, through the plate glass window as Marty marched stiffly down the sidewalk.

"And here I thought Maddie kept the whole family's supply of sticks up her butt. What's gotten into your little sister, girls?"

"I guess we're all a little tense." I turned my attention to my cousin. "Seeing a body hung up like the Monday wash will do that to people."

"That, and watching your sister narrowly escape death from the razor-sharp pieces of an exploding light," Maddie added.

Henry motioned with his coffee cup toward Mama. Still making the rounds, she'd just stuck a fork into a neighbor's plate for a sample of egg and sausage scramble. "Your mama seems to be handling the stress pretty well."

"She might tell you she's just playing a part, Henry, now that she's Himmarshee's own Kelly Conover," I said.

Just then, the cowbells jangled on the diner's door. "Speak of the devil," Maddie whispered.

"Oh my god," Henry breathed.

"Looks like the alarm clock just rang on Mama's fifteen minutes of fame," I said.

As the diners became aware of who had just made an entrance, whispers spread like ripples in a pond. One of the waitresses dropped a plate of ham and red-eye gravy. Then, complete silence descended. The cashier stopped in the middle of ringing up a check, hand hovering over the keys on the cash register. The fry cook left the kitchen, wiping his hands on his apron and smoothing his balding head. One of the younger patrons fumbled for her cell phone and started snapping pictures. An older diner, the wife of the Rotary club president, slapped her hand.

"Put that camera phone down, Brianna! Miss Conover has a right to privacy. Who do you think you are? One of those smart alecks from *TMZ*?"

Maddie put her hand to her mouth and whispered, "And who do you think has the Hollywood gossip page at TMZ.com bookmarked on her computer? Mrs. Rotary herself."

Kelly's eyes met mine, and I waved her over. Henry, meanwhile, still hadn't uttered a word. He took the napkin out of his collar, straightened his tie, and unrolled the cuffs on his light gray dress shirt. As the movie star approached, he nearly knocked over his own chair as he leapt to pull out one for her.

After everyone was settled, and Henry had mopped the drool from his chin, Kelly asked what I knew about Toby's close call in the parking lot.

"Jesse and I had just found him, shortly before you came walking along the path," I said. "He stumbled out of the woods right where we were riding."

"How convenient," Kelly said.

"What's that supposed to mean?" Henry's sharp, defense-attorney self was warring with his bedazzled male adolescent, because he immediately grinned and added, "I'm Henry, by the way. I'm a lawyer, so I'm used to asking questions. I don't mean any offense, Miss Conover."

"Call me Kelly." As she turned those money-green eyes on him, Henry melted.

"Okay, then: *Kelly*. I'm a big fan."

"You're a big something," Maddie harrumphed.

"Anyway . . ." Kelly said, "I just think it's weird Toby got hurt, and then managed to get to the exact spot where you and his little girlfriend would find him."

"Maybe not so much weird as lucky," I said. "He needed to be checked out, and we were able to do that, and then get him to the medic."

"But his injuries weren't serious, right?"

"He was pretty banged up."

I was feeling strangely protective of the teen star. Maybe it was because I had watched Jesse rip out his heart and stomp on it. That had to hurt as much as his injuries from the parking lot incident.

Kelly persisted, "But it wasn't anything life-threatening."

I nodded, "Right."

"Whose idea was it to go riding?" she asked.

I knew Jesse and I had talked about how I didn't want anyone hurt with the horses, but I couldn't actually remember whether she'd asked or I'd offered to give her a horseback lesson.

I shrugged.

"Well, who wanted to ride through that particular stretch of woods?"

I got a quick flash of Jesse admiring the

woodsy hammock. *Is it safe to ride through there?*

I must have had a funny look on my face, because Kelly said: "I knew it! It was Jesse's idea!"

"So?"

"Mace is right," Maddie said. "Why should that make a difference?"

It was Kelly's turn to shrug. "I'm not sure. When you've been in Hollywood as long as I have, you always question what's made out to be the truth."

Chin on his hands, Henry's face was moony. "Kelly, you don't look a day older than when you starred in the *Teenaged Detective.*" Had he heard a word of what we'd been saying?

"Thanks," Kelly said, "but that was a lifetime ago. I've learned over time not to trust public images, and I don't for a minute buy that clean-cut Disney-star crap surrounding Toby Wyle."

I thought back to him strutting out of Jesse's trailer, zipper undone, that first day Mama and I saw him on the set. Definitely not Disney. What about Jesse? Was she playing me? I wasn't going to share my thoughts with Kelly, though. She might be the one fooling all of us.

"So, are you suggesting Toby or Jesse may

have something to gain by making Toby appear to be a victim?" Courtroom Henry was back, thank goodness.

"I think one or both of them had something to do with the murder. They're trying to confuse everyone by diverting suspicion away from Toby."

Kelly turned those eyes on him, like deep green pools in an enchanted forest. Horny Adolescent Henry looked like he wanted to jump in for a swim.

"I don't buy it." Maddie reverted to her usual role, skeptical principal. "What's Toby's motive? His manager is Barbara Sydney. She's also the ex-wife and was the current business partner of Norman, the murder victim. Toby was reportedly golden with both of them. Why would he risk that? What would he have to gain?"

Mama had crept up to the table again, and was listening. Unnaturally quiet, she seemed aware her audience was now transfixed on a much bigger star. "I'll tell you what Toby had to gain. Publicity," she finally said. "We actors breathe it like oxygen. Isn't that right, Kelly?"

"I'm sorry. Have we met?"

Kelly's voice was cool, all Hollywood superiority. Mama's cheeks pinked. For a moment, I thought it served her right, but then I felt sorry for her.

"That's my mama, Rosalee," I reminded Kelly, a little sharply. "She's playing Ruby, the prostitute."

"Dancehall girl." Mama smoothed her coiffure.

"Oh, I'm sorry, Rosalee. Of course! It's nice to see you again."

Mama's face glowed, even though everyone else at the table could tell Kelly was only being polite.

"That's a good point you make about publicity, Rosalee. But Toby and Jesse have more publicity than they can handle right now. Negative publicity. What are the tabloids calling them? To-se? Jes-to?"

Mrs. Rotary President leaned in from the next table. "Jeby."

Kelly dipped her head slightly, like a queen recognizing a loyal subject. Then she continued, "Anyway, the same thing about publicity doesn't hold true with . . ."

As her words trailed off, she studied the hands she folded on the tabletop.

"Publicity with what?" I asked.

She lowered her voice. "*Who* not *what,* and I don't want to say. We go way back."

"Don't worry, we won't tell anyone," Henry said. "I'm used to respecting lawyer-client confidentiality."

What Henry didn't say was: if you're not a client, watch out. There's not a more enthusiastic participant in the Himmarshee Gossip Hotline than Henry Bauer, Esq.

Kelly glanced around the café. All the diners suddenly seemed fascinated by their food. Forks scraped plates. Spoons clinked against coffee cups. Conversations resumed. No one wanted to look like a nosy rube. She leaned in close. We did, too.

"Greg Tilton." She whispered his name. "He needs publicity, bad. The tabs don't even bother following him around anymore. He needs a big picture."

Maddie said, "This picture seems pretty big."

Kelly regarded her hands again. Finally, she raised those green, liquid eyes to her audience.

"Yes, it is. And Norm Sydney was hacking Greg's role to bits so Toby could emerge as the new big star of this very big film."

TWENTY-FOUR

Perched on the top rail of the horse corral, I watched across the way as Jeb and one of his ranch hands worked about two dozen head of cattle. Jeb's cow dog gave a couple of yips, helping to drive the animals toward their pen.

It was late morning. After breakfast, my sisters and I had separated, as they had errands to finish in town. When Mama and I arrived at the movie location, she'd vanished into the hair and make-up trailer. She was probably regaling the stylists right now with her beauty tips.

Now, Jeb leaned into the small herd from the saddle of his bay gelding. He and the horse seemed as one. The animal pivoted and side-stepped, pushing against the cows and easing off as needed. It was like a dance, where all the partners knew their steps. In one fluid motion, Jeb turned and flicked his cow whip over the rump of one recalcitrant steer.

My heart thrummed, keeping time with the hoof beats. Damn if that man wasn't a beautiful sight in the saddle.

Finally, the dog barked and snapped at the heels of the straggler. The cow trotted to catch up with the rest of the herd. The ranch hand swung shut the gate as the last animal entered the enclosure, the dog still in pursuit.

Jeb spun and galloped toward me, stopping his horse inches from the fence where I sat. He grinned, and saluted me with an index finger to the brim of his cowboy hat. His white teeth gleamed in his sun-browned face. A smear of dirt, or maybe dried manure, crossed his angled cheekbone.

"I see you're still riding that sorry nag," I said. "How old is poor Cheyenne now, about a hundred and ten?"

He lifted the whip and pointed it at me, a smile belying the menacing gesture. "You should know better than to poke fun at a cowman's horse. He's twenty, and he can run circles around horses half his age."

He turned the horse in a couple of tight circles to demonstrate. I jumped off the rail to give the hardworking horse a pat on the neck.

"So Cheyenne's just like you, huh? Twice

as good as cowpokes half your age?"

Jeb laughed. "Yep, I'm just like that Toby Keith song." He started the verse. I chimed in, singing about how he might not be the man he once was, but he's still as good once as he ever was.

We grinned at each other. Were we remembering the past? Or were we anticipating the future? Maybe it was neither. Maybe we both just liked that barroom song.

Suddenly, I noticed Jeb's eyes had strayed from mine. He stared over my shoulder, his grin now a frown. I turned to see where he was looking. There was a man in the distance, crouched down low by the gate of the cattle pen.

"Hey, what the hell are you doing?" Jeb's shout was sharp, angry.

The man rose. It was Greg Tilton, seemingly noticing us for the first time. The glare of the setting sun made it difficult to see his expression.

"That's a bad place to be, buddy." Jeb's voice was still raised to carry, but I could tell he was aiming for friendly. "Cattle can be unpredictable."

Tilton gave us a cheerful wave. Then he looped his thumbs in his waistband and ambled away, whistling.

"Weird Hollywood people." Shaking his

head, Jeb turned his attention back to me. "Now, where were we?"

"I believe you two were doing a Dogpatch version of a duet." The voice came from behind us. It held a slight accent, and a blizzard's worth of ice.

I felt the color drain from my face. Jeb must have noticed my stricken look.

Ignoring Carlos, he tipped his hat to me. "Looks like you and Miamuh here have some business to discuss." Then he turned the reins on Cheyenne, and nudged the horse with his heels.

As Jeb galloped off, silence stretched out between Carlos and me. Then, both of us started to say something at the same time.

"Jeb and I are just friends . . ."

". . . I can't believe the way you . . ."

I quickly motioned him to speak. "You go."

"I can't believe the way you act when that cowboy is around. Yesterday, you were cuddled up to him at lunch; now he's back, and the two of you are flirting out here. It looks to me like you never really got over him." He leaned against the fence, avoiding my eyes.

"You know that's not true."

"I don't know anything. Are we together? Or would you rather be with him? Say the word, and I'm gone. I'm not desperate. I don't want to force myself on someone who doesn't want to be with me."

The ground was solid, but I felt unsteady. I grabbed his arm. "You can't seriously believe I don't want to be with you."

He pulled away, arms folded tightly over his chest. "That's the way it looks. Or, maybe you want to be with me; but you want to be with him, too."

"You're overreacting. I've known Jeb forever. I won't deny there's history. But it's ancient. I've told you that, Carlos. Why won't you believe me?"

He reached out to me, brushed some hair from my eyes. A shiver of desire ran up my backbone. That's love, isn't it?

"I want to believe you, Mace. But I'm not blind. I see the way you look at each other."

I wasn't sure what to say to that. Hadn't I just been watching Jeb, thinking he looked purely gorgeous? But admiring the way he sat his horse and worked his cattle wasn't the same as wanting him, was it? It wasn't the same thing as being in love.

Thinking, I dug at a rock in the dirt with the toe of my boot. Carlos stroked my hair. My whole body went hot at his touch, and my heart melted with tender feelings for him. That was love. Now, I was sure.

And I was just about to tell Carlos so, when Jeb whistled, and yelled for his dog.

"Here, Nip. C'mon boy."

I glanced over, watching Nip squeeze under the bottom rail of the cow pen and lope toward his master. The dog's tongue lolled from his mouth like he was smiling with the pure pleasure of his work. The sight of Nip looking so happy brought a grin to my face, too.

Carlos let the strand of hair he'd been caressing slip from his fingers. "I think that smile on your face is my answer."

Jamming his hands into his pockets, he turned to go.

"I was looking at the dog, Carlos," I called after him. "Nip was grinning, so I was, too."

He didn't look back.

"The dog's name is right out of the book *A Land Remembered.* Every cowman in middle Florida names his dog Nip or Tuck." I raised my voice. "Don't you think that's funny?"

Head down, Carlos didn't laugh, and he didn't answer. He just kept walking.

Hurricane-force winds roared. Sabal palms thrashed. Jesse, rain-soaked and desperate, struggled to make her way across a pasture in the raging storm.

Mopping water from her eyes, she stared at the whipping branches of a downed oak. The frilly hem of a child's white dress peeked out, barely visible under the massive tree. With each step forward, the wind buffeted Jesse a half-step back.

Closer now, she stumbled to the ground and crawled the final distance. Her hand went out to touch the white hem. Lightning flashed, revealing the emotions contorting Jesse's face: fear, grief, and an ice-cold rage. Lifting her face to the sky, she let out an anguished scream.

"And . . . Cut!" Paul Watkins said. "Nice, nice work, Jesse."

Unconsciously, I'd been holding my breath. I exhaled, slowly. Mama, standing beside me, heaved a deep sigh.

"My stars and garters! Jesse absolutely nailed that scene."

"Whew!" I said to Mama.

I knew it was make-believe. A fire hose sprayed "rain" from a 5,000-gallon tanker truck. Generator-powered wind fans with six-foot blades whipped up the tempest of the "hurricane." A control box triggered movie lamps to produce dramatic "lightning" strikes.

And the small child, crushed by the storm-felled tree? That was a stunt dummy, outfitted in a white dress.

Yet, Jesse's emotions seemed so real, I was caught up in the story. The scene had her searching for her character's little sister, lost in a hurricane. My mind went back to the day my little sister, Marty, narrowly escaped the venomous bite of a rattlesnake. Watching Jesse, I felt the same clutch of fear in my stomach that I'd felt that day: What if I couldn't save my sister?

I remembered how Jesse had quizzed me about feelings, and said she used them in her acting. I could understand the terror on her face when she saw her "sister" crumpled and broken, and the grief when she realized she was dead.

What I didn't understand was the dark place Jesse went to pull up that chilling flash of rage.

Twenty-Five

A crowd milled about base camp. I hurried over to find out what was going on, peering over the head of a vertically challenged woman from the wardrobe department.

Johnny Jaybird stood in the middle of the huddle, immaculately dressed in pressed trousers, a navy blazer, and crisp white dress shirt. He looked like he'd just stepped out of a men's store along Palm Beach's ritzy Worth Avenue. Preening, he basked in the attention of cast and crew, bobbing his head toward each corner of the crowd. His smile seemed genuine, absent the arrogant smirk I'd seen on the set the first day.

Getting shot must have agreed with him. Or maybe it was surviving getting shot.

Greg Tilton stood beside the bench seat of a folding table on the fringes of the crowd, watching Johnny. He had what looked like a sandwich wrapped in tin foil in his hand, and a smirk on his face. His fellow cast and crew members seemed to give him a wide berth. It appeared he was alone in his own world despite being surrounded by people.

Paul Watkins stepped from the crowd to approach his first assistant director. Smiling warmly, he clasped Johnny Jaybird's small hand in a two-fisted shake. "How you feeling, Jonathan? Did you get the flowers we sent to the hospital?"

Johnny bobbed in deference. "They were beautiful, Paul. Much too extravagant, though."

"No cost is too great, buddy." Paul put a tentative hand on the younger man's back. "We're just glad you're okay. Right, everybody?"

The crowd murmured in assent.

"You going to be up to working again, bud? I have plans for you to shoot some more action scenes. I was absolutely right about your talent in that area. I've been doing this long enough to know a budding genius when I see one."

Paul's assessment seemed a bit excessive to me, but Johnny stretched his neck upward, as if letting the director's praise rain down upon his head.

Paul, the affectionate smile still plastered on his face, seemed like he was going to continue on with the appreciation fest. But Barbara sidled up through the crowd to whisper something in his ear. His face immediately turned serious. She crooked her arm through his and whisked him away.

"Gotta go," he called over his shoulder. "It's always something, isn't it? Good to have you back, buddy!"

I had to wonder where Paul's solicitous attitude was coming from. It wasn't as if he'd shown a lot of concern for Johnny Jaybird before. Did he want something from the young assistant director? And if he did, what was it?

I worked my way to the inner circle of the crowd, intent on getting those questions answered. When there was a pause in the well-wishing, I smiled at Johnny. He gave me what seemed like a genuine grin in return. I was encouraged. "How's the wound?"

"I was lucky."

"You sure were," I agreed. "Listen, I've been wondering about something."

He raised his eyebrows, offered an inquisitive head bob.

"Where was the director that morning you shot the horse scene? I thought he was supposed to be in charge?"

The arrogant mask fell back over his face.

"The inner workings of film-making can be extremely complicated. You're the animal wrangler, right? Maybe you should just stick to animals."

Someone in the crowd snorted a laugh. I was actually amused, too. He was such a ridiculous snob, it was funny. But Mama had found her way to my side, and she failed to see the humor. She pulled herself up to her full height, which was almost equal to Johnny's.

"My daughter is no dummy, Mister. Mace was valedictorian of her college class at University of Central Florida."

He leveled a cool look at my defender. "Isn't that the school that has a special program to study Disney World? Never been there. I did graduate work at the American Film Institute. Maybe you've heard of it?"

He sneered, waiting for Mama to answer. She held her tongue, surprisingly.

"Before that, I was at Princeton," he added.

Mama crooked her wrist, fancy style: "Well, la-di-da-da. You know, I dated a boy from Princeton once. He had an impressive diploma, but no common sense. Couldn't find his own butt with his hands in his back pockets."

A chuckle made its way around the crowd.

"Princeton doesn't mean you're any smarter than my middle girl, Mace."

As Johnny narrowed his eyes at Mama, and she crossed her arms over her chest, I settled in for what I hoped would be a good show. But the crowd started stirring. A wave of whispers rippled from one end to the other. People moved aside, making way. Toby shuffled his feet and kept his eyes on the ground as he trailed behind Greg Tilton. Tilton stepped up smartly, front and center. A hush grew. Soon, there was silence.

Toby, head down, looked like he'd rather be anywhere but at the center of that crowd. A loud whisper came from the rear: "Better duck. It's Toby Take Aim."

"He's got some nerve," said someone else, not even bothering to whisper.

Some shushes circled around the crowd, but then another voice chimed in. "Yeah, Toby could have killed him."

Tilton held up his hands, cleared his throat. The crowd stilled.

"Listen up!" He sounded competent, take-charge. Just like in the movie where he was an anti-terrorism task force leader. "Toby has something he wants to say."

He nudged the young star forward. When Toby's voice came out, it was barely audible. I was right next to him, and I couldn't make out a word. Tilton poked him hard in the back.

"Speak up. Be a man."

"I'm sorry I shot you." His voice grew louder, and he raised his eyes to meet Johnny's. "I didn't know the ammunition was live. I thought it was the prop gun, loaded with blanks."

Johnny waved a hand. "I know you didn't mean for me to get hurt. Apology accepted."

I didn't like Johnny much, but I thought the fact he didn't make Toby grovel made him look like a gentleman. The assistant director took three steps toward the young star, coming so close that Toby backed away. He grabbed at Toby's wrist, and forced the teen's hand close to his side.

"You can feel the bandages, right there. That's where the bullet entered and exited."

Toby, face reddening, tried to pull his hand away. Johnny Jaybird held it in place with an odd mixture of intensity and intimacy.

"All our actions have consequences." Johnny stared, trying to catch Toby's eyes. The young star dropped his gaze to the ground. "The doctors say it's healing pretty well, but it'll leave a scar. Guess I'll never have a career as an Armani underwear model."

Toby's head snapped up. Glaring, he snatched his hand away. Did I remember reading something in People that Toby got his start modeling underwear?

"Not cool, dude!" the young star said.

"I'm not making fun of you, Toby. You stepped up and admitted what you did. I just wish you'd be as forthcoming about everything in your life."

Toby's face was scarlet — whether from anger or embarrassment, I couldn't tell. He turned and stomped into the woods. Johnny followed him more slowly, holding his side and walking gingerly. Everyone watched them go.

"Cue the ominous music," some wisecracker said, and several people laughed.

I glanced toward Tilton, who had returned to the picnic table. He was unwrapping half of his sandwich, but his eyes were fixed on the retreating figures of Toby and Johnny. His expression was hard to read. Was he interested? Amused? Did he like being a troublemaker?

"I'm going to talk to Tilton," I said to Mama.

She automatically reached in her pocket and offered me her Apricot Ice. "And smooth some of those snarls out of your hair, honey. That rain has left you looking like my little dog, Teensy, before the groomer gets a hold of her."

"I'm not trying to get a date, Mama."

"Oh, I can see that, darlin'."

I stalked away, leaving Mama standing there with the lipstick tube in her outstretched hand. She might have followed me, but Sal was coming into the camp at the same time. She Apricot Iced her own lips, and ran to meet her husband.

Tilton was still staring off in the direction Toby and Johnny Jaybird took. He didn't seem to notice my presence.

"What's up with those two?" I asked him.

He turned to me, a blank look on this face. He put down the sandwich. I nodded in the direction the two men had taken.

"Jonathan's obsessed with trying to get young Toby to be honest; to get in touch with who he really is. We're all waiting to see how long it's going to take."

"For what?" I asked.

"For Toby to admit to himself that he's gay."

I lifted my jaw from the ground. "Gay? Does Jesse know about that?"

He gave me a knowing smirk, and bent his head toward the edge of the crowd. Jesse had just arrived, accepting praise and compliments on her performance as she made her way toward her trailer.

"Why don't you ask her?"

A few minutes later, I was doing just that. The adoring crowd was dispersing. Someone had handed Jesse a cold soda from craft services. "Got a minute?" I asked.

"Hi, Mace. What'd you think?"

For a moment I wasn't sure if she was referring to Toby and Johnny. Of course, she meant her scene. "You nailed it! Really outstanding. I believed every word you said."

Her face lit up. I guess even when you're famous, you never get tired of hearing you've done a good job.

I quickly caught her up about the strange encounter between Toby and the assistant director. "I thought you and Toby were a couple, Jesse. I saw the way he looked at you after the incident in the parking lot. He told you he loved you."

She sipped at the soda, shrugged. "Toby's confused about his sexuality. It happens."

"But, I thought that day you two came out of your trailer . . ." I was going to say he didn't seem the least bit confused then, strutting as he zipped his jeans. She interrupted me.

"There's real life and then there's Hollywood, Mace. We're all about fantasy and make-believe."

She took a long swallow of soda. And then she was silent, seemingly examining the nutritional rundown on the back of the can. I watched her, trying to figure out what she was thinking. Her face was blank. Finally, she raised her eyes to mine.

"Toby's mistake is thinking I can save him. I am nobody's savior."

Twenty-Six

"I wonder if Jesse would give me some notes on my character's motivation. Do you think I should ask her, Mace?"

I was half-listening to Mama's dissertation on everything Jesse had done right in playing her big scene as the terrified, bereaved older sister. Of course, I was far more interested in some of the other roles she'd been playing: Toby's sexual conquest; a sworn enemy of Norman; supplicant to Norman's ex-wife and business partner, Barbara.

Mama nudged me in the arm. "Well, do you, Mace?"

"Do I what?"

"Think that Mama should go bother one of Hollywood's most famous young actresses for tips on how to read her one line," Maddie said.

Mama sniffed. "It's actually two sentences, Maddie."

"That's right. And Rosie's part is essential to the plot." Sal looked adoringly at Mama.

"I stand corrected," Maddie said.

My sisters had finished their business in town. They met up with Mama, Sal, and me under some shade trees in base camp. We hid from the late afternoon sun, as we waited out one of the many delays on the set. Now that I knew a little bit about film-making, I realized it was amazing that any movies ever made it to the theater. Hurry up and wait.

Marty suddenly clutched my hand. "Don't look now. Carlos is headed this way."

Everyone except me immediately shifted or turned in their chairs to watch him approach. Subtle.

"Sal, I need a word." He nodded, unsmiling, at the rest of us.

"No problem." Sal started to rise, when I saw Mama place a restraining hand on his tree-trunk-sized thigh.

"Carlos, honey, why don't you have a seat and rest a bit. You look like something the dog dragged up from under the porch."

He offered Mama a weak grin. "That bad, huh?"

I thought he looked gorgeous, if a bit tired. I wanted to smooth the frown line from his brow, and kiss the tension off his lips. I resisted an urge to reach over and straighten his hair. Whenever he was deep in thought, he scratched at each side of his head near the temples. It left his thick hair sticking out in peaks over his ears.

I interlaced my fingers on my lap so I wouldn't be tempted. I was still angry about the way he'd left me standing at the horse corral, calling after him like a desperate, needy girlfriend.

Marty slid over on a bench seat, patting a space for Carlos. "Mama just means you look tired. You've been working so hard. Why don't you take a break?"

Marty looked up at him with that sweet, imploring way she has; the way I don't have.

He glanced at me, raised his eyebrows in a question.

I shrugged. "It's a free country."

I immediately felt a pinch on my thigh hard enough to leave a bruise: Maddie.

Mama said, "Ignore my middle daughter, Carlos. She was raised by wolves."

"Sorry. Do have a seat," I mumbled. "We'd love to have you join us."

"Don't mind if I do." Ignoring the frost I tried to put in my voice, he squeezed in next to Marty, sitting across from me. "Where's your good friend, Jeb?"

I could feel my blood pressure rising. "I

tried to explain, Carlos. I recall you stomping away and refusing to listen, as usual."

A worried look passed between my sisters and Mama. Even Sal looked concerned.

"Jeb Ennis?" Maddie snorted. "That broken-down, no-account, ex-rodeo cowboy? He doesn't have a pot to piss in. I saw him getting coffee this morning; probably after a drunk last night. His looks are going, too."

"No, they're not, honey. Jeb is still one fine-looking man." Mama winced a bit, and I knew from her glare that Marty must have kicked her. "You're right about the pot, though. I heard Jeb lost everything he owned, again."

"Well, he still has his cattle dog, right Mace?"

I narrowed my eyes at Carlos. What kind of game was he playing? Did he want to get a rise out of me? Was he trying a lame joke in an attempt to make up? I couldn't tell. He had his cop face on. So, instead of saying the wrong thing, I said nothing.

"Mace, the man asked you a question!" Mama swatted my folded hands. "I didn't teach you to ignore people when they speak to you."

I jerked out of her reach. "Stop slapping on me, Mama. I'm a grown woman!"

229

"Then start acting like one!"

"Ring, ring . . . Kettle, it's the pot." I offered her a pretend phone. "Who's the one simpering around the set, pretending to be a movie star? Who's the one playing dress-up, like she's in her second childhood?"

Sal slammed one of his bear-paw-sized hands on the table. "Enough, Mace! Don't talk like that about your mudder. She earned a speaking part, and she's good. She's going to steal the whole movie!"

He beamed with pride at Mama, who planted a kiss on his cheek. "At least I know how to keep my man happy, don't I, Sally?"

Sal nodded, grinning like a fat man at an all-you-can-eat buffet.

I heard Marty's quiet voice. "Mace can't help it if she doesn't express her feelings well. Not everybody wears their heart on their sleeve." She looked pointedly at Mama, and then turned to my estranged boyfriend. "She cares so much about you, Carlos. We've never seen her like this with anyone she's ever dated."

"That's right," Mama chimed in. "Mace loves you."

My cheeks burned. I must have been blushing, which was totally embarrassing. I didn't dare raise my eyes to see Carlos's reaction to my family trying to patch up our romance. But I was listening to every word; including the next ones, when Maddie managed to put her foot in it.

"She was crazy about Jeb Ennis, of course. But Mace only thought that was love." Maddie leaned to grab at both shins. "Ouch!"

"Jeb is history, Maddie. I was a kid. I tried to tell Carlos that, but he didn't want to listen. Now, if y'all are through dissecting my sorry love life, I need to go check on the horses."

I propelled myself away from the table, fighting the urge to look over my shoulder to see if Carlos would come after me. I could almost feel my skin scorching where five pairs of eyes were aimed at my back. I was debating whether to swallow my pride and return to get Carlos, when I saw Greg Tilton watching me from another table, a plastic-wrapped sandwich in his hand. Maybe he lacked the Hollywood obsession with calories, because I'd already seen him eating lunch, and this was his second extra sandwich of the day. Dropping it on the table, he fell into step beside me.

"Hey, want some company?"

"Not really."

A look of surprise flitted across his face. "I thought we could talk about what's been happening around here. Somebody mentioned you're really smart. They say you're some kind of super amateur detective when it comes to solving murders."

He had me at "smart."

"I'm not much in the mood for talking," I said, "but you can tag along with me to the corral."

As we made our way through the woods, Tilton must have caught on to my black mood. I was pleasantly surprised that he didn't yammer at me, or insist I turn my frown upside down to a smile. I hate when people say that. I saw him watching a cardinal as it flitted from branch to branch. "Pretty redbird, huh?"

" 'Cardinalis cardinalis,' " Greg answered.

You could have knocked me over with a *cardinalis* feather. He gave me his patented movie-star smirk.

"I was quite the birdwatcher when I was a kid," he said. "Guess that makes me a dork."

"Not at all," I said. "I wish more people were aware of the natural world around them."

"When I was a boy, I used to escape to the woods for hours. I felt safe there."

"Me, too." I raised my head to take in the green canopy of trees above us. "Still do."

We were silent for a while, just standing together on the path, enjoying the sights and sounds of the woods. Something small scurried through the undergrowth, and we both turned to follow the noise. It was probably a squirrel, or maybe a snake. He spotted a hawk in a tall pine, and pointed it out to me without a word. I showed him the resurrection ferns growing on an oak's branches, green and lush now after yesterday's rain. It felt good, companionable, to share my love of nature with somebody who appreciated the outdoors like I did.

I was scanning the ground, still searching for any little critters moving through the brush, when I realized Tilton had gone motionless beside me. He wasn't checking out the trees or the undergrowth or the birds anymore. He was checking out me.

"You know, the way that dappled sunlight hits your face is really stunning. And you have this serene expression as you look at the woods. You're a beautiful woman, Mace. It makes you even more desirable that you don't seem to realize it."

Uh-oh.

I started to protest that he shouldn't get the wrong idea, that I was involved with somebody, but he put a finger to my lips.

"Shhhh, don't speak." He'd lowered the tone of his voice into the seduction register. "Just accept the compliment."

I felt like Sandra Bullock in a plain-Jane role, at the moment the dashing hero shows an interest.

He rubbed his finger suggestively over my lips. That sandwich must have been tuna fish, because I could smell it on his hand. I jerked back my head, and shook it with force. "No."

"No?" He raised his brows, surprised. Then his face contorted with anger, and he grabbed my wrist. "I know you're attracted to me. What's your problem?"

An image of Carlos's face appeared in my mind. "For one thing, I'm seeing somebody. For another, I'm not attracted to you."

He gave a snort of laughter at the very idea of that. "Yeah, right. Anyway, I'm not asking you to marry me. Wouldn't you like to be able to say you got it on with the great Greg Tilton?"

He still had a bruising grip on my wrist. He pulled my hand to the fly of his jeans, forcing me to stroke him through the fabric. Apparently, he was ready. But I was far from willing.

I struck as fast as a Florida panther, using my free hand to grab his ear. I twisted it, hard. At the same time, I brought my knee up with a solid shot to his groin. Dropping my wrist, he doubled over. He clutched one hand to his ear. The other cupped his crotch, as he gasped for breath.

He stepped backward, stumbled over a marlberry shrub, and landed on the ground. "Bitch!" His face was crimson, either from groin pain or rage.

"You asked for it."

"Nobody treats Greg Tilton like that, especially not some country mouse from Hicksville, Florida."

"Well, I guess you're wrong about that, because this country mouse just kicked Greg Tilton's ass."

Grimacing, he tried to get up. I put my boot to his shoulder and sat him back down.

"Touch me again," I said, "and I'll knock your teeth down your throat just to watch you spit 'em out, single-file."

What happened wasn't funny. Still, I was grinning as I walked away because of the last sight I'd had of him. The "great Greg Tilton" was sprawled on his ass, smack dab in a patch of poison ivy.

TWENTY-SEVEN

I was still shaking, not from fear but from anger. *Hicksville?* Who the hell did Greg Tilton think he was?

I was on my way back to base camp, to warn Mama and my sisters about him. I didn't even want to think about what might have happened if he'd tried the same thing on Marty, who is as sweet, and about as fragile, as a child's heirloom doll. Passing by where Tilton had been sitting, I noticed a raccoon had jumped onto the table. He'd gotten past the plastic wrap on the sandwich Tilton left, and was feasting on half of it. I must have been right about the tuna fish. Raccoons can't resist the strong smell.

Paul's wife, Savannah, was talking with my family. She was animated, gesturing with those graceful hands. Sal had left, probably to have that word that Carlos wanted. But my sisters and Mama leaned forward, listening eagerly. Savannah noticed me first, and waved me over. As I got closer, her smile changed into a worried frown.

"Where's Greg?" she asked.

All eyes were on me, expectant.

"Gone, thankfully."

"What did you do, Mace?" Mama tsk-tsked. "Don't tell me you managed to scare him away, too."

"Oh, I scared him all right; but only after he scared me first."

Savannah nodded. "I told you so," she said to my sisters. "Did he force himself on you, Mace?"

Mama's eyes got round. Marty gasped. Maddie reached out a hand to touch my cheek. "Did he hurt you?" my big sister asked.

I shook my head, uncomfortable now with all the attention on me. "He did try something, but he didn't get very far. I'm fine."

Maddie patted my face with relief. "He's not nearly as big as he looks in the movies. If anything, you probably hurt him."

"Well, not permanently," I said with a smile.

"I'm just happy to hear you took care of it," Savannah said. "Just so long as it wasn't his face. Paul's shooting Greg's close-up scenes this afternoon."

"Oh, it wasn't his face." I told them what

Tilton had done, and how certain he'd seemed that I'd be willing to play along. "I kicked his butt, and left him sprawled in a patch of poison ivy."

"Well, I'd say that's right where he belongs, honey. Not that I approve of violence, but you had every right," Mama said. "See if I ever ask him for his autograph!"

Savannah reached into her purse. She slid a wrapped candy across the table. "I was saving this for later, but you need a treat from 'Savannah City Confections' more than I do. The pralines are good, but this chocolate's to die for. They're from my hometown."

I thanked her, and then asked, "When I first walked up, you said 'I told you so.' What did you mean?"

She brushed back a thick lock of her graying hair. She really was pretty. She had Meryl Streep's dignity, crossed with the perky Southern charm of Reese Witherspoon.

"Your mama had gone off to the little girl's room when I sat down, but your sisters told me Greg followed you off into the woods. I had a bad feeling . . ."

Marty said, ". . . and you were right."

Savannah's nod was grim. "He fancies himself a ladies' man. When a lady doesn't agree, he's been known to get really ugly, really fast."

"Is that personal experience talking?" I asked.

She cast her eyes down, her long lashes feathery against milky skin. Her voice was a whisper. "I'm not the only one."

Mama put a hand on Savannah's arm. "Now, I'm doubly glad Mace gave him what for."

Maddie said, "How come we've never read about this side of Greg Tilton in *People* magazine?"

Savannah lifted her shoulders. "There have never been formal charges, as far as I can tell. Women know if they come forward against a famous star like Greg, their whole lives become open for examination. Nobody wants to be hounded by paparazzi, or become the lead story in the *National Enquirer.*"

Marty shook her head. "That's not right. He shouldn't be allowed to get away with it."

Savannah waved a hand. "Everyone makes excuses for him. And he did have a terrible childhood. His mom was an abusive drug addict who abandoned him, basically selling him for a pipe full of crack. He lived in a whole series of foster homes; most every one of them was worse than the last."

"How old was he?" Mama asked.

"Four or five when his mom sold him."

"Old enough to realize what happened," I said.

"I can see how he might want to feel loved," Marty said.

Maddie balled her fists and rubbed pretend tears from her eyes. "Oh, boo-hoo-hoo. None of that gives him the right to go forcing himself on women who aren't interested in 'loving' him. He's not the only person in the world who had it tough as a kid. A troubled childhood excuses nothing."

Savannah nodded. "You're right, Maddie. There is no excuse. But it does help explain why he's the way he is. And living in the bubble of Hollywood has just amplified it. When you're a big star, you come to expect special treatment. No one *ever* says no."

When it comes to the word no, I was finding out that Hollywood people are a lot like spoiled toddlers, screaming for more in the checkout line at Toys "R" Us.

Nerves always stimulate my bladder, so it was time for me to make a visit to the honey wagon.

Dispensing a butt-kicking, though, gooses my appetite. So, I made a detour on my way back by the craft services truck to check out the snacks. I grabbed an oversized brownie for myself, and two more, plus a cookie for the table.

I ducked my head into the catering tent, which was nearly empty between meals. I noticed Jesse in a corner, talking to Paul. I wondered if she was looking for praise from him about how she handled her scene. Unlike their aversion to hearing "no," these people loved to hear about how great they were. Big egos and a lack of self-control seemed like a dangerous combination.

Toby and Johnny Jaybird sat at another table. Johnny, leaning in toward the younger man, was doing most of the talking. Though Toby's eyes were aimed at the ground, his head was inclined toward Johnny. He seemed to be listening intently.

Mama's husband was bonding over a cup of coffee with a tall, red-headed Teamster. The man had a New Yawk accent to rival Sal's. I'd seen the teamster earlier in the week, radioing instructions to a driver arriving with an 18-wheeler filled with movie-making equipment. I had a fleeting urge to stop at their table and ask Sal if he'd spoken with Carlos. I didn't want to seem so desperately female in front of two tough guys, though.

Excuse me, does my boyfriend still like me?
Outside, the raccoon had finished off the first half of Tilton's sandwich, and was now working on the second. The animal seemed to be having some trouble with the plastic wrap, though. Raccoons are extraordinarily clever and dexterous, so I was confident it would prevail.

Back at our table, Mama's face brightened when she saw the sweet treats.

"Just what we need!" She clapped her hands. "Eating chocolate is much better than talking about Greg Tilton. What a disappointment. I still remember him, guns blazing against the bad guys, in the first Western I saw him do. What a hero he was."

"Acting, Mama," Maddie said.

As I sat, my gaze returned to the raccoon. It had dropped the sandwich, without managing to peel free the wrapping. In fact, the animal's behavior was strange. It tumbled from the bench seat, and then had trouble righting itself on the ground. The coon zigzagged toward the woods, like a drunk trying to follow a straight line at a DUI checkpoint.

"Mace?" Mama's voice sliced through the air.

"Hmm?" I said, turning to her.

"Pay attention! Maddie and I asked which

brownie you wanted. What is so darned interesting over there that you can't answer your mama?"

"The big brownie is mine." I turned back toward the animal, now walking in circles. "There's something wrong with that raccoon."

"It's a pest; that's what's wrong with it," Maddie grumbled. "I'm cutting this biggest brownie in half for Mama and me. I left you the second-biggest one."

The raccoon seemed dizzy, off-balance. As I got up for a closer look, convulsions started racking the poor thing's body. Then it stiffened, and plopped over on its side. By the time I got there, the raccoon was dead.

TWENTY-EIGHT

Kneeling next to the raccoon, I brushed at my eyes.

"Why are you crying?" Jesse stood over me. "You warned us over and over to stay away from them. You said they can carry disease. You called them beggars, no better than thieves."

"Yeah, I know what I said; but I think this raccoon was poisoned. None of God's creatures should have to suffer like that."

"Poisoned?" Her eyes went wide.

I glanced over my shoulder at the bench. "We need to call the police over here to take a look at that sandwich. Meanwhile, we can't let anybody get near enough to touch it, or take it."

I quietly asked her to sit at the table, so she could guard it from the curious, or maybe the nefarious. Before she went, Jesse pulled aside a production assistant. "You better let Barbara know about this."

The PA hurried off toward the production trailer.

Meanwhile, my sisters and Mama had joined me by the raccoon's body. Murmurs moved in waves through the gathering crowd. I looked around, searching in vain for Tilton. In fact, I didn't see any of the stars, aside from Jesse. Savannah had disappeared, too. If it was Tilton's sandwich that killed the raccoon, I hoped he hadn't eaten any. I didn't like him, but I didn't want him dead.

"What makes you think it was poison?" Mama asked.

"Remember when that pack of wild dogs got into the strychnine at our cousin Bubba's?"

"The Bubba in jail, or the other Bubba?" Maddie asked.

"The good Bubba."

"Right," Marty said. "He had it for the ranch where he was working; for the rats."

I nodded. "This animal showed the same symptoms those dogs did."

We all redirected our gaze to the dead raccoon. It had vomited. A bit of white foam still clung to its mouth.

A breathless voice came from the edge of the crowd. "Barbara sent for the detective. She wants him to examine the raccoon."

I looked up to see the same production assistant. While I was glad Carlos was being summoned, I was surprised Barbara hadn't come back with the PA. I fully expected her to push me out of the way so she could take over. Even if the dead raccoon would likely be the first raccoon she'd ever seen up close, Barbara didn't seem like the type to miss a chance to be in charge.

Soon, a stir in the crowd signaled Carlos's arrival. People moved aside to make way. He wore his authority like a suit of armor. Was his armor also to keep me out? His face was steel; not even a flicker of recognition when he saw me. I felt the chill like an icy wind. Mama and my sisters must have felt it, too.

"Mace is the one who noticed the raccoon acting like it was poisoned," Marty told him.

"She's made sure no one has come near it," Maddie added.

"And she made Jesse stay over there with what's left of the sandwich until the crime scene folks can come collect it and test it for what might have killed the coon," Mama said.

He glanced toward Jesse. She sat at the table, faithfully guarding the sandwich. He gave me a curt nod, like I was a helpful stranger. "Everybody move back, please.

This is police business. Just go back to whatever you were doing."

The crowd started to shuffle this way and that. Sal arrived, adding his voice as high-volume backup to Carlos's order. "Dat means go, people. Move along. Nuttin' to see here."

Sal physically pushed against some of the more reluctant looky-loos. Between his natural Bronx megaphone, and his broad chest, he was a one-man crowd deterrent. When Mama, my sisters, and I made no move to leave, Carlos focused those black lasers on me.

"You and your family go away, too. Please." His voice was drained of emotion. "We need to clear this area."

I tried to fight the resentful remark making its way up my throat. I lost the battle.

"If I hadn't noticed the way the raccoon died, you wouldn't even know to suspect poison," I said.

"Yes, your powers of observation are quite keen, when it comes to animals."

That didn't sound like a thank-you to me.

Marty tugged at my arm. Sucking the Apricot Ice off her bottom lip, Mama regarded Carlos and me with worry in her eyes. Maddie said, "C'mon, honey. Let's go back and finish our brownies. I saved the last cookie for you."

Carlos turned his back, dismissing me. He squatted down to examine the raccoon. I started away. "Thank you, Mace," he said coolly.

"You're welcome." Relief flooded my body. I turned to him. "I figured it was best to keep people away from the raccoon and the sand . . ."

"No," he interrupted. "I meant thank you for leaving."

A knife twisted in my heart.

I pushed my untouched cookie in a circle around a paper plate. My appetite was gone.

"Mace, don't play with your food, honey. Someone else could still want that cookie, if you'd keep your dirty fingers off it."

I didn't even snap at Mama to stop treating me like a six-year-old. When she got no rise out of me, Mama furrowed her brow at Maddie and Marty. "We have to fix things, girls. Mace and Carlos are meant to be together. They just happen to be the two most stubborn people on God's green earth."

"You better take things into your own hands." Maddie's voice was soft. "You do not want Mama trying to fix things."

She tucked a lock of my hair behind my

ear. Such unaccustomed tenderness from my big sister made my eyes sting with tears.

"Oh, honey!" Marty offered me a tissue. "Swallow your pride and tell him you're sorry about Jeb."

Running my knuckles under my eyes, I waved away Marty's tissue. "No. There's nothing between Jeb and me. I don't have anything to be sorry for. Carlos is the one who should apologize to me, for being such an overly sensitive wuss."

Maddie gazed across the way at Carlos — his chest broad, his jaw firm, his black eyes smoldering with intensity as he considered where the dead raccoon fit into his puzzle. "You can call Carlos a lot of things, Mace, but no one in their right mind would ever use the word 'wuss' to describe that manly specimen."

Shaking her head, Mama rose from the table. She walked over to Sal, who was still doing crowd duty. Pointing toward me, she stood on tiptoes and whispered in his ear. Oh no, what was she cooking up?

As she returned, Sal dutifully did her bidding. I watched him from the corner of my eye as he approached Carlos. They had a short conversation, and then Sal looked at me with an expression that seemed pitying.

The big man shuffled back, looking like a

child heading to the doctor for a shot. In his most blaring voice, he reported to us, and to anyone else within a fifty-yard radius, what Carlos had said.

"He said he's too busy right now to worry about some on-again, off-again relationship. He's got more important things on his mind, what with a murder investigation, a poisoned raccoon, and an army of Holly-wood reporters breathing down his neck."

"That's fine, Sal. Thank you." Mama patted his hand, glancing nervously at me. "You can tell us the rest later."

Sal plowed ahead, a rookie officer unde-terred from finishing his first verbal report. "Carlos said, and I quote: 'Mace is going to have to get her head on straight without my help. I'm sick of trying to deal with a woman with the emotional maturity of a seventh grade girl.' "

Sal looked at me. The expression *was* pity-ing, with a bit of apologetic thrown in.

"That part about the seventh grade was his words, not mine. Sorry, Mace."

I winced. The truth hurt.

"I'd say you're at least as mature as a high school girl," Marty said.

Maddie nodded loyally, and then nar-rowed her eyes to a spot over my shoulder. "What are *you* doing here?"

I turned my head. I'd been so focused on what Sal was saying, I hadn't noticed Jeb Ennis come up. How much had he heard?

"Howdy, Maddie." He tipped his hat to my sister. "Always a pleasure. You know, that Carlos fellow must have left half his mind in Miamuh. He doesn't know what he's turning his back on."

I guess Jeb had heard enough.

"Any man in his right mind would be happy to have Mace, hang-ups and all."

As I sat there, surely blushing with embarrassment, Jeb put a hand on my shoulder. It seemed like a friendly gesture, but I could feel him caressing my skin through the fabric of my blouse. He looked at me, desire sparking in his blue eyes. The fire must have been catching, because I began to think along those same lines.

Maybe I needed something more simple than what I had with Carlos. What did I have with Carlos, anyway? Hadn't he just dismissed me without a backward glance, and then disrespected me on top of that?

Jeb had some problems, no doubt about that. With him, though, all his hang-ups and shortcomings were out in the open. Jeb wasn't complicated. He wasn't moody. He wasn't Carlos.

"I've got a cooler in my truck. What say

you and me go grab a few beers and sit by a cow pond?" A devilish smile lit Jeb's face. "I'll even collect some rocks so you can toss 'em into the water."

Why not, I thought. Why the hell not?

Standing, I ignored Mama's disapproving glare, Marty's worried frown, and Maddie's loud tsking. I didn't even try to scoot away as Jeb tossed a casual arm around my shoulder.

As we left, I turned my head ever so slightly to steal a glance at Carlos. He seemed completely unaware of my presence . . . or absence. Instead, he glowered at the poor raccoon, as if he blamed it for being poisoned and complicating his homicide investigation.

Carlos was so intensely focused on the problem at hand, I doubted if he realized I was granting him his wish. I was walking out of his life.

TWENTY-NINE

The cab of Jeb's pickup smelled like a vat of mosquito repellent. With dusk coming on, the insects were ravenous. We'd fled the banks of the cattle pond for the relative shelter of his truck. But it was hot, so we had to crack the windows. We'd both bathed in the stuff to ward off the biting swarms.

The bugs buzzed at us in frustration, seemingly determined to find a patch of unprotected skin. They wouldn't find it on me. Even my earlobes were coated with the spray.

Jeb leaned in and gave me a kiss. I stiffened. He sat back against the bench seat, wiping his sleeve across his mouth to get rid of what must have been the acrid taste of repellent. He slapped his neck, where one of the insects landed on a spot he must have missed.

He lifted a lock of my hair, and then ran his finger down my neck and into the V of my blouse. I wanted to feel a shiver of desire for Jeb. Instead, I got a picture in my mind of the last time Carlos's fingers had traveled that same trail. A deep longing for what Carlos and I had shared hit me like a kick in the gut.

I pulled away, snapping the top button closed on my Western-style blouse. Jeb and I shifted, each edging as far as possible toward our respective doors on the truck.

"Late in the year for the mosquitoes to be so bad," he said.

"Rain didn't help," I answered.

Despite our long history, an uncomfortable strain hung in the air between us like a thick fog. Maybe it was the close quarters of the truck. Or maybe it was the fact that Carlos's scowling image slid in front of my eyes every time I looked at Jeb.

"How's the ranch doing?"

"Okay, but it's been hard to get ahead," he said. "I'm still paying off debts from that trouble I had a while back. The movie people hired a cattleman out of Osceola County to supply the stock, but he had a family emergency. Bad for him; lucky for me. I can sure use the extra cash."

"Still gambling?"

He traced a pattern on the steering wheel. "No way. That bad habit of mine about ruined my life."

Neither of us spoke. The truck was so quiet, I could hear him breathing. I watched the second hand of his wristwatch jumping away the seconds on a luminous dial. Finally, I took a breath and said, "This isn't going to work, Jeb."

He sighed, and it sounded more like relief than disappointment.

"I was wondering which of us would be first to say it." He patted my knee, friendly like. "Can't blame a guy for trying. Of course, I might still be game for a little somethin.' Truth is, I think your mind is on someone else."

I stared out the window. It would be dark in an hour or so. The woods around the parking area were already filled with deep shadows.

When I didn't respond, Jeb said, "Why don't you try to make it right with Miamuh? It's as plain as the balls on a bull that you're in love with the guy."

"It's complicated."

"Hell girl, love usually is." Laughing, he brushed a hand through his hair. "And speaking of that, I thought I was going to be Dr. Love tonight. Looks like I turned into Dr. Phil instead."

When I looked over at him, he gave me a

wink. "I know a lot about love, see. I'm usually the one to 'complicate' things up."

"How is that girlfriend of yours, anyway?"

"She left me. Again. I've been thinking maybe a fling with Kelly Conover would make her jealous enough to come running back."

I snorted. "Good plan. Why don't you try something for a change that doesn't involve you cheating on your girlfriend? Besides, do you really think you've got a shot with every man's Hollywood fantasy woman?"

"Like I said before, can't fault a guy for trying."

We both chuckled, our laughter like sunlight burning off the tense fog between us. Impulsively, I slid next to him, threw my arm around his neck, and pulled his face close so I could kiss his cheek. Jeb looked startled, and then gave me a sweet goodbye kiss right on the lips.

I drew away, and started to make a joke about how Dr. Phil probably wouldn't accept a kiss as his pay. The words died in my mouth. Carlos's car was parked on the driver's side of Jeb's truck. He'd chosen just the wrong moment to come retrieve something from his front seat. In the flash of his dome light, I could see him watching us. The look he shot me was pure disgust.

"Shit," I said.

Jeb turned and saw him, too. "You can say that again."

Carlos grabbed a bag from his floorboard and slammed the car door. I was certain I'd have felt the ground shake if I'd been standing there. He stalked off, something he'd been doing a lot of lately. I resisted the urge to jump out of Jeb's truck and follow. Really, how could I explain away what Carlos had seen with his own eyes: me and my old beau in the front seat of his pickup, kissing and hugging like high school sweethearts? I could tell him I'd just informed Jeb that things wouldn't work between us, but Carlos wouldn't believe it.

I was defeated before I could even try.

"Mace, I'm sorry . . ." Jeb started to speak, but I held up my hand to stop him.

"I don't want to talk about it. Let me just sit here for a minute and calm down. I need to get my head straight. I'm expected at my mama's for pizza in a half hour or so, and want my game face on."

I sat there, wondering what was wrong with me. Why couldn't I get this love thing right? Even with her record of lousy marriages, Mama had managed to do it perfectly at least twice, once with my daddy and now with Sal. Both my sisters were happy, in long marriages with men who adored them. Why couldn't I commit? Why couldn't I find contentment like that?

Jeb picked at a cracked piece of vinyl on his dashboard. Finally, he looked at me, his face worried. "Do you want me to say something to Carlos? I can explain how you were just letting me down easy."

"God, no." I thought of how proud Carlos was, how it would gall him to have Jeb butting in. "That'd just make it worse."

I took a few deep breaths, trying to calm the awful gnawing in my stomach. I told Jeb goodbye, and had my hand on the door to leave when a cell phone shrilled nearby.

There was just enough light in the sky to make out Barbara Sydney. She was striding with purpose toward a fancy Jaguar, parked a couple of vehicles away from us. She barked out a hello in that harsh Boston accent. "This is Barbara," she confirmed. "Hang on a minute."

Shifting the phone away from her mouth, she looked to the left and to the right. We must have been hidden from her view by the shadow of a tall van that was parked right next to us. We could see her, but apparently she couldn't see us.

"Okay, I cannot be the source of this information, right?" She glanced over each shoulder, and continued walking. "I'll sue your ass to Sunday and back if you quote me by name. This is strictly on background."

Barbara's voice paused as she listened to the caller. Jeb raised an eyebrow at me. I put my finger to my lips.

"I wanted you to know the latest news from this nightmare of a project," she said. "There's been an attempt to poison someone in the cast."

She kept walking, phone to her ear.

"Nobody, so far. But a raccoon keeled over dead today. Our redneck animal wrangler says it ate a poisoned sandwich . . ." she paused, listening for a moment.

"How the hell would I know what kind of sandwich? My fear is Toby Wyle might be the target."

Toby Wyle? I mouthed the name to Jeb. He mouthed back at me: *Redneck wrangler?*

"The cops are looking into it, right."

That was the last thing we heard Barbara say as she opened the door and climbed into the driver's seat of the pearly white sedan. The interior light stayed on for a moment or two after she shut the door. It was just long enough to tell she was still talking full speed into the phone, as she gunned her engine and roared out of the lot.

As the Jaguar sped past us, I wondered: Could Barbara have been the mystery driver of the light-colored vehicle that nearly killed Toby in the parking lot?

THIRTY

"Hurt her again, and I'll kill you!" The sound of a sharp slap — and the frantic yelping of a Pomeranian — punctuated the angry words.

"Ouch, Jeez!"

"Shhh, Sal, you're not supposed to say anything. Use your actor's physicality. React."

Physicality? Surely the book Mama checked out about the Actor's Studio must be due back at the library by now.

The yapping grew louder. On the other side of Mama's front door, I could hear her and Sal, along with the scrabble of pedicured paws clicking against the tiled entryway.

"I can't help it, Rosie. That really stung. I think you're supposed to pull your punches, honey."

I stood on the front stoop, debating whether I was up to the Mama-Sal-and-

Teensy circus. The promise of Pizza Night enticed me onward, though. I may have been lovelorn, but I was also hungry. Not counting the brownie, I'd barely had a bite to eat since breakfast.

I opened the door, nudging aside Mama's pet with the toe of my boot. Of course, Teensy was extremely put out. The little Pomeranian high-tailed away from me, taking a flying leap onto the back of Mama's peach-colored sofa.

"Teensy! You know better than that," she yelled. "Get off of that couch."

As usual, the little yapster paid no mind to his mistress. Burrowing deep between two lemon-sherbet accent pillows, Teensy made himself comfortable. Head resting on his front paws, he lay on the couch and fastened his eyes on Mama and Sal.

They stood, center stage on a wide expanse of peach-colored carpet. Sal rubbed his cheek. Mama gave me a cheery wave. "Hey, darlin'! We're running my lines."

"Line, Rosie. There's just the one."

"Well, not if you count it by sentences, Sal."

I walked over and lifted Sal's chin. In the peach-colored glow coming from Mama's Lucite chandelier, I could see a hand-shaped outline starting to show on his cheek.

"That's got to smart." I leaned closer for a better look. "You should know by now, Sal. Mama's never been one to pull her punches."

She pouted, prettily. "I surely did not mean to hurt him. But the scene has to be believable. Some drunken cowpoke has just gotten fresh. I'm angry. I've had all I can take with all these men pawing at me."

"*Ruby*," Sal said. "Ruby has had all the pawing she can take."

"Well, of course, Sal! We all know I'm not Ruby. I'm ACTING here."

Mama stood on tip-toes and put a hand toward his cheek. Sal bobbed out of reach like a glass-jawed boxer. His palms went up in surrender.

"Don't come any closer! I'm okay."

"So," I said, "Sal's the stand-in for the drunken cowpoke?"

He bowed from the waist, pretending to doff a cowboy hat. "At your service, purty lady."

Mama harrumphed. "You can offer to serve Mace all you want, darlin', but she won't take you up on it. She prides herself on being independent; not needing anyone. Plus, she's as stubborn as Grandpa Pete with a pork chop."

"We don't have a grandpa named Pete."

"It's a saying, Mace."

"Well, it doesn't make any sense. Why would a pork chop make someone stubborn?"

Rolling her eyes, Mama heaved a dramatic sigh: "See what I mean, Sally? Mule-headed."

He ignored her, a defensive tactic he'd picked up from my sisters and me. "Any progress on Carlos?" he asked. "Are the two of youse getting along any better?"

My response was a scowl, which must have been surly enough to scare him. Sal pressed his lips together, scurried over to the couch, and scooped Teensy up from between the pillows. Without another word, he and the dog hastened to the safety of the kitchen.

Mama looked at me, her face creased in sympathy. "Oh, honey!"

A part of me wanted to collapse into tears, and fall into her comforting embrace. But when she leaned over to brush the bangs from my eyes, I jerked my head away. Old habits die hard.

She tsked. "You surely do make life a lot more difficult than it has to be, Mace. Why do you try to push away everyone who loves you?"

That was a pretty good question. I was still searching for some way to answer, when Teensy let out a yip and tore out of the kitchen. The little dog threw himself at the front door like he'd been shot from a cannon. Each time Mama had a visitor, Teensy believed he was the sole defense against whatever invading force was about to overrun the helpless humans inside. Right now, he was barking at a pitch high enough to make my ears bleed.

A shout came through the window from the front walk. "Mama! If you don't muzzle that animal, I swear I'm going to skin him alive and make him into a clutch purse."

Mama swooped down and put her hands over the dog's ears. "Hush, Maddie! You'll hurt Teensy's feelings."

Sal followed the dog to the door. As Mama opened it, he took a pizza box from each of my sisters' hands. Once Mama and Sal got married, he started taking part in our weekly tradition. It had always been Girls' Night, but neither my sisters nor I minded him joining in. He helped us keep Mama in line. Lord knew, we needed all the help we could get.

After we'd fixed our drinks and settled

into our usual chairs, we divvied up the pizza. I piled three everything-but-anchovy slices on my plate. Between Maddie and Sal, I never knew if I'd get the chance to eat my share. Marty cut her slice of plain cheese into tiny pieces, and slid her crust onto Maddie's plate. Mama rolled up her slice like a cigar, and took a nibble from the end. Sal covered his with a gale of red pepper flakes, and then ate half the piece in a single chomp.

When he swallowed, he held the remainder of his piece up for our inspection: "I know you girls don't like to hear this, but this sure ain't New York–style pizza."

"That figures," I said, "since we don't live in New York."

"Thank you, Jesus," Mama added.

"Funny, the fact that Himmarshee pizza is substandard never seems to stop you from eating it," Maddie said.

He finished the first slice, and shook pepper flakes on a second. "I'm just saying . . ."

The sound of chewing and drink-sipping rounded the table. Teensy skittered from chair to chair, seeking the softest touch. He bypassed Maddie and me entirely, focusing on Marty, Sal and Mama. At least Marty dropped her morsel for Teensy on the floor;

Mama fed the dog from her hand, and then kept eating with the same hand.

"Mama, that's just gross. Dogs' mouths are filled with bacteria," I said.

"So are people's mouths, honey. That doesn't mean I'd run and wash my face if you gave me a kiss."

"So now you're saying your daughter has the same standing as your dog?"

Even though I knew what Mama meant, I was in a bad mood and itching for a fight. She gave me a long look, like she was weighing whether to rise to the bait.

"Well, honey, I'm not saying you and Teensy have the same standing. Some days, I like the dog a little bit more."

"Ooooh, snap!" Maddie said.

Marty, the family diplomat, smoothly changed the subject to one she must have known would effectively keep Mama and me from bickering. "Sal, you've been helping Carlos and the police. Who do they think killed the movie producer?"

We all went quiet as Sal licked pizza grease from his fingers. Mama handed him a napkin, which he folded, unused, and placed beside his plate. "They don't have a whole lot yet, to tell you the truth. It's still early in the investigation. They do know the victim was killed where he was found."

"Really?" I said. "Out in the open like that?"

"Well, there was no blood trail. You and Rosie might have walked right in on a homicide in progress if that morning's horse scene hadn't taken so long to film."

An image of Norman splayed on the fence ran through my mind. Who had brought about such an undignified end for such a powerful man?

"I'm surprised nobody heard the shot," Maddie said.

"Suppressor." A quartet of puzzled looks were aimed at Sal.

"Commonly called a silencer," he clarified. "And the weapon was small caliber."

I digested that detail, along with the pizza.

"What about all the other strange things that have happened on the set?" Mama asked. "Does Carlos think they're related to the murder?"

Sal extracted another piece from the "everything" box. "That's still unclear."

"Did the cops find out where that sandwich Tilton had came from?" I asked.

"Tilton told them a whole basket of food was left in the fridge in his trailer. He assumed it was from the production office," Sal said. "He ate one of the sandwiches in the morning, with no ill effects. The second one was the one the raccoon got."

Sal shoveled the pizza slice into his mouth. With her usual precise timing, Maddie asked him a question just then. "Is Carlos still looking into whether someone tampered with that light that nearly killed Mace?"

He put up a hand until he could swallow. "All I know is he's considering every aspect. He's under an awful lot of stress, Maddie. It's not the best time to ask him about Mace."

Mama must have pinched him under the table, because Sal suddenly clapped a hand over his mouth. "Jeez, sorry Mace. I meant stress from the case. I wasn't implying you're the reason for his stress."

The four of them looked at me with sad cow eyes. "I don't need your pity." I pushed an uneaten slice and a few stray black olives around my plate. "I couldn't care less what Carlos thinks about me. I'm doing fine."

Glances were exchanged, but no one challenged me on that flat-out lie. Mama topped off her glass with sweet pink wine, and then offered the box to me. I waved it away.

"Well, let's see if you are doing fine." Maddie began to tick off points on her fingers. "You've managed to piss off a man who loves you, punch out one who doesn't, and all while someone else might have tried to kill you. Oh, yeah, and that devil Jeb Ennis keeps hanging around like a pit bull after a bitch in heat."

Maddie displayed her hand, with the pinky the only digit left un-ticked. "I'd say you're doing just Jim Dandy, Mace."

Raising her brow, Mama hefted the wine box toward me again. This time, I motioned her to tip that sucker over and keep on pouring.

THIRTY-ONE

Dew sparkled on the pasture as if God had tossed out a diamond to adorn every blade of grass. Early morning light glinted off the water in the horse trough. At this time of day, the sun was as welcome as an old friend. By noon, I'd be cursing it as a fiery sweat-ball sent straight from hell by the devil.

As I neared the corral, the horses nickered a greeting. It wasn't so much that they were ecstatic to see me, as it was the buckets of feed I carried. Still, I gave them a loud how-do whistle in return.

I was all alone this morning, which was fine by me. I'd exhausted my patience for family fun at last night's pizza dinner. And if I never had to cater to another Hollywood type, I'd be a happy gal. I had a break on that front. Jesse's next lesson wasn't until the afternoon; and no horse scenes were planned for the morning.

Even though the animals weren't needed for filming, they still needed to eat. So here I was: hefting hay and measuring out sweet feed and supplements for my equine charges.

A good-natured Appaloosa mare nosed my shirt collar as I tried to open the gate. A little pony banged its head against the slats of the fence, trying to reach into the feed bucket.

"Go on, get back, now!" I shouted. "Y'all better show me some manners, or nobody eats."

They knew my threats were hollow. Like Mama with her beloved Teensy, I was a soft touch for the big, pitiful eyes of begging horses.

When I was done distributing breakfast, I returned to the trailer with the empty buckets. I spent some time straightening tack and seeing what supplies were needed. When I came out, the horses had finished eating. They were shifting nervously around the corral. I stopped and closed my eyes, trying to hear what they heard: A crow cawed from a fence post. Cattle lowed in their pen across the pasture. The horses circled the enclosure. Their hooves striking the sandy ground made the sound of muffled clapping.

Then I heard a murmur of distant voices, human voices. Across the way, at the cow pen, I saw Kelly Conover and her mysterious protector, Sam. Her mouth was moving, and her palms were raised to the sky. Sam stood with his head bowed and his hands in his pockets, a short distance from Kelly. I couldn't distinguish her words, but from her posture, it looked like she was praying. I'd certainly seen her utter a curse, and finish it off by spitting on the ground. I couldn't believe she was now seeking an audience in the opposite spiritual realm.

Sam waited until she finished, and then he wrapped his arms around her in a tight embrace. She rested her head for a moment against his chest, and then pushed away. When one of the horses gave a loud whinny, both of them looked over toward the corral.

They couldn't have missed me, standing by the fence and gawking at them like I was at a carnival sideshow. I gave a halfhearted wave, and then turned my attention to the horses.

I hoped my lack of enthusiasm would signal I didn't want company. But the idea she wasn't wanted wasn't likely to occur to a woman like Kelly. She started toward me across the field, Sam trailing at her heels like a faithful pet. I boosted myself up onto the fence's top rail to await my audience with Hollywood royalty.

"Morning," Kelly called cheerfully.

Sam offered a wave that was at least as heartfelt as mine.

"It's Mace, right?"

I nodded at Kelly.

"These horses are really beautiful. You do a great job taking care of them." Kelly's smile was brighter than the morning sun. I felt myself warming to her. "We're lucky they hired you on as wrangler. Believe me, not everyone is as conscientious as you are about the job."

I knew I was grinning like an idiot. It turned out flattery from a mega-star worked just as well on me as it did on most other people. I tipped my cowgirl hat and scuffed at the rail below me with my boot heel, playing up my yokel's role. "Aw, shucks, ma'am. Thanks!"

A sly smile transformed Sam's face — the first time I'd seen any expression aside from a frown of worry or concern. So it seemed there *was* a personality there, behind those studious eyeglasses and steadfast devotion to Kelly.

"I couldn't help but notice you over there with your palms raised. I don't mean to get personal, but were you praying?"

I expected her to burst out laughing. Hollywood wasn't exactly known for its godly devotion.

"That's exactly what I was doing. Praying for forgiveness, in fact."

"Don't look so shocked," Sam said. "Not everyone in the movie industry is a godless heathen."

"I didn't think they were," I lied.

"Right," Kelly said. "In fact, Sam was just about born in a pew. His dad was the pastor of a little storefront church."

"Part-time," he said. "He worked full-time as an electrician. He always liked to say that the church fed souls, but it was electrical work that fed the family."

Kelly smiled at him. "Sam played the piano in their church."

"Badly," he said. "But I enjoyed it. My father and I were close. We did everything together."

"Did he pass away?" I asked.

He nodded. "My senior year in high school."

"I lost my daddy, too," I said. "I always wonder how life would have been different for us if he hadn't died."

Sam regarded me with dark eyes, full of intelligence and compassion. I could under-stand why Kelly wanted him as a friend, even if she didn't love him the way he so obviously loved her.

"I'm sorry about your father, Mace. Losing a parent stays with you your whole life, doesn't it?"

I nodded, grateful for the hat brim that kept my face in shadow.

"Well," Kelly said, "I know one thing that'd be different. Sam probably wouldn't be a Hollywood film editor if his dad had lived. Right, Sam?"

From under my hat, I saw him nod.

"My father was convinced Hollywood was a modern-day Sodom and Gomorrah. Some days, I think he had it right." He chuckled. "Besides, I planned to work with my dad after high school. He even had the signs made up before he died: Dobbs and Son."

"Sam's a brilliant editor." Kelly beamed at him. "One of the best in the business. Most of his magic is created after the film is shot."

"So that's why you haven't been that busy on the set," I said.

"Right. I come to locations when I can," Sam said. "I like to watch out for Kelly."

"I don't know what I'd do without Sam." She patted his arm. "He's my best friend."

Sam looked like he could listen to her brag on him all day. But I was curious about something else besides film editing and their one-sided relationship.

"You said you were praying for forgiveness, Kelly. What for, if you don't mind me asking?"

She raised those glorious green eyes to the sky. Her lovely face was open, guileless. She didn't look like she minded at all the personal nature of my question.

"You know God sent his son to redeem our sins, right?"

Her question made me think of all my Wednesday nights and Sunday mornings in church; of singing hymns and memorizing scripture. Maybe I didn't spend as much time in the pew these days as Mama or Maddie did, but I still considered myself a believer.

I quoted John 3:16: *"For God so loved the world, he gave his only begotten Son, that whosoever believeth in him should not perish, but have everlasting life."*

Kelly's eyes shone. "So you know then. I was asking forgiveness for damning Norman's soul to hell."

"You mean when you spit on the ground."

She nodded. "Only God has the right to decide who is rewarded with eternal life, and who suffers the fires of hell."

Sam gave her arm an encouraging pat.

"I'm not big enough to forgive Norman for what he did to me, and to others. But I can ask God to help me get there; and to forgive me when I fall short."

Shortly after Kelly's surprising revelation that she'd been saved, she and Sam said they had to go.

"Why don't you come with us to breakfast?" she asked.

"Thanks for the invite." I waved an arm at the horses in the corral. "I've still got lots of work to do, though."

So I wouldn't feel like such an antisocial liar, I did get to work. As they left, I began brushing down the horses. By the time I got to the pony, Sam and Kelly had disappeared from sight.

Combing out the little guy's mane, I stared into the empty pasture. Across the way, the cow pen caught my eye. That started me thinking about how Mama and I found Norman's body on the fence. I thought of what Kelly had said about asking for God's help.

All my life, I'd learned that God hears you no matter when or where you pray. I wondered what made Kelly traipse all the way out here to have her conversation with God.

Why did she want to stand in the same

spot where Norman was murdered to seek forgiveness?

THIRTY-TWO

I know what you did to my daughter.

Omigod, I thought. Not again.

"That's the way I think it sounds better, but my husband Sal likes it the other way. Mace says she can't tell the difference, either way. Which way do you think has more emotional weight, Jesse?"

Mama had cornered the young star outside her trailer. Jesse sat in a camp chair, a floppy sun hat protecting her fair skin. The brim was turned up, so she could watch Mama's repeat — and repeat — performance. On the empty chair next to Jesse sat Mama's library copy of *An Actor Prepares*, sticky notes marking several pages.

"Try it the first way again, Rosalee." Holding a hunk of bread, she pointed at Mama, like a conductor signaling with a baton.

Now I was certain Jesse was on drugs. There was no way she could listen to one more rendition of Mama's line without resorting to violence. Unfortunately, I didn't have a stash of happy pills in the back pocket of my jeans.

I called out to Mama, and she whirled at the sound of my voice. "Honey! You're just in time. I'm getting acting tips from the most talented, most beautiful young star in Hollywood."

She picked up her autograph book, hidden by the thick acting text, and waved it at me. "Jesse gave me her John Hancock, too. I'll treasure it forever and ever."

Mama was really stirring it up.

"Sorry, Jesse," I said. "You'll have to forgive my mother, if she's bothering you. She's not used to being on a movie shoot. Her enthusiasm runs away with her manners sometimes."

Jesse winked at me. "No prob. I don't mind at all. I expect to be coaching her next on how to accept her Academy Award."

"Speaking of coaching, are you still up for a horseback lesson later?" I asked.

"Don't think so," she said. "I broke down and confessed to Paul that I'm not very good at the horse thing. He says we may not need me riding; just sitting in the saddle will do."

"Lucky," I said.

"You know it. I'm a pretty good actor, but

I don't think I could sell having grown up galloping on horseback through the Florida wilds."

Mama shook her head. "I bet you could, honey. Jesse won an Oscar when she was just eleven years old, Mace. You were the youngest winner ever, weren't you, honey?"

Jesse absent-mindedly picked off pieces from the bread and tossed them on the ground. "Not quite," she said. "Tatum O'Neal was younger."

"Oh, that's right. I saw that on IMDb."

I looked blankly at Mama.

"Internet Movie Database, sweetheart. You really have a lot to learn about the Wide World of the Web."

While Mama crowed about all she'd learned on the "Wide World of the Web," I was wondering how winning that prize affected Jesse. How do you live up to achieving that kind of success before you've even hit puberty? Maybe you're so afraid of failing, you don't even try.

A few mourning doves and a blue jay had discovered the crumbs. Jesse studied the birds as they edged closer to us. Suddenly, they startled and scattered. Mama's face brightened at something over my shoulder. I turned to see Paul Watkins's wife coming from around back of Jesse's trailer.

"Yoo-hoo," Mama sang out. "Over here, Savannah!"

Jesse let out a sigh of what sounded like exasperation. But when I looked at her face, all I saw was a cool smile.

"What's this?" Savannah's drawl was music to my Southern ears. "Are y'all having a hen party without me?"

"What the hell is a 'hen party'?"

"It's an old-fashioned term from our generation, Jesse," Mama explained. "Think of it as *Girls Gone Wild,* without the going wild."

"It's not that old-fashioned."

Savannah sounded miffed, and Mama seemed to catch her tone. "I didn't mean to say *we're* old, honey."

Savannah arched a perfectly groomed brow. "Who's this *we,* Kemo Sabe? I'm at least fifteen years younger than you are, Rosalee."

I saw on Mama's face that she was weighing whether to argue that point. But since it would involve her having to state her own age, I knew she'd decide against it.

"Whatever you say, Sugar."

That "sugar" didn't fool me. The temperature in the air between Mama and the normally sweet Savannah had just dropped by ten degrees. Maybe the director's wife had gotten up on the wrong side of the bed. Or, maybe she'd looked over to see Paul's pillow hadn't been slept on at all. Whatever, she was in some kind of mood.

Jesse smirked as she shredded more bread. The birds were returning, cautiously. "Wise decision not to challenge her, Rosalee. Savannah likes things her way."

"Yes, I do. Especially when my way is the right way."

"Oh, I forgot: Savannah is always right, too."

"About some things I am. Yes."

"About some things, oh yes!" Jesse cupped her hands under her chin and put on a mocking drawl.

Mama's head swung back and forth between Savannah and Jesse like a one-eyed dog in a butcher shop. I probably looked the same way, trying to decipher what the two of them really meant behind the words they spoke. I caught Mama's glance. She shrugged.

Savannah took a couple of steps toward Jesse. The star tossed the rest of her bread to the birds. "I have to go."

"Don't, Jesse . . . Please." Savannah reached a hand to the younger woman's cheek; Jesse swatted it away.

"Don't beg, Savannah. It's so unattractive."

Getting up, Jesse folded the hat brim to shield her face from view. "I'm going inside. I need to rest, and I don't want to be bothered." The three of us watched as she flounced up the steps to her trailer.

"Thanks for the autograph," Mama called after her. "Does that mean our rehearsal is over?"

The door slammed shut behind Jesse. The birds took flight.

"Guess so," I said to Mama.

"Well, that was rude," she said.

"What did you expect?" Savannah snapped. "You had no right to bother Jesse with your stupid lines. She's a big star."

Mama looked like she'd been slapped by one of her fellow teachers at Sunday School. Then she got peeved.

"For your information, Jesse offered to help me with my lines. And I don't recall her getting all ticked off until *you* arrived on the scene."

Savannah stared at the door of the trailer. I thought I saw some movement behind the window blinds, but the door stayed firmly shut. Savannah marched up the steps and banged at it. Once. Twice. A third time. In between, she called out Jesse's name, pleadingly. Not a sound came from inside. Finally, she gave up, backing down the steps. She didn't say a word to us as she left, never even glancing our way.

"My goodness, who licked the red off of Savannah's candy?" Mama asked.

I shrugged, keeping my eyes on Jesse's trailer. "There's no figuring out these Hollywood people, Mama. They're like aliens from another planet. I'm not even sure they breathe oxygen."

Now, I was sure I detected the blinds move. A moment later, the door inched open. Jesse's smooth cheek and upturned nose appeared around the edge.

"Is she gone?"

Mama and I nodded.

"Thank God!" She came back out, clutching the sun hat to her breast, her red hair pulled back in a casual ponytail. She looked like the teen-aged girl she'd so recently been.

"What was that all about?" I asked.

"You don't have to say, if it's private," Mama added. "We're not gossips."

Well, I thought, at least one of us isn't a gossip.

Jesse sighed. "I stopped caring about gossip a long time ago, Rosalee."

I didn't believe that for an instant. Jesse,

and the rest of this Hollywood pack, seemed to thrive on drama. And gossip was a big part of that. Still, I wanted to know what had just happened.

"Well, then?" Mama prodded.

"Savannah thinks she's in love."

"With her husband?" Mama's brows V-ed into a frown.

"Not even close." Jesse winked at me.

Things were becoming clear, but Mama wasn't seeing.

"How long?" I asked.

"Not long," Jesse said. "We hooked up right before I got the part."

"Don't tell me: Savannah helped influence her husband to hire you," I said.

Another wink.

"Would one of you please tell me what's going on?" Mama asked.

"Savannah's in love with me, Rosalee."

I saw the satisfaction on Jesse's face, as she watched Mama pick up her jaw from the ground. If shock was what she'd wanted, that was what she got.

"Buh . . . buh . . . but you're both women," Mama sputtered. "And Savannah is married!"

Jesse waved the sun hat. "Your daughter and I already had this conversation about

287

sexuality in Hollywood. It's fluid, right Mace?"

"What's that supposed to mean?" Mama asked.

I wasn't about to go there. Mama would start reciting Bible verses right and left.

"Hollywood is a different world, that's for sure," I said. "My attitude is you can live your life however you want, as long as no one gets hurt. Fact is, Savannah looked hurt to me."

Jesse shrugged. "Don't be so sure about that. The reason I backed off wasn't because Savannah is too old for me. It was because she's crazy. Believe me, beneath that sugary Southern exterior beats a cold, vengeful heart."

With that, Jesse looked toward the sky. Clouds were rolling in, but there was still sunshine enough to give Jesse a bad burn. She stuck the hat back on her head, and settled herself again in her camp chair.

"Now," she pointed at Mama. "Time to rehearse!"

I hurried away, with the aspiring actress's umpteenth line reading echoing in my ears.

Thirty-Three

The wind moaned. Sheets of rain slanted down sideways from a dark gray sky. With each furious gust, the plastic panels of the catering tent flapped and shuddered.

"Are we having a hurricane?" Paul Watkins peered out nervously at the storm-tossed sabal palms. Fronds were shaking loose, blowing end over end across a sodden landscape.

I added a couple of packets of sugar to the cup of coffee in front of me. "This is nothing; just a little thundershower," I said. "They're as common this time of year as the splat of love bugs on windshields in springtime."

When the storm kicked up, most of the stars had sought shelter in their trailers. I'd found refuge in the food tent, where I spotted Paul. He was alone, for a change. I decided to take advantage of that fact, and invited myself to sit down. Talking about the weather was a good way to work up the nerve to ask him what I really wanted to know.

"Say, Paul . . ."

"Hmmm?" He was still focused on the fury outside.

"Something's been bothering me."

"There's nothing wrong with the livestock, is there?"

"No, the horses and cattle are fine."

Turning, he raised an eyebrow. I forged ahead. "Where were you the morning that Norman Sydney was murdered? Why was Johnny Jaybird shooting that scene with the galloping horse?"

I knew what Savannah had told me. I wanted to hear what her husband would say. Seconds ticked by as he stared at me, the storm outside the window seemingly forgotten.

"Do you work for the police in addition to being an animal wrangler?" he finally asked.

I shook my head.

"Has the studio hired you to look into the case?"

"No."

"Then it's really none of your business, is it?"

"But . . ."

He grabbed my wrist. His grip was surprisingly strong for such a skinny guy. "But nothing," he said. "It's not your business. Do you understand?"

I nodded, and tried to pull away. He tightened his hold. "I asked you a question."

"Yes," I said. "I understand."

He let go, leaned back in the chair. I rubbed at my wrist as he returned his attention to the storm. Paul's reaction made me even more suspicious about his whereabouts. There was more than one path to that answer, though.

I stole a quick glance at Carlos, nursing a soft drink in the corner of the tent. He sat with his back to the wall and his cop shield up. He didn't meet my eyes. From his closed-off body language to the hard set of his jaw, everything about him signaled he wanted to be left alone by everyone, and most especially by me. The message was unspoken, but clear: Walk through the force field at your own peril.

I wasn't about to take the risk. I'd just have to find another way to discover what Paul had told the police.

The director jumped as a deafening thunder clap rattled the cups and spoons on the table. He looked so spooked, I felt a little sorry for him.

"Don't worry," I said. "The storm will blow itself out in a couple of hours."

"Hours?" He put his elbows on the table and dropped his head into his hands. "Why did I ever think I should shoot this film in Florida?"

"Y'all should have come down during winter. That's the dry season. We hardly ever get rain in the winter."

"Figures. This production and I have been cursed since Day One."

"Cursed, huh? Norman Sydney might say the same thing. But he can't, seeing as how he was murdered."

I shot Paul a dark look.

"You're right." At least he had the sense to look chagrined. "I need to keep things in perspective. It's not life and death. It's just a movie . . . and the last chance I'll ever get to resurrect my career."

His head fell back into his hands.

"Why so glum, chum?" Mama's tone was chipper, as she placed a plate full of biscotti on the table between Paul and me. "These cookies are as hard as the gravel they're using to patch State Road 70. That's how they're supposed to be, C'ndee claims. Watch out you don't lose a filling, Mace."

When Paul didn't raise his head to acknowledge her, Mama seemed a bit put out.

She was not used to being ignored by men. I, on the other hand, was becoming quite accustomed to it.

"Have a seat, Mama."

Still she stood. I knew she was waiting for Paul to pull out a chair. When he made no move to do so, she huffily seated herself.

"Don't mind if I do sit, darlin'. Isn't this rain something?"

Paul finally looked up. "It's something, all right; something that's burning through buckets of money with weather delays."

"Can't you just change things around to shoot some inside scenes?" I asked.

"We've shot all the interiors. The whole reason we're here is to get the exterior shots. I wanted this film to look like authentic Florida. No glimpses of mountain peaks or California redwoods where they aren't supposed to be."

He stared outside to the rain-battered palms again. "What is that scraggly, ugly-looking tree anyway?"

"It's a sabal, also called a cabbage palm," I said. "It's Florida's state tree."

"Better watch out, Paul. Mace takes the symbols of her native state seriously. She doesn't like to hear them criticized."

"Right," I said. "I can poke fun at Florida, but you can't, as an outsider. It's like family. I can say my big sister is bossy, and my mama's a little ditsy. But no one else better say it."

Mama narrowed her eyes. I dunked a biscotti into my coffee and swirled.

"And I might call my daughter a stubborn mule who doesn't know how to keep a man happy, but that's only because Mace knows I'm saying it out of love. She knows I only want her to be the best she can be."

Paul looked over at Mama. She gave him one of her adoring smiles, and added an eyelash flutter, too. He rewarded her with a leer.

"I bet you know how to keep a man happy, don't you, Rosalee?"

Reaching across the table, he covered her hand with his. I could see him stroking one of her fingers suggestively.

"Now, Paul, don't be a bad boy!" She leaned away, neatly sliding her hand out from under his. "I'm a married woman."

He lowered his voice to seduction register. "And I'm a married man. So what? Maybe the two of us could make each other happy for a little while."

I cleared my throat. "Would you two like to get a room?"

Mama laughed. "Don't be silly, Mace. Paul is just doing what he thinks he has to do to keep his Hollywood reputation intact. Directors always come on to actresses. They don't mean anything by it."

"Since when are you such an expert on Hollywood's morals, Mama?"

Paul chuckled. "Nope, she has it pegged exactly right, Mace. I'm known as a rogue and a ladies' man. It's hard for a tiger to change his stripes, even when his stripes are getting gray."

He ruffled Mama's hair and patted her on the cheek. "I like a woman who tells it like it is."

Mama aimed a superior smirk at me. "See? I told you so!"

What unfolded next happened fast. Paul cupped Mama's face in both hands. He pulled her out of her chair, so that she was standing between his legs. He planted a big, wet kiss right on her lips, and then patted her on the rear end. He must have added a pinch, because Mama's eyes widened and she gave a surprised little hop.

I hadn't even seen Sal approaching, but suddenly there he was. As he loomed over our table, his eyes looked murderous. "Take your filthy hands off my wife."

The words were ice-cold, and all the more threatening because of their lack of passion. Sal held himself under tight control, making the prospect seem more terrifying that this behemoth of a man might explode.

Paul looked up at him like a rabbit facing a wolf.

"No need to get mad, Big Guy." He scooted his chair as far from Mama as he could, and placed his hands on the table where Sal could see them. "I was just having a little fun."

"That's just how people in Hollywood act, Sally."

"We're in Himmarshee, not Hollywood." Sal's voice was full of menace as he glared at Paul. "Now, I want you to apologize for manhandling my wife. And then I want you to pick yourself up and leave this tent."

People at other tables were starting to look our way. Conversations paused. Eating stopped. Eyes turned toward the big man and the movie director.

"I have no problem saying I'm sorry. My bad." Paul's smile had lost a shade of its devilish quality. "I have no intention of leaving, though. It's pouring outside."

"That's not my problem," Sal said. "Look at it this way: You can use the rain to cool yourself off."

Paul crossed his arms over his chest. "I'm not going out in a downpour just because you're insanely jealous. Besides, if you knew anything about Hollywood, you'd know the director is like a king on his movie set. You can't order me around. I do the ordering."

"Like I said, we're not in Hollywood. Now, are you going, or do I have to throw you out?"

"You can't be serious.' "

"As a heart attack. Get up."

Sal crooked his finger, motioning for Paul to stand. Paul clutched hard at the arm rails of his chair, giving his head a defiant shake.

"No way," the director said.

"Your choice."

In a flash, Sal lunged at him, hooking Paul's neck with one of his beefy arms. He pulled the director backward across the floor, chair and all. *Bounce-drag, bounce-drag, bounce-drag.*

Paul hung on. People darted out of the way, overturning tables and trays of food. Sal kept tugging. The threesome — Paul, the chair, and Sal, now red in the face — got closer and closer to the exit. No one stepped in to try to stop them.

"Mace, do something!" Mama's tone was urgent. "Sal's going to mess up my movie debut."

I wasn't as concerned about Mama's debut as I was about my paycheck. If Paul truly was the King of the Set, I didn't want him to evict me from the kingdom. I'd earned my pay, putting up with these people. I wasn't about to get fired before I got it.

As I threaded my way through the tent toward Sal, I noticed Carlos doing the same. We arrived at the big man's side at almost the same moment. I'd heard Sal panting from several yards away. His face was now three shades beyond rosy, and the veins were popping out on his neck from exertion. If we didn't do something fast, Mama had a good chance of becoming a widow again.

"You've made your point, Sal." Carlos put a restraining hand on his friend's arm. "Let go of the chair."

He was using his calming voice, the one for talking suicides off a bridge — or retired tough guys out of a fool's mission.

I grabbed Sal's opposite elbow, and leaned in to whisper in his ear. "Mama is positively swooning because you stood up for her. She says if the two of you go home right now, she'll find a special way to show you her love and appreciation."

He hesitated, just long enough for Paul to release his death grip on the chair's arms, and leap out of the seat. The director scooted quickly away from Sal, glancing around the tent to see how many people had witnessed his humiliation. Pretty much everyone had. As Sal's breathing slowed to normal, Paul tugged at his ponytail to straighten it. He smoothed his safari jacket, trying to regain some of his dignity.

"You've got to be crazy if you think I was really coming on to your wife, man. She's way too old for me. And she's not even that pretty."

Mama gasped with hurt feelings. That did it. Sal hauled back and hit Paul in the jaw. The force of the big man's punch sent the director reeling. He staggered backward into one of the serving tables, lost his balance, and tumbled to the floor, taking the table-cloth with him.

Brownies and biscotti rained down, pelting the director in a downpour of dessert.

THIRTY-FOUR

Barbara finger-combed a hunk of baklava from Paul's ponytail. She brushed shattered biscotti from the shoulders of his bush vest. She blotted with a napkin at a glob of brownie frosting hanging off his left ear.

"Who does that New York asshole think he is?" she asked, loudly. "He probably has a hundred pounds on you, Paul."

The "New York asshole" had stormed out of the tent after his dust-up with the director. Mama had to run to keep up with her defender's long strides. My last sight of Sal and Mama was out the tent's plastic panels, as they ducked under a trailer's awning to wait out the rain.

"That man is a menace." Paul rubbed his jaw. "I ought to file charges against him."

Carlos looked him up and down. His clothes were stained with chocolate, which would be hell to get out in the wash. But aside from that, Paul's ego seemed the only thing that had suffered any real damage.

"You could do that," Carlos said. "But we might have to get into what you'd been playing at with another man's wife that provoked him to lose his temper."

Barbara leveled a cold look, taking in both of us. "Oh, *please*. That hillbilly can't keep her hands off Paul. He was just responding, the way any red-blooded male would."

"Why don't we just say that both of them like to flirt, and leave it at that?" I said. "And the insult you want in Florida is 'Cracker.' No hills here, hence no hillbillies."

I didn't tell her a lot of Floridians, with roots deep in our sandy soil, wear the Cracker label as a badge of honor. I know I do.

People lined up to pay their respects to Paul. A sympathetic murmur moved through the ranks of cast and crew. I heard someone mutter, "That New Yorker has a lot of nerve. Did you see the way he pounded Paul?"

Carlos and I took a few steps back, so we'd be out of the way of the sycophants and well-wishers.

Someone else chimed in, "Yeah, Paul wasn't even doing anything. That huge guy attacked him for no reason."

Carlos leaned close to me and whispered,

"Nothing like getting your butt kicked by a big guy to make people forget you're a jerk."

I nodded. I couldn't do more because I was busy inhaling my ex-boyfriend's distinctive male scent: sandalwood and spices, and a trace of strong Cuban coffee on his breath. God, how I missed this man!

"So, that was smart of Paul, no?" he asked.

I took one last deep breath, hoping the smell would hold me for a while. "No. I mean yes. It was smart of Paul. Surely a man who can't even defend himself couldn't be a murderer, right?"

"Are you asking me if Paul's a suspect?"

"Are you telling?"

"Not a chance," Carlos said.

"Tease!"

He was stonewalling me, as usual. But I didn't even mind, because we were talking. He was even grinning at me. I studied his face. Despite the crooked smile, there were fatigue lines around his eyes and mouth. Stress was taking a toll.

"You look tired, Carlos."

"Flatterer."

"No, you're still devastatingly handsome. I just meant you look physically beat. Are you sleeping okay?"

He shrugged. The closed look descended over his features again.

"Listen," I said, "even if you don't want us to be a couple anymore, that doesn't mean I've stopped caring. Who else will watch out for you if you freeze me out?"

"Perdóneme. Forgive me, *niña."*

His eyes softened, and he reached toward me. I thought he was going to caress my shoulder. I steeled myself for the shiver of desire I always felt at his touch. But the touch didn't come. Catching a glance at his wristwatch, he stuck his hands in his pants pockets instead.

"Am I keeping you from something?"

"Sorry," he said. "I do have to go. The police chief's been holding regular news conferences to occupy the media. He's trying to keep them in town, and away from the movie set and crime scene."

"Good luck with that. The ranch road looked like a parking lot for TV live trucks when I drove in this morning."

"Yeah, I get dozens of shouted questions every time I come and go. Anyway, the chief wants me in town to talk to reporters at this afternoon's briefing, notwithstanding the fact I have absolutely nothing new to report."

The expression of dread on his face was almost comical. He looked like he'd just been gowned and prepped for a colonoscopy.

"You'll do fine," I said. "I've seen you dance around questions. Just give them the Martinez Glower. You'll terrify those reporters into submission."

"This is the national media, Mace. They're sharks, and sharks don't get scared. Just this morning, the muscle guys on the movie's security team found a reporter from NBC's *Today* show nosing around. They tossed him out, none too gently. He just laughed and said he'd find another way to get on the set."

He glanced over his shoulder at Barbara and Paul.

My eyes followed his. The director was accepting handshakes and back pats. Barbara stood at his side, whispering occasionally into his ear. Otherwise, she watched him with the adoring gaze of a political spouse. Everyone was treating Paul like he was lucky to have survived an unwarranted attack by a crazy man.

Sal *was* a little crazy, which I chalked up to him being married to Mama. But giving the obnoxious director a punch in the kisser was warranted, as far as I was concerned. I felt a smile on my lips as I thought of Paul tumbling over that table. It was a shame about the ruined desserts, though.

Suddenly, I sensed Carlos staring at me. I quickly ran my tongue over my teeth to check for chocolate traces. I'd scooped a brownie off the floor and eaten it, in accordance with the five-second rule. Carlos's face was unreadable.

"What?" I asked him.

"I was just remembering something."

Something good? Something bad? I wanted to ask him to elaborate, but I didn't. Maybe he was remembering why he'd been so angry at me.

"I'd like to continue this conversation later," he said.

"That sounds ominous."

"Not at all."

Well that had to be good, right?

"I'd like that," I said.

"Me, too. Very much."

As I watched Carlos leave, my heart swelled with something like hope.

I'd taken a seat in the food tent away from the lunch crowd to make some phone calls. I checked in with my boss at Himmarshee Park, to see how the place was surviving without me. Rhonda said, a little too quickly, that everything was going great.

I called my Aunt Jo to check on one of my two cousins named Bubba. This was the

Bubba who couldn't stay out of trouble. He'd gotten out of jail, only to land in the hospital with a broken arm. He flipped his all-terrain vehicle doing donuts on the football field at Glades High.

"You know what a redneck's last words are, right, Mace?" my aunt asked on the phone. " 'Hey, y'all . . . watch this!' "

The fact his mama was cracking jokes told me bad Bubba's condition wasn't critical.

By the time we finished chatting, the sun was coming out. The rain was barely a drizzle. I was about to leave the tent when I heard Barbara's voice, a harsh whisper. She'd cornered Johnny Jaybird in the shadows, away from center stage where Paul still held court.

The assistant director's head was cocked toward Barbara, who towered over him. Her hands were stuck on her hips, scolding-style. I stepped behind a towering stack of canned sodas to listen in.

"You have no right . . ."

"I'm Toby's manager, Jonathan," she hissed. "I have every right."

"This is his personal life, Barbara. It's none of your business."

"That's the key word, 'business.' What you want for him is bad for his business and it's bad for mine."

"That was yesterday's Hollywood. Things are different today. I just want him to be honest. He should respect who he is."

"Oh, grow up! How many action heroes can you count who are out of the closet?" Barbara rounded her fist into a goose egg, and shoved it under his nose. "Zero."

Johnny Jaybird stumbled back, arms flapping to protect his wounded side. "Maybe Toby doesn't want to be an action hero."

"Toby is too young to know what he wants. It's my job to tell him. You're probably just after him for sex anyway."

"God, Barbara! He's a minor." Johnny's lip curled with disgust. "I'm 'after him' to make him stop living a lie. Besides, Toby's your client, not your slave. There's still a little thing called freedom, even in Hollywood."

She sneered. "Freedom? I don't think so. Not freedom to be a mega-star as well as a *faggot*."

He absorbed the ugly slur like a slap.

Before he could respond, Barbara stuck her face inches from his. "Keep your faggot hands off him." The words dripped venom. "If you don't, there *will* be consequences. Maybe the next person who fires a loaded gun at you will be a better shot."

His eyes widened; his mouth dropped

open. Johnny's face showed the shock that surely mirrored my own.

THIRTY-FIVE

I rapped on the door of the production trailer.

Inside, I could hear Barbara on the phone, but I couldn't make out the words in her rapid-fire Bostonese. Maybe she was reporting the latest brouhaha on the film set to some Hollywood gossip columnist. I could just imagine the headline:

Cursed Project Director Pummeled by Big Apple Bully.

I figured I'd better intervene before she painted my mama as the Hicksville Hussy who started it all. I banged harder on the side of the trailer.

"Come!"

As I entered, she looked up, covered the receiver with one hand, and pointed to a chair in the corner. "Sit!"

What's next, Roll Over?

Barbara made nice on the phone, saying her goodbyes. It was strange to hear a pleasant tone coming out of her mouth, just like a normal person.

"Mmm-hmm, okay . . . I'll be home in time for your father's funeral, just as soon as the authorities release his body." She reached out and gave a framed photo on her desk a tender stroke. "Give my darling granddaughter a big hug and a kiss."

So Barbara had not only been Norman's wife, she was a mother and a grandmother. For some reason, that surprised me. I hadn't known Satan's female twin was capable of human reproduction.

Hanging up, she glared at me. "So, it's Marsha — the hillbilly offspring; daughter of the town slut. Have you come to apologize for your mother?"

"Not exactly," I said. "And my name is Mace." I didn't bother reminding her about the hills.

"What can I do for you, *Mace?*" Barbara made a show of looking at her watch.

No time for a preamble: Good. I sat in a chair in front of her desk and summarized what I'd overheard between her and the assistant director. "It sounded to me like you were threatening him."

Her eyes went round, a caricature of innocence. "Me? I don't make threats, dear."

"I know what I heard."

"Well then, you must have misunderstood. That can happen when you become involved in things that are none of your business."

"Anyone should make it their business to try to stop a crime, or to see that the person who already committed one is caught and punished."

She sneered. "Aren't you the good citizen!"

"How much do you want to keep Johnny Jaybird away from Toby?" I asked. "Enough to plant a loaded gun when you knew they might rehearse that scene? Enough to shoot Johnny yourself?"

"Everyone knew Toby had the scene, and he'd definitely rehearse it," she said. "The schedule on a movie set isn't a secret. As for me ever shooting someone? That's patently ridiculous. I don't know one end of a gun from the other."

Her tone and her face signaled the line of questioning was closed. She tapped her fingers on the desk, then looked at her watch again. I decided to take a shot at my other suspicion about Barbara. "I hope I'm not keeping you from making your regular phone call."

The tapping ceased.

"You know, the call you make to the media to get out information about all the

311

trouble the movie is in."

She waited a beat before answering. I monitored her face, but couldn't detect anything beyond annoyance.

"I have no idea what you're talking about."

"My friend and I saw you sitting in your Jaguar in the parking lot, talking on the phone. You made a threat that what you revealed could never be traced back to you."

Her expression remained impassive.

"Are you hoping negative publicity will help shut down this project?" I asked.

"Now, why would I want that? You must have heard someone else talking to a reporter."

"We were looking right at you," I said. "My friend will also say he's certain it was you."

"Ah, friends. One of you lies, and the other swears to it." She shrugged. "Or, maybe you're the one feeding information to the gossip sheets. And now you're running around spreading malicious lies about me to deflect the blame. You didn't happen to have a recording device with you, did you? Some actual evidence that would help prove this unfounded allegation against me?"

My silence must have given Barbara the answer she was after.

"Didn't think so." She smirked. "If you want to play in the big girls' sandbox, Marsha, you should be sure to bring along some big girl toys."

"It's Mace," I said.

"I know."

We stared at each other across the desk. The superiority on her face jangled my last nerve. "What do you think that grandbaby of yours would think about how you treat people?" I asked cruelly. "Would you like to hear her use the kind of hurtful word that you slung at Johnny Jaybird?"

Her eyes flicked to the photo on her desk. I saw the chink in her armor.

"Is that your grandchild?" I gestured at the picture.

Nodding, she handed it to me. It captured a dark-haired child in a pink dress, standing in front of an imposing old church. A sweet smile dimpled her cheeks. Chubby, toddler arms stretched up toward an unseen photographer.

"That was taken at the Salem Witch Museum."

I restrained myself from asking Barbara if she was a visitor or an exhibit.

"The girl is adorable," I said, looking at the picture.

Barbara's arrogant smirk softened to a

smile. "She is," she agreed. "Her name is Taylor. She's the best thing in my life."

The emotion that thickened her voice made me feel a little guilty. I handed back the photo. She gazed at it, pure love radiating from her face. With a sigh, she gently replaced it on her desk.

"Her mother was a difficult child. We were estranged for years. But when Taylor was born, my daughter came back into my life. Norman's, too. He cared so much about our little granddaughter; he wanted to become a better man for her." Her eyes got a distant look, and she touched the photo. "He took this picture."

She brought a knuckle to her eye. Ohmigod, was she going to *cry?*

"Taylor keeps asking why she can't talk to Pop-Pop on the phone. She doesn't understand that her grandfather Norman is gone."

Tears glistened. She took a shuddery breath. "I'm really not the bitch you think I am, Mace. Hell, that everyone thinks I am." Making an *O* of her mouth, she touched the tips of her index fingers beneath her eyes, trying to stop the tears before they dissolved her mascara.

"Sorry," she said. "These last few days have been pretty awful."

I fumbled through the pockets of my jeans

314

for my cotton bandana, and handed it to her. She used it to blot. The scarf was probably covered with horse hair. I hoped she wasn't allergic. A few moments ago, I would have relished the idea that she was.

"You cannot imagine how tired I am of being Barbara Sydney. When I was coming up in Hollywood, a woman had to be tough, and more so than a man in every way to succeed. More cruel. More cut-throat. More heartless."

She sighed. "I was good at pretending to be all those things, until finally I wasn't pretending anymore. That's who I became."

She blew her nose into my bandana. Luckily, I had another in the horse trailer.

"You're a strong woman, too, Mace. I can tell."

She looked at me. I wasn't sure what she wanted. Agreement? Commiseration? I simply nodded, choosing neither.

"It's different for women your age, though. You don't have to be hard to be strong." She sniffled. "I'm so sick of being hard."

"Well then, change," I said. "If you don't like the way you are, become someone different."

"At this point, I don't think I can." She looked down at the desk, and her voice got soft. "That's what scares me."

Now, her tears started to really flow. I sat there, squirming in my seat. A crying jag was the very last thing I expected when I set out to question Barbara. What was I supposed do now, pat her on the back and murmur, *There, there?*

The truth was, I did see a bit of this woman in myself. And I didn't particularly like the resemblance. Barbara offered a cautionary tale of how needing to always be in charge can close you off to human feelings. I made a silent vow to work harder at showing Carlos how much I cared for him. As long as I was making promises, I also decided I'd try to be nicer to people in general.

There was no time like the present to start.

"There, there." I reached across the desk and patted Barbara's hand, taken aback when I didn't detect either scales or a cloven hoof. "Everything is going to be okay."

"You're putting us on, Mace." Maddie leaned back in her chair, arms crossed over her chest. "Is this a practical joke?"

"Hand to God." I raised my right hand. "Barbara was blubbering like a baby."

My sisters, Mama, and I had gathered at base camp. We sat around a picnic table in the common grounds between the rows of work trailers and stars' quarters. Marty and Maddie had come to the location again, in case I needed help.

If the afternoon sun got strong enough to dry out the soaked landscape, Paul might want the horses to shoot a scene so far delayed by the rain. There was still standing water on the ground, but the sky was trying to clear. While we waited, I caught them up on my encounter with Barbara in her trailer.

"Well butter my butt and call me a biscuit," Mama said. "I wouldn't have believed that woman was capable of shedding tears."

"Humph," Maddie said. "Maybe crocodile tears."

"Did you believe her, Mace?" Marty asked.

I hesitated. When I was sitting there across from her, I'd been a hundred-percent convinced she was emotionally wounded. Given time to replay the scene in my head, I wasn't so sure.

"You know how a killdeer acts around its nest?"

Mama and Maddie offered up matching blank looks. Marty, a student of animal behavior, like me, nodded. "Of course," she said. "The wounded-wing routine."

"Right. The bird hops around, dragging a wing, to deflect attention from what she really wants to protect."

"So what's Barbara protecting?" Maddie asked.

"Herself, that's what. That woman has self-preservation written all over her." Mama applied fresh lipstick and fluffed her hair. "Mace, did Barbara happen to mention me at all? I'm a little worried that after that crazy scene in the food tent, Paul might decide to cut my part."

Leave it to Mama to work the conversation back to her. I'd given them the condensed version of Barbara's breakdown, knowing enough to leave out the names she'd called Mama. If I hadn't, we'd be in the middle of a half-hour dissertation on how other women were always jealous, and how Mama never could help the way men responded to her.

"Your name never came up," I told her.

Technically that was true. Barbara had only referred to her as a slut and a hillbilly.

As Mama recounted in detail for my sisters how Sal had defended her honor, my attention wandered. Birds splashed on the ground in puddles left by the rain. The wind was picking up again, rustling the cabbage palms and blowing more clouds our way. I looked over toward Jesse's trailer. The blinds were drawn. I thought about Savannah standing there knocking at the door. Despite Jesse's claim that Savannah was nuts, I liked her. And if she truly was in love with Jesse, I felt sorry for her.

Several birds had gathered again near the young star's trailer. She'd probably scattered more bread on the ground. One particularly bold cattle egret stalked through the small flock with purpose. Its spindly legs propelled it past the other birds, as it snatched up crumbs with its sturdy yellow bill. It strutted closer and closer to the trailer, as the other birds hung back.

I almost laughed out loud, imagining the bird hopping up the steps to peck at Jesse's door, demanding more bread. I elbowed Marty so she could watch the bold egret, too. Just then, the bird stepped even closer, and stretched its neck out to snatch a soggy chunk of bread in a puddle at the bottom of the trailer's steps.

Electrical sparks spit and flashed. The cattle egret rocketed backward through the air. The acrid smell of burned feathers reached my nose. The bird was dead before it hit the ground.

Almost before I'd had a chance to process what happened, the door to Jesse's trailer swung open. The pointy toe of her boot appeared on the threshold. Like jigsaw pieces, several images instantly combined and shifted through my mind: the long-beaked bird, the puddle, and a black electrical cable snaking through the water from under the star's trailer.

"Don't move, Jesse! Stay where you are," I shouted. "Somebody's trying to kill you."

THIRTY-SIX

"You saved my life, Mace."

Jesse's face was pale. Her hands trembled. She kept looking over her shoulder at her trailer as a crew member examined the cable that had charged the puddle at the bottom of the steps. After the bird was electrocuted, the generator that provided power to the trailers in base camp was cut off.

"Actually, that cattle egret saved you. If I hadn't seen the poor bird get fried, I'd never have known to warn you not to come down the steps."

"I'm just glad I listened."

"For a change," Greg Tilton said. "You picked a pretty good time to start heeding sound advice, Jess."

She narrowed her eyes at him. But he was smiling, and his voice had a gentle, teasing note. It seemed to defuse her will to fight. She chuckled softly. "You got me there, Greg."

I noticed him scratch at an ugly red rash on his wrist. I should have felt bad about the poison ivy, but I didn't.

Jesse glanced over her shoulder again. A second electrician had joined the first. He donned a pair of reading glasses and bent over at the waist to get a better look at the power cord by her trailer. She returned her attention to us.

"What you said is true, Greg. And there are a lot more things about me that could use changing, too. I guess a near-electrocution sparks thoughts about personal improvement."

Once I'd realized what had happened to the bird, all hell had broken loose. My sisters and Mama joined me in shouting to Jesse to stay in the trailer. Greg Tilton had come running when he heard the commotion. He quickly summed up the situation. While my sisters, Mama, and I fanned out to keep people from straying too close to the puddle, he raced off to find somebody on the electrical crew to cut the power.

"What the hell?" Barbara had stormed out of her office, yelling from the top step. "Everything went dark. Did some asshole forget fuel for the generators? Whoever it was, he's fired."

I thought it was odd that even after Barbara learned why the power was off, she didn't stick around to make sure Jesse was okay. She'd stomped away toward the parking lot. She was probably sitting in that Jaguar right now, phoning some reporter with details of the latest deadly development.

Jesse sat now on top of a picnic table, cupping a mug of hot tea to keep her hands from shaking. The rest of us surrounded her on benches and outdoor folding chairs.

My sister Marty had barely said a word. Finally, she asked Tilton: "Are electrical accidents common on movie sets?"

"Nothing like this," he said. "There are a lot of backup safety measures so people don't get hurt."

Maddie said, "But Jesse could have been killed."

The young star's hands trembled. She put her cup on the tabletop, liquid sloshing over the sides.

"Do you suppose it was intentional?" Mama asked.

Jesse glanced at the electricians, whose faces were etched with deep frowns. She looked at me, her eyes full of questions. I shrugged, unsure about the answers.

"Can you think of anybody who'd want to hurt you?" Maddie asked.

Jesse and Tilton exchanged grins. "Where should I start?" she said.

"I'll get a box of pens and a carton of paper to make the list," he added.

"Well, like who?" I pressed them.

They looked at each other again. Were the two stars closing Hollywood ranks against the outsiders?

Finally Jesse said, "I'd rather not speculate until we're sure of what's happened. It could have been just an innocent accident."

From my vantage point, I could see the two men at the star's trailer. As one shook his head, the other snuck furtive looks at Jesse. When he saw me watching, he averted his eyes.

"Speculation or not," I said, "it seems somebody's targeting the stars of this movie: Toby in the parking lot; that sandwich Greg had; and now you, Jesse."

Mama gasped, "What if I'm next?"

Maddie snorted. "I'd say Kelly Conover has more to worry about than you do."

"I just hope I'll still get to do my scene," Mama said.

"Putting aside my mama's narcissism for a moment, what do y'all think?" I asked the two actors. "Will this shut down the movie?"

"No way," Jesse said.

Tilton agreed. "Not with just one day of

filming left. There's way too much money tied up in the project to shut it down now." Grinning, he pointed at me. "You better stick around, though. No telling who you'll have to rescue next."

Was he making fun of me? I searched his face for that trademark smirk. It wasn't there.

"I'm serious," he said. "You saved Jesse's life."

She beamed at me. Tilton's eyes were full of respect. Marty and Mama proudly clutched their hands to their chests. Even Maddie looked impressed. Outwardly, I cringed at the attention. Inwardly, it fed my savior complex. It felt good.

"I'm not surprised my sister saw the bird. She always sees things no one else does," Maddie said. "It's because she spends so much time alone, thinking instead of talking. Mace isn't a people person."

I was actually thinking at that moment — thinking I'd like to change the subject before Maddie moved on to more personal details. I could just hear her telling them next about my sorry love life: not a "people" person, not a romantic person, and apparently not a "relationship" person.

"Honestly, it was nothing," I said. "Anyone would have done the same thing."

"I'm not so sure about that," Jesse said. "I owe you one, Mace."

Tilton scratched at his elbow, and then whispered in my ear. "I do, too. The other day, I acted like a complete jerk. Thanks for putting me on my ass. You knocked some sense into me."

Both my sisters had tensed up when he moved in close. I gave my palm a tiny lift, our barely perceptible sisters' signal to stand down. I wasn't sure how this change had come over Tilton, or even if it was a real change. Still, I wanted to play it out to see where it led.

Besides, if worst came to worst, I already knew I could whup him.

Watching him with Jesse, it was easy to forget how crude he'd been with me. He seemed now like an older brother: both teasing and caring.

He nodded at her cup, empty on the table. "You want another one, Jess?"

When she hesitated, he said, "It's no trouble. I promise I won't tell everyone that you were like some junior diva, ordering me to run and fetch it."

"Takes one to know one, Greg." She gave him a playful punch, and then handed over the mug. "Thanks, dude."

"No worries." He smiled, showing acres

of teeth. "Want to walk with me, Mace?"

He couldn't have missed Maddie shaking her head and Marty biting her lip. Mama said, "Mace, don't you need to get to the corral to check on the horses?"

His finger traced an X over his chest. "Cross my heart and hope to die, I'm on my best behavior."

I wanted to talk to him alone. Before Mama and my sisters could lasso and hogtie me, I stood up. "I could use a cup of coffee."

My big sister got to her feet. "I'll come with you, Mace."

"I'm fine." I pointed toward the food tent, just across the grass. "You can see us from here. I'll bring you back some of C'ndee's *tiramisu*."

Marty tugged at our big sister's sleeve. Maddie sat, either because Marty had curbed her protective instincts, or because I'd bribed her with the promise of sweets.

She narrowed her eyes at Tilton. "We'll be right here," Maddie said.

"You bet we will," Mama added.

"Right here, watching," Marty echoed.

As we neared the tent, the rich scent of brewing coffee perfumed the air. Were those fresh-baked sugar cookies I smelled? Even though my mouth watered, I had some business to attend to first with Greg Tilton. He seemed to want to be my new *BFF*, as Mama would say. I decided to take advantage of our new "Best Friends Forever" status.

I touched his arm. "Hold up a minute, would you?"

He stopped, head cocked at me in a question.

"You and Jesse got really quiet when we asked who might have fooled with that electric cord. Why was that?"

"Like Jess said, guessing doesn't really serve any purpose until we know what caused that bird to be shocked."

"It seems pretty clear," I said. "The way that electrician with the reading glasses . . ."

"Gaffer," Tilton said. "That's what we call the chief electrician on the set."

"Sorry, it seems clear from the way the *gaffer* reacted, there was something wrong with that cord, and somebody put it in the puddle."

"You can't assume that, Mace. Cables and cords run everywhere on a movie set."

"Then you're saying it wasn't intentional."

"No. I'm saying we don't know enough to theorize." Glancing back toward the trailer, he lowered his voice. "I will tell you, Jesse's made a lot of enemies for someone so young. She's hurt people, and that's all I want to say."

I thought of Savannah pounding on the young star's door, face tight with anger and pain.

Suddenly, I heard Tilton chuckle beside me. "Something funny?" I asked.

"Not really, in light of what almost happened to Jesse. But I was just thinking of how much faster everything moves in Hollywood these days. In just a few years, she's managed to make more mistakes — and enemies — than I made in decades."

"So who are your enemies, Greg?"

He gave me a half-smile, so familiar from his movies. "I'm not worried about the enemies I can name. I'm worried about the ones I can't."

THIRTY-SEVEN

I watched the ground, trying to dodge the deepest rain puddles in front of the food tent. When I looked up, Tilton was staring at me.

"I meant it, you know."

"What?" I asked.

"Everything. That Jesse was really lucky you were there; that I'm sorry for coming on so strong in the woods. You clearly weren't interested, and I had no right to try to force it. I don't expect you just to forget, but I hope I can convince you to forgive me."

I must have looked skeptical, because he quickly tried to explain himself. "Seeing how close Jesse came to getting hurt, maybe dying . . . Norman's murder . . . everything else that's been happening on the set. All of it has made me realize how short life is. I don't want to spend the time I have left being an asshole."

I think I opened my mouth. No words came out. I was that stunned.

"I'd like it if we could be friends, Mace."

Friends with a Hollywood legend, especially one begging me for forgiveness? Gee, I thought, let me study on that for a while.

"Okay, with a caveat," I said. "Everybody oversteps a line at some point. But if forcing yourself on women is a pattern with you — and I've heard that it is — you need to get some help."

A flicker of anger lit in his eyes. "Who told you it's a pattern?"

"*Who* is not important; w*hy* is. Are you denying there's a pattern?"

He stopped walking and looked off to the left at the distant trees. I turned to wait for him.

"Are you?" I finally said.

"No, I'm not denying it. There's some truth there." He brought his gaze to mine. "You know, I had a pretty screwed-up childhood. It left some raw wounds."

"Which is all the more reason you should get help. Get yourself straightened out. The way to heal isn't to hurt everybody else."

He put his hands in his pockets and studied the ground. "I know that."

"What is it, then? The power?"

He looked at me, brows raised in a question.

"The first day we met, you mentioned you'd been in and out of lots of foster homes. You must have felt pretty powerless, being pushed around all the time. Maybe you need to feel like you can dominate someone."

"So you're an animal wrangler *and* a psychologist?"

"Can't help it. My big sister psychoanalyzes me all the time. I think I caught it from her."

He showed me the blisters on his forearm and gave a rueful grin. "Well, if that's what's going on in my head, dominating you sure didn't work."

"I'm serious," I said.

He shrugged. "Honestly, I don't know where it comes from. I've always resisted getting therapy. I guess I've played too many tough guys. I never wanted to seem weak."

"How's that working out for you?"

"Pretty bad."

"That should tell you something." I started for the tent again, shooting a question over my shoulder. "Besides, doesn't everybody in Hollywood have a therapist?"

"Ah, yes. The emotionally troubled movie star. It's such a cliché, right?"

"It's not a cliché if it's your life."

In the tent, we picked up Jesse's tea and Maddie's *tiramisu*. I also slid a half-dozen of the still-warm cookies onto a plate. I took a bite from one, and then stirred three packets of sugar into my coffee.

"Not big on counting calories, I see."

"I'm a growing girl," I said. "Besides, this is Himmarshee, not Hollywood. They've had to put in steel bars to reinforce the pews at half the houses of worship in town. Nobody counts calories in Himmarshee."

"Well, you look great."

I gave him a sidelong glance.

"I'm not hitting on you. I'm stating a fact. You look healthy, and I can attest to the fact that you're strong. It's a simple compliment, Mace."

"Yeah? Well, that's one of *my* psychological issues. Everybody tells me I don't know how to take a compliment. I'm never sure if the person means it; I never know how to respond."

"Just say thanks."

"Okay." I grinned at him. "Thanks."

"You're welcome. See how easy that was? I gave a beautiful woman a compliment, without expecting anything in return. You accepted it without overanalyzing what it meant."

His smile crinkled the corners of his eyes. I saw real warmth there.

"While we're talking so freely . . ." he said.

Uh-oh, I thought. Here comes the left hook.

"You should see your face. You look like you swallowed spoiled milk."

"That obvious?"

He nodded. "All I was going to ask is if it'd be all right for us to talk again. It's normally hard for me to open up to people."

"Yeah, I know how that is."

"How about tomorrow afternoon?"

When I hesitated, he showed me his open palms; nothing hidden. "Don't worry, we'll make it a public place. Let's say the catering tent. We can grab something to eat and two seats in the back."

Still, I didn't answer. His eyes turned pleading. "I just feel like *talking* about getting help might make me more likely to finally *get* help. I know it's wrong how I've treated women."

That's what finally did it. I love to hear someone admit they're wrong, as long as the someone isn't me. "Okay, let's make it for dinner, right there." I pointed to a table just inside the tent's entrance.

I was surprised at the relief that flooded

his face at my decision. I hoped I wouldn't
regret making it.

THIRTY-EIGHT

Tilton walked me back to the picnic table. He handed Jesse her tea, gave my shoulder a friendly squeeze, and then started away. Suddenly, he turned. In what seemed like an impulsive gesture, he bent and kissed me. It was a glancing brush, but still on the lips. "Thanks, Mace."

Maddie's mouth dropped open. Mama's eyes went wide. Marty's top teeth were making their way to the bottom row, right through her lower lip.

I was relishing their shocked expressions until I noticed Carlos at Jesse's trailer. The gaffer was talking to him, but for the moment, at least, Carlos's glare was aimed at the departing Tilton and at me. I wondered if a scorch spot was forming at the spot where the movie star had kissed me.

When I waved, Carlos scowled. He said something to one of the men, and then shifted to turn his back to me. The gaffer lifted the cable and pointed to the puddle, as the first electrician on the scene nodded.

"Well, you've done it now, Mace." When Tilton was out of whisper range, Maddie started in. "Are you trying to convince Carlos you're the town floozy?"

"It was a friendly kiss."

"From Hollywood's most notorious womanizer," Marty said in a hushed tone.

"Not smart, girl." Even my new best friend Jesse piled on.

I looked at Mama, who was tsk-tsking me. "When I told you it was good to keep your man guessing, I didn't mean for you to rub his face in all your affairs."

I broke off a piece of a sugar cookie. The whole thing crumbled in my lap. "I'm not having any affairs, Mama. Tilton was just thanking me for agreeing to talk with him tomorrow. He said he wants help with his issues about women."

"Oh, please." Jesse blew on her tea. "He wants something, but it's definitely not help."

I turned to watch Tilton walking through base camp. He was smiling and whistling. He didn't look emotionally troubled. Just as I was about to tell Jesse she might be right, I noticed Carlos watching me from the corner of his eye. Of course, he would catch me at the very moment I was staring after the movie star like a love-struck fan.

Marty said, "You should go talk to him."

"Yes, you should," Jesse said. "But could you do it after he's finished finding out if someone intentionally tried to murder me?"

"Carlos! Wait up."

He walked faster. I had to run after him to catch up. "Didn't you hear me?"

"I heard you."

Thunder rolled in the distance. It looked like another storm was headed our way. I gathered my breath from my sprint across the pasture.

"Well, why didn't you stop?"

"I don't have time." He still hadn't broken stride.

"Right," I said. "The investigation."

"No," he said. "It's not that. I've got at least an hour to wait before the Florida Department of Law Enforcement can get here to process the crime scene at Jesse's trailer."

"Crime scene?"

"The electrician showed me where somebody skinned the cable."

"The gaffer," I said.

"What?"

"Never mind. What about the cable?"

"The rubber was nicked, leaving live wire exposed. It was intentional."

I digested that word — *intentional.* I'd been right, which in this case didn't make me feel happy. Then the other thing Carlos said registered in my mind.

"What'd you mean before? You said you don't have time. For what?"

He finally stopped. "For you."

"Excuse me?"

We stood right outside a family cemetery, created by the movie company for the location shoot. The tombstones were made of polyurethane foam, grayed and weathered to appear old. An ancient live oak, real and weeping with Spanish moss, threw long shadows across the make-believe graves.

Carlos grabbed my arm, guiding me through an opening in a split rail fence newly built, but designed to look rustic. "Let's duck in here for a minute. I owe you that much."

Those ominous words made the solid ground feel like a rolling ocean beneath my feet. I almost wished one of those fake graves would gape open and swallow me. At least then I wouldn't have to hear what I knew Carlos was about to say. Placing his hands on my shoulders, he turned me so he could look me full in the face.

"I can't do this anymore, Mace. I need to be with someone I can trust."

"You can trust me. You keep getting jealous for no reason."

He shook his head. "I'm not jealous, I'm exhausted. Will you, won't you? Loves me, loves me not."

"You're jumping to conclusions. What you just saw with Greg Tilton? I did him a favor, and he gave me a friendly kiss. There's nothing — *nothing* — between us."

He picked a few strands of moss from one of the low-hanging branches; rolled them between his fingers. "But you see, I'm not sure. I'm never sure. Maybe it's the cowboy. Or it might be the movie star. Or maybe it's somebody else. I'm constantly wondering, who are you getting together with that I *don't* see?"

His dark eyes searched my face. "You put up walls, Mace. And I'm tired of trying to knock them down."

Tears stung the back of my eyes. I tried to swallow. I couldn't speak. It seemed my heart was filling up my throat.

"I want a woman who loves me completely."

I found my voice. "Like your late wife? I can't replace her."

"I never expected you to. She was my

whole life, and I was hers. I do want someone, though, that I am certain is mine."

I took a deep breath. "See, that scares me when you say that, Carlos. You make it sound like I'm something you want to possess. I don't want to feel trapped."

"Trapped? So you think of me as your jailer?"

I reached out to touch his cheek. He backed away from my hand. "Do you?" he asked.

I toed the dirt around one of the gravestones. A small one, it said *Baby James Burroughs, Asleep with Jesus.*

"I don't feel trapped by you. I feel trapped with you," I said. "Suppose I do commit myself one-hundred percent to you. You do the same with me. Then, suppose it doesn't work out? That's what I'm scared of."

He cocked his head. "So, is this the part where I'm supposed to reassure you? The part where I say, 'Don't worry, Mace. Nothing will ever happen. We'll be together forever.' "

I didn't trust myself to speak. So I studied the graves. The stone next to Baby James belonged to his older sister. For the movie, the children died on the same day: January 6, 1893.

I watched a black swallowtail butterfly,

mired in a muddy puddle left by the earlier storm. The creature was dying, its wings fluttering ever more slowly.

Finally, he answered his own question. "I can't give you that reassurance, Mace. I know better than most that nothing is forever. Someone murdered my wife, and took her away from me. Your father died, and left you. Your mother has been married five times. Each time, she probably thought it would be forever. Nobody can make that guarantee. And frankly, I'm tired of dancing around the fact that you expect me to."

He looked up to the darkening sky. Black, heavy storm clouds were massing overhead. Lightning streaked across the edge of the fattest cloud.

"We'd better get in before that storm breaks loose," I said.

He gave me a sad smile. "Ah, yes. The weather. Always a safe topic when you don't know what to say."

"We should go," I said. "The rain is really going to come down."

"Is that it, then?" he asked. "Are we broken up?"

I pressed my lips together. What did he want to hear? Did he want me to beg him not to break up? I wouldn't do it. Wasn't he the one who said I wasn't worth the trouble?

There was no getting around that simple fact.

The silence stretched between us until the first fat raindrop splattered on one of the tombstones. *At Peace,* the inscription on the marker said.

As the skies opened, and we lit out for shelter, I knew that peace was easier said than found.

THIRTY-NINE

The music throbbed. The sound of cowboy boots pounding the wooden floor in time to the Charlie Daniels Band hurt my head. I took another long swallow from the Budweiser in front of me. The Eight Seconds Bar was offering a bucket of beer, five bottles for five bucks. I was getting my money's worth.

Toby Wyle was on the dance floor, surrounded by a bevy of young beauties. I recognized the rodeo queen, and a runner-up for the Swamp Cabbage Festival's royal court. His lips were locked with the princess from the Speckled Perch Festival, who was the prettiest and the blondest of the bunch.

Johnny Jaybird seethed from a seat with a ringside view of the dance floor. A peanut bowl went untouched on the tabletop in front of him. A bottle of cheap whiskey was getting a workout, though. Pouring himself a hefty glass, Johnny looked as miserable as I felt. It's a bitch when the person you care about doesn't care about your feelings.

"Mind if I sit?" Savannah stood at an empty barstool beside me.

"It's a free country." I slid the peanut bowl her way. I'd already made a small mountain of shells on the barroom floor.

She settled on the stool, and waved a five-dollar bill at the bartender, an older man I didn't recognize. He hustled toward us with another ice-filled bucket of beer.

"These are on me." She plucked out the first bottle, and twisted off the cap. "I feel like an idiot for making such a fuss at Jesse's trailer."

I wondered if you calculated the distance in the barroom between Johnny, Savannah, and me, would it form a perfect triangle of crushed hearts? I gave her a shrug. "Love makes people do strange things."

Face reddening, she studied her hands. I realized I'd overstepped.

"Sorry, Savannah. Jesse told us about the relationship between you two."

"Jesse has a very big mouth."

I noticed she didn't deny it. Silence settled between us like a long stretch of empty road. The jukebox switched to an oldie by Freddy Fender, "Before the Next Teardrop

345

Falls." The pounding boots turned to a slow shuffle.

She slid a plastic-wrapped praline toward me on the bar. I read the label: *Savannah City Confections*. I placed it in my top pocket, and then clinked my bottle to hers. "Here's hoping for better luck in love for the both of us."

The corners of her mouth crooked into a grin. "Trouble with the police detective?"

"You do not want to know," I said.

I glanced over at Toby again. Savannah's gaze followed mine. He had an arm draped around one beauty; another nuzzled his neck. The third playfully snatched the cowboy hat off his head. Perching it atop her own blond locks, she tugged at Toby's collar to pull him close for a sloppy kiss.

"Poor Johnny Jaybird doesn't look like he's enjoying the floor show," I said.

"It's sad. He has tender feelings for Toby. He'd probably be a good protector, if Toby would come out. But Hollywood makes people hide who they really are." She raised her bottle to take a sip. The enormous diamond on her wedding ring winked in the blue glow of a neon beer sign.

"People in Hollywood seem to hide a lot of secrets," I said, leadingly.

The thought ran through my mind: What

else might Savannah be hiding?

"Give the detecting a rest, would you?" I thought I heard a hint of irritation, but when she spun a half-turn toward me, she was smiling. "Speaking of secrets, what's the deal between your mama and my husband?"

"There's absolutely nothing between them." I hoped I sounded reassuring. "Mama is happily married."

She took another swallow, and turned her back to the room. "It doesn't matter, Mace. Paul is married to me in name only."

I wanted to tell her it mattered a great deal to Sal, who had nearly pounded her husband into dust defending Mama's honor. Instead, I asked, "How long has Paul known about you and Jesse?"

She waved a graceful hand. "Jesse's not the first. Paul's known I was into girls since before we got married. He wanted a wife who wouldn't care if he played around; I wanted a husband who would give me nice things and not ask too many questions."

"Is that what you got?"

Her eyes met mine in the mirror behind the bar. "He doesn't ask and I don't tell; and vice versa."

"So you ask no questions about Paul and Barbara Sydney? Maybe her husband Nor-

347

man didn't subscribe to the same policy."

She rolled her eyes and shelled a peanut.

"That whole mess between the Sydneys was more dysfunctional than anything I've ever been involved in. Barbara is stone-cold crazy. There's no telling what that woman is capable of."

I didn't mention that Jesse had said the same thing about Savannah. "Dysfunctional, how?" I asked.

She pressed her lips together. "I'm not going to speak ill of the dead. Let's just say Paul made a pact with two devils to get this picture done."

"But . . ."

She made the lip-zipping motion. "Not to be rude, but it's none of your business. Ask Barbara or Paul if you want to know more about their relationship."

"Why . . ."

She cut me off. "Don't try to weasel it out of me, Mace. I'm not that drunk."

I looked at her in the mirror. Her serious expression and the stiffness of her spine told me she was right. She wasn't at all drunk.

"Okay then," I said. "So what about the 'nice things' part of your bargain with Paul?" I leaned close to her hand to admire the diamond. "Looks like he came through on your ring."

She held her hand to the light. "He did. I also got a little ranch out near Jackson, Wyoming. I'd always wanted to be a cattle-woman."

"We had a ranch when I was young, but my daddy made some bad business decisions. We lost it." I took a slug from my beer. "He died not too long after that. Everybody said the stress of losing everything brought on his heart attack."

"I'm so sorry." She patted my knee. "Tell you what, you can come out to Wyoming anytime you want. The two of us will saddle up and work the cattle together. Sound good?"

I gave her a sideways glance. She laughed and shook her head. "Don't worry. No strings attached. You're a little too masculine to be my type."

I didn't know whether to be relieved or insulted. I was curious though. "So, is Kelly Conover your type?"

Savannah snorted. "Hardly. She's too girly."

"I don't know. She's part Gypsy. Very hot-blooded."

Savannah cocked her head. "You didn't really believe that load of crap she tries to sell, did you? The woman's family roots go back generations in Fort Wayne, Indiana."

"You're kidding."

"Nope; she's a hundred-percent, milk-fed Midwesterner. You gotta be careful, Mace. Stick with the Hollywood people who *don't* lie. Like me. Just as friends, of course."

"What the hell?" I finally said. "Working cattle in Wyoming sounds pretty good."

I tipped my bottle to hers. We clinked to seal the deal.

The hands on the bucking bronc clock behind the bar were almost at midnight. Suddenly, I felt the weight of the day's events dragging me down toward exhaustion. I still had a long drive ahead of me to my cottage.

I yelled down the bar. "Can I get a Coke over here?"

The bartender brought me a tall glass with ice, and two cans of soda. "Drink 'em both, Mace. I want you wide awake driving way out there on State Road 98."

I peered at his face. His cheeks were ruddy. Broken veins crisscrossed his bulbous nose. He had a lot of miles on him. If I had to guess, I'd say a lot of them had been driven drunk.

"I'm sorry." I smiled. "Do I know you?"

"Name's Clyde, from down in Clewiston. I used to date your mama."

"Who didn't?"

The activity at the bar was winding down. Savannah was about to depart. "I have to be up early to pack," she said. "The shoot's almost over. I'm leaving in the morning."

Toby had abandoned the girls on the dance floor. He sat now at Johnny's table, leaning close and listening to the assistant director. Toby's presence made Johnny look so absurdly happy that I felt sorry for him. I hoped the young star decided who he wanted to be before he broke the poor guy's heart.

An excited murmur moved through the bar, heralding the arrival of a Hollywood VIP. Poised at the open door, Kelly Conover prepared to make a dramatic entrance. Stealing a glance at himself in the mirror, the bartender spit on his thumb and then used it to smooth his unruly unibrow. Too bad he didn't have time to trim the stray hairs from his nose and ears, too.

I wondered just how long ago it was that Mama dated him.

I was just about to tease the barkeep about his Kelly crush — No fool like an old fool — when I saw her grin over her shoulder. She laughed, that famous sweet-dessert-and-a-side-of-sex giggle. Whoever was behind her, holding the door open, must have said something really funny.

A moment later, I saw Kelly's companion, hand placed possessively at the small of her back. If I hadn't grabbed the bar rail, I would have tumbled off my stool from the shock.

FORTY

Kelly either didn't know or didn't care that she was with my painfully recent ex-beau. She sent me a cheerful wave across the Eight Seconds barroom. Carlos seemed too captivated by the radiance of this star to even glance my way.

I felt all those peanuts melding into an iron cannonball in my stomach. Offering Kelly a curt nod, I turned back to count the ice cubes in my glass of soda.

Please, God, don't let them come over here.

The man upstairs must have taken pity on me because the two of them headed for a booth in the back. Most people stared openly as they passed. Only one other patron in the bar watched as surreptitiously as I did. From his vantage point a few stools down, Sam Dobbs also tried to make it look like the last thing he was doing was following Carlos and Kelly's progress in the mirror.

As soon as they ducked into a high-backed booth, I caught Sam's eye. Leaning past a tattooed redhead next to me, I lifted my glass to him. Sam returned my toast, and added a dejected shrug.

Poor Sam. Poor me. What a couple of saps.

On the jukebox, Willie Nelson began to croon "Always on My Mind," stirring up all kinds of memories. Carlos and I danced to that tune at Mama's wedding, which was just about the last time things felt right between us.

The movie star and my ex got up to dance to what had been "our song," I felt like the mule in the movie company's corral had just kicked me in the gut. When the song ended, Savannah left me with a pat on the back and a pitying look.

I'd had all I could take. I left a five for shaggy brow, and scooped my keys off the bar. I cut across the far edge of the dance floor, but it wasn't far enough to avoid the sight of Kelly gazing up into Carlos's face with adoration. His hand low on her back pulled her close, as he stared dreamily into those famous green eyes.

I couldn't compete with her body or her looks. But she was Hollywood-style nutty, wasn't she? Would Carlos really choose a shallow, mixed-up starlet over me?

Of course he would; especially when the starlet was the same All-American beauty who once gave a come-hither smile from a poster on the wall of his bedroom. Kelly was older, maybe, but she was just as beautiful as the teenaged boy's fantasy she used to be.

As I pushed open the barroom door, I thought I caught a reflection in the small porthole window. I thought Carlos was watching me leave. I spun around, only to realize he wasn't looking after all.

A breeze brushed my face as I stepped outside. I was grateful. Maybe the clean night air would help dry the tears that had begun to wet my cheeks.

I stumbled over a chunk of rock in the gravel parking lot, nearly falling on my butt. I wasn't drunk. I'd ordered light beers, which went down like water. Nope, I was blinded by tears. I brushed them away, angry at myself for letting Carlos get to me. Of course he'd prefer a screen idol. Who wouldn't?

Well, me for one. Greg Tilton had been interested. But all I could see was Carlos when the movie star looked at me. I wished I could take back that moment in the fake graveyard, when Carlos asked if we were truly broken up. I wanted to say no. Instead,

I said nothing. If only I could have a do-over, I'd make things right again.

Wending my way through the rows of parked vehicles, I looked for my Jeep. That's when I spotted Barbara's gleaming Jaguar at the lot's far corner. Among the beat-up cars and mud-splattered trucks, it looked as out of place as a high-fashion model at the Walmart.

The driver's door was open, and the interior light lit. Barbara leaned against the door, facing me. Even though Paul had his back to me, I recognized him by the long gray ponytail snaking down the back of his motorcycle jacket.

Her arms were crossed over her chest as she listened to him, a scowl painted on her face. Taking cover behind a hulking Chevy Silverado four-by-four, I inched close enough to hear them. The cab on the massive truck was taller than me.

"The fact you're throwing away money isn't even the main thing, Paul. You've lost your touch."

"But . . ."

She hissed, "The dailies look like crap. You've lost your touch. You may have been a great director, once. But you've become a no-talent hack."

Paul's face reddened. He leaned into her.

"How would you know? The only talent you ever had was for marrying the right man way back when."

"You've pegged one thing: I did marry right. And my ex-husband would have never stood for what's been happening on this set. Over budget. Bad PR. Out-of-control stars . . ."

He stepped menacingly toward Barbara, his face inches from hers. "Well, Norman's not here anymore, is he?"

Drunken laughter carried our way. Paul stepped back, and both of them turned their heads toward the sound. Two cowboys wove through the parking lot. The shorter of the two propped up his buddy, who was about to lose the straw Resistol teetering on his head. As the men passed by, Paul and Barbara glared at each other, eyes spitting sparks.

A truck door slammed nearby, and then the short cowpoke came back alone. His buddy was probably already snoring from the front seat, sleeping it off.

Barbara, still staring at her lover, seemed to be assessing him. Disgust — and something else — was written on her face. "No," she finally said. "Norman is not here. And isn't that lucky for you?"

■ ■ ■ ■

I hit the Play button on my answering machine. As soon as I heard the voice, I knew I'd regret not waiting until the morning.

"Hello, Mace. It's your mama."

She took a long, pre-lecture breath. I went to the kitchen and grabbed a bag of tortilla chips and my homemade salsa. Might as well be fortified for what was coming.

"Honey, your cousin Bubba called here tonight. Not the good Bubba. Aunt Jo's boy. Did you know he broke his arm? Anyhoo, Bubba said he saw you crying in your beer at the Perch while Carlos danced with Kelly Conover. Bubba said she looked as fine as chrome rims on a Ford F-350, by the way. Funny, I completely forgot to ask him what Kelly was wearing . . ."

I knew Mama must have a point in mind, somewhere.

"Bubba said he would have come over to check on you, but he was getting lucky with some gal he just met."

Sounded like Bubba.

"But what I called about, honey, is you and Carlos. Have you even tried talking to him? I just know if you tell him how you really feel, you'll be able to iron out things between you."

Wila meowed from her spot under my bed.

"My sentiments exactly, girl," I said. "Who'd take relationship advice from a woman who's been married five times?"

"Now, Mace, I can picture you rolling your eyes about now."

How does she do that?

"But honey, you know I've seen you happy with Carlos. All I want is for you to be happy. I think he could give you that, if you'd just let him. Why won't you let him?"

The chip in my mouth turned to ashes. I couldn't swallow, given the lump in my throat. I told myself it was the jalapeno peppers I'd chopped into the salsa bringing tears to my eyes.

"Okay, honey, the machine is telling me to quit now. You're a beautiful girl, every bit as pretty as Kelly. Well, you would be with a little make-up, anyways. Remember that. I lov . . ."

The beep cut her off, mid-word. I sat there for a moment on my couch, staring out the window into the night. Wila padded into the living room from her hiding spot, and jumped up next to me. We're not normally a cuddly couple, but the cat seemed to sense I wanted company. Her warm body was a comfort beside me.

"I screwed up, Wila." Whispering, I stroked her velvety coat. "It's my fault Carlos is fooling around with Kelly. If I'd tried harder to let him know how I feel, that would have been me dancing with him tonight."

Wila purred. Did she agree? Was she contradicting me? Maybe she was just enjoying the massage.

The last explanation was most likely. Still, it felt good to unburden myself. I wasn't Catholic, so the cat was the best confessor I was likely to get.

"What should I do, Wila?"

A knock at my bedroom window put a quick end to my conversation with the cat. I jumped up; Wila leapt to the floor. As she scurried under the couch, I grabbed Paw-Paw's shotgun from the closet.

FORTY-ONE

My cottage is tiny, and I could see the window of my bedroom from the living room, just a half dozen steps away.

It was inky dark in the backyard. Whoever had knocked was outside the glow of the light from the front porch. A shiver worked its way along my spine. Could the intruder see me, while I couldn't see him, or her? Another knock sounded, more insistent this time.

"Who's there?"

Taking cover behind the bedroom doorframe, I quickly loaded and racked the shotgun. That dramatic sound everyone knows from the movies ricocheted out the screened window.

"*¡Dios mío!* Don't shoot! It's me, Carlos. I didn't want to wake you in case you were sleeping."

I exhaled the breath I'd been holding, pulled back the slide and ejected the shell.

"Well, I'm not sleepy now." I went to the window. "What are you doing out there?"

"I'm checking to make sure you're safe." He tapped at the glass. "I've told you about this. I really wish you wouldn't leave the window open, Mace. Anybody could push through this screen."

His overprotectiveness was about to make me bristle, as usual. I counted to five instead. Maybe it meant he still cared about me, at least a little.

"Want to come in?"

"I was hoping you'd ask."

Once he was inside, and settled on the couch, I got him a soda. I grabbed my salsa, found a couple of napkins, and transferred the chips I'd been eating straight from the bag into a glass bowl. Mama would be proud.

"What brings you way out here?"

"I wanted to talk."

"Ever hear of a phone?"

He cocked his head at me. I hoped my smile stripped the words of any sting.

"I wanted to see you in person. I was afraid if I called first, you'd say I couldn't come."

"Fair enough," I said. "Let's talk."

I put the bowl between us on the couch and sat down. He took a long swallow from his can of Coke.

"No games?" he finally asked, as he looked into my eyes.

I showed him my hands, holding no tricks.

"I'm sorry about how I was acting with Kelly tonight. It was childish. I wanted to make you jealous."

"Mission accomplished," I said.

"I'd like to give things another try, Mace. Give *us* another try."

I searched his face. His eyes held mine. I felt like I was floating in those dark chocolate pools. And then I remembered how just a couple of hours earlier, he'd been staring just that same way into Kelly's eyes.

"I don't know, Carlos. You seemed awfully cozy with the movie star."

He shrugged. "It was just one dance. The main reason I called Kelly tonight was business. I needed to ask her some questions regarding the investigation."

I sat up straight. "Why? Do you think Kelly's involved?"

He shook a finger at me. "You know I'm not going to tell you that."

"That means you do."

"No, it means I'm not going to tell you. So quit asking." He leaned closer, brushed a lock of hair behind my ear. "Besides, this is about us. Do you think what we have is worth working on?"

Judging by the way my skin sizzled at his touch, I did. For once, I didn't hesitate.

"Yes, I absolutely do," I said. "Can we start working on it right now, please?"

His eyes went all hot and liquid. I felt a shudder of desire. We moved toward each other, and kissed. His mouth tasted sweet, like cinnamon breath mints overlaid with Coke. He laced his fingers into my hair, and pulled my face roughly to his. Willingly, I went. Fingers fumbled with zippers and buttons. The bowl tumbled off the couch. We tore at one another's clothes.

Anger. Confusion. Love. Lust. All the emotions that had been racing through my body crystallized, and then melded into one powerful urge. We became one, and the flame of hurt I'd felt when I saw him with Kelly was extinguished, right there on the couch. Just to be sure, we put the flame out again.

After we were spent, he chuckled.

"Not exactly the after-glow response I'd hoped for." I gave his shoulder a playful punch.

He picked a crushed tortilla chip from my hair and showed it to me. I had to smile, because I had spotted a big glob of salsa on his bare chest. I swiped the salsa onto my finger, and then dabbed it on the chip. He popped the combination into his mouth.

"Not bad," he said.

"I've got a leftover slice of Mama's butterscotch pie in the fridge," I said. "Want something sweet?"

"I just had something sweet." He gave me an exaggerated leer.

I was about to ask if he was ready for thirds on that particular treat, when I heard the sound of country music floating through the night air. Outside, a truck was jouncing into my yard. Carlos raised his eyebrows at me. I shrugged, grabbed a long T-shirt, and went to the window to look out.

Uh-oh. The pickup was big, white, and very familiar. The engine stuttered to a stop. A door squeaked open, and then slammed.

"Mace! You home, darlin'?"

The words were slurred. The accent was country, and also familiar.

"It's me, sweetheart. Jeb Ennis!"

Boots shuffled on the gravel path outside. *Step. Stumble. Stumble. Step.*

"I told you I could still find my way here." Jeb's shout was slurred. "I'm a little drunk, but not too drunk to get busy."

A knock sounded at the door. Carlos had already put on his pants and shoes. He was gathering his keys and wallet.

"Please stay," I told him. "I'll get rid of Jeb."

He stood in front of the mirror on the dresser in my bedroom, buttoning his shirt. He wouldn't meet my eyes.

"I had no idea he was coming out here, Carlos."

The knocking turned into pounding at the front door.

"Open up! I reconsidered our little chat in my truck. I love you. I'm gonna change, just like you always wanted. That's a promise."

Carlos slipped his wallet in his back pocket, patted it. "That sounds like a pretty good offer to me. I'd take Jeb up on it. Like he said, it's what you've always wanted."

"I'm not interested in Jeb. I'm interested in you. I thought I'd just proved that."

I glanced at the couch, its pillows all askew. I hoped I wasn't blushing.

He focused those lasers of his on me. "That was just sex, Mace." His voice was ice. "Anybody can do that."

The knob on the front door rattled. "I'm tellin' you, sweetheart: I love you!"

Carlos unlocked the door and yanked it open. The surprise on Jeb's face when he saw him standing there was almost comical. But I wasn't in a laughing mood. As Carlos stalked past Jeb, I followed him out onto the porch.

"Please, don't go."

I hated the desperate note I heard in my voice. I hated it even more when Carlos coldly shook off the hand I'd placed on his arm. He didn't bother to answer as he hurried down the steps. I ran after him into the yard, leaving Jeb standing on the top step with his mouth hanging open.

"Carlos . . ." I called as he got into his unmarked cop car.

"Your cowpoke is waiting for you." I heard the sneer in his voice. "Maybe you two can saddle up and ride off together into the sunrise, after he sobers up."

With that, he swung the door shut and gunned the engine. The Crown Vic spit grass and gravel as Carlos tore out of my yard and out of my life.

Watching him go, I caught sight of Jeb weaving drunkenly on the porch steps. As Carlos roared past, Jeb turned his head to look. That made him lose his balance, and he tumbled backward to the ground.

"Hey, darlin', how 'bout a little help?" Smiling a dopey grin, Jeb reached out a hand for me to pull him up.

I stepped over him without a word, somehow resisting the urge to aim a kick at his head. I stomped up the stairs and through my front door. Then I slammed it on my drunken first love and the rest of my regrets.

FORTY-TWO

The next morning, the mood on the movie set was subdued. Long faces, hushed voices, very little chatter. Maybe everyone was feeling the effects of the previous night's bash at the Eight Seconds Bar.

Or maybe I was just looking at the world through depression-gray glasses.

I'd been holding a private pity party since Carlos peeled rubber out of my yard. Jeb must have gotten tired of banging at the locked door. When I peeked out the window, he was snoring on the front porch. I heard him start his truck and drive away just after six a.m.

Good riddance. I was furious at him for ruining my reunion with Carlos. Jeb's timing always was better in the rodeo than it was in real life.

"What's wrong, Mace? You haven't even touched your breakfast."

Marty's soft voice brought me back to the

present, and the table outside the food tent where I sat with my sisters. She picked up my fork and handed it to me. I laid it down again beside my uneaten scrambled eggs.

"Are you going to finish those home fries?" Maddie asked.

I pushed the plate her way. "Knock yourself out."

The sight of Maddie dousing everything with ketchup made the coffee I'd swallowed roil around my otherwise empty stomach. "I'm not feeling very well." I started to rise, when Marty tugged at my sleeve.

"Sit down, sister. Tell us what's wrong."

"Nothing wrong with these potatoes," Maddie said around a mouthful of mostly ketchup. "What's put you off your feed this morning, Mace? Not that I'm complaining."

"I don't want to talk about it."

"Carlos?" Marty asked.

To my horror, I felt the sting of tears behind my eyes again. I don't think I'd cried so much since we had to put down my favorite dog when I was ten.

Passing me a folded napkin, Marty waited for my answer. Her blue eyes were full of sympathy.

Finally, I nodded yes to her question.

"Oh, honey!" She scooted close and rubbed my back.

"Could you pass the salt, please?" Maddie said.

Marty slammed a hand down on the table-top.

"What?" Maddie looked up from her — formerly my — breakfast plate. My dejection finally seemed to register on her radar.

"Well, why didn't y'all say something? I'm not a mind-reader."

Marty rolled her eyes. "Honey, tell me what happened with Carlos. I bet it's nothing that we can't fix."

"Well, that's one bet you're going to lose, Marty," I said.

I filled them in on everything that had happened, beginning with Carlos dancing with Kelly at the bar. I continued through the romantic make-up session at my cottage, minus the multiple X-rated details. Then, I ended with the interloping ex-beau plummeting off my porch.

"So, did you invite Jeb to sleep over then?" Maddie picked at a few remaining pieces of greasy, charred onions on the plate. My stomach clenched.

"I don't love Jeb, Maddie."

"That hasn't stopped you before."

When Marty saw I wasn't rising to our big sister's bait, she stepped in. "Can't you see Mace is really hurting? She needs

371

encouragement, Maddie. Not criticism."

"I wasn't criticizing," Maddie said. "I was stating a fact."

"Well, cut it out!" The heat of Marty's glare was so unaccustomed, so intense, it raised a guilty look like a welt on Maddie's face.

"Sorry, Mace," Maddie said, adding an awkward pat of my hand.

I shrugged and then heaved a big sigh. I hated this sad-sack version of me, but I couldn't seem to help it. All I wanted was to go back home and pull the bedcovers over my head. But I couldn't. The horses had to be cared for. If Jeb was still on a toot, or sleeping it off, he might not show up to handle his cattle. I might have to do that, too. Not to mention, Mama's dancehall scene was scheduled for shooting later in the day. She'd kill me if I missed it. I may be miserable, but I didn't want to be murdered.

I sighed again.

Now, both my sisters were staring at me in that sad way you look at someone in the hospital who you know won't be coming home. Suddenly, Marty brightened. "You need a distraction!"

Maddie clapped her hands, like a first-grade teacher promising finger-painting.

"Exactly! Let's see if we can figure out who killed the producer."

"I don't care who killed him," I said.

"Really? You don't care if a murderer gets away with it? You don't care that the same person may have tried to kill you by rigging that light to blow?"

Maddie searched my face. "Aha!" she cried. "I saw that spark of interest in your eyes just now. Of course you care."

I toed the dirt under the bench seat with my boot. "Maybe a little."

"Excellent," Marty said. "Let's survey the suspects." Her head swiveled to all sides of the base camp. "Greg Tilton, at fifty paces."

Maddie and I shifted to follow the direction of her nod.

Tilton was talking to a couple of crew members, a cup of coffee in his hand. When he noticed us looking, he saluted with the cup and gave his trademark smirk. All of us quickly looked away.

"Well, I for one don't trust him." Maddie spoke under her breath. "What's he hiding behind that annoying grin?"

"You're still mad because of the way he tried to force himself on Mace," Marty said.

"Aren't you?" Maddie asked.

Before Marty could answer, I said, "The man has problems. He's said he's sorry. He probably never meets anyone who says no."

"Excuses!" Maddie said.

Marty sneaked another glance at Tilton. "He even stopped me on my way in this morning. He wanted to tell me how sorry he was. He said he's changed, and asked me to make sure Mace knows that."

"She's been there, heard that," Maddie said. "I wonder why he didn't talk to me?"

"Probably scared off by the way you scowl at him. Kind of like you're doing now," I said.

Maddie snapped her head back toward us. "Why does everyone say I scowl?"

"Because you do." Marty patted our big sister's cheek. "Anyway, he was a perfect gentleman."

"Humph," Maddie said. "So was Ted Bundy."

"It was so weird this morning," Marty said. "I stood there, staring at the guy I daydreamed about all through middle school. I must have filled a whole notebook, practicing my future signatures: Marty Tilton. Mrs. Greg Tilton. Greg and Marty Tilton."

Maddie said, "I drew lace-bordered hearts around the name of my crush: Scott Baio."

I groaned. "Not the guy from *Joanie Loves Chachi*?"

"He was adorable," Maddie said. "Whose name did you practice, Mace?"

"John W. Jones Jr."

My teen crush garnered blank looks from both sisters.

"Three-time world champion rodeo bull-dogger in the 1980s," I said. "Plus, he had dreamy eyes."

They laughed, and I joined in, feeling a bit more like myself again. I looked around, and my gaze settled on Sam Dobbs, knocking on the door of the production trailer. Kelly wasn't with him. I tried not to imagine her off somewhere, keeping company with a certain detective.

"Are you thinking of him as a suspect?" Maddie's eyes followed mine to Sam.

"Honestly, the guy's barely said two words to me. I don't know much about him, except he's crazy about Kelly."

Maddie said, "Well, he's a man, so that makes sense."

"I was just remembering last night; he was trying to pretend he didn't care if Kelly was cuddling up to someone else at the bar. He was acting, just like I was."

As Sam disappeared into the trailer, some small scrap of information about him tried to surface in my mind. All I kept seeing, though, was our eyes meeting in the mirror behind the bar, two sorry-ass kindred souls.

"What about that guy?"

Marty's whisper forced me to refocus. Being lovelorn was distracting me from sleuthing. She pointed out the dapper assistant director, head bobbing as he talked into a cell phone.

"How much do we know about Johnny Jaybird?" Maddie asked.

I knew quite a bit, at least about his sexuality. I didn't share it with my sisters, though. Maybe I identified with the way the poor guy was being jerked around by Toby.

"Getting shot makes Johnny seem more like a victim than an aggressor," I said.

"Maybe he got shot because he *was* the aggressor," Maddie said.

Johnny slipped his phone into his pocket, and cocked his head across the camp toward Jesse's new trailer. After her close call, the police commandeered her former trailer as a crime scene. A temporary trailer was hauled in. Toby and Jesse sat in front of it now, in camp chairs.

"I've got my eye on Toby," Marty said. "That parking lot 'accident' seems fishy."

I raised my brows at my little sister, who rarely suspects anybody of anything.

"For one thing, the timing was too perfect," she said. "For another, nobody else saw or heard a thing."

I recalled Toby looking artfully disheveled after the near-miss. The question was, how artful?

"Toby's not the murderous type," Maddie said with her usual certainty. "Remember that movie where he played a Cub Scout? He was as sweet as speckled pup."

"Acting, sister," I said.

"Maybe." Maddie nodded thoughtfully. "But a certain innocence, even purity, shines through."

"He didn't look so pure strutting out of Jesse's trailer the first time I saw him," I said.

"What about motive, though?" Maddie asked. "Greg Tilton might have wanted Norman and Toby both out of the way, so his role wouldn't get cut. But what would Toby's motive be? You said Norman liked him; and he's clearly the apple of Barbara's eye."

"Hmmm," I said.

"What?" both sisters asked at once.

"About Norman . . ." I looked around, saw no one listening in. "Savannah told me he was a predator, and he wasn't fussy about gender. Maybe he forced Toby . . ."

Marty picked up my thread. ". . . and Toby hated him for it. Maybe he shot Johnny as a way to explain away his fingerprints on the gun. Maybe Toby used that same gun to kill Norman."

"Was it the same gun, Mace?" Maddie asked.

"How should I know? Carlos isn't even talking to me. Even if he was, he wouldn't share ballistics details." I made my tone a little less peevish. "It's a good theory, sisters. But Jesse and Toby made a big deal of letting everyone know they were 'shagging' all that morning that Norman was killed."

"So they said." Marty looked pointedly toward the young pair.

They giggled and tussled together, as cute as a couple of kittens.

"They do look awfully chummy," Maddie said.

Were they chummy enough to provide each other with alibis for murder?

FORTY-THREE

"Rolling." The camera operator was ready to film.

"Action." Paul spoke in a normal tone of voice, and his command was relayed via headset to the assistant director, who repeated it to the scrum of cast and crew members surrounding Mama.

"I know what you did to my daughter." Mama leaned close to the actor playing the drunken cowboy. Her eyes spit fire; her voice was low and threatening. In her flaming red wig, movie make-up, and dancehall-girl gown, she looked gorgeous. "Hurt her again, and I'll kill you."

The actor playing the drunken cowboy backed up a step. His face registered shock and surprise.

"Cut."

Mama looked off the set of the pretend dancehall to where Paul sat in his director's chair. He was studying the scene on a video monitor.

"Did I do something wrong?" she called.

Johnny Jaybird patted her arm. "You were great," he whispered. "Paul will have us do take after take. That's normal. Each time, you hear 'Action,' just act like it's the first time you've done it."

I thought it was kind of him to reassure her. As the crew set up to repeat the shot, she glanced over to where Sal, my sisters and I were watching. I flashed a thumbs-up; Sal mouthed, *Beautiful!* Beaming with pride, Maddie blew a kiss. Marty clasped both hands over her heart.

As filming continued, more spectators drifted over to the dancehall set. Mama performed her lines over and over. I had to admit, she hit it right each time, energy never flagging.

"She's really good," Marty said, as the camera crew stopped to change positions for the second half of Mama's Hollywood moment.

"You sound surprised." I smiled at her.

Mama's enthusiasm seemed contagious. Maybe it was just because it was getting close to the end of the last day of filming, but I did notice more smiles and fewer scowls on the set. Even Barbara nodded and poked me in the ribs after one of Mama's takes.

"Can't argue with Paul's eye," she said. "Your mother's good as the dancehall girl, even if it will cause me problems with the union. Anybody from the Screen Actors Guild asks, your mother should say she's weighing whether to join."

"Action," Paul said, and Johnny Jaybird relayed the command.

Mama hauled off to slap the cowboy, and pulled her punch just before connecting. Poor Sal bore the bruises of those practice sessions, but they'd helped her master the choreography of fake movie-fighting. Once they'd filmed the male actor's recoil, and added the sound effect of hand hitting skin, the audience would never be the wiser. They'd feel the sting of Mama's palm on the cowboy's cheek; imagine the welt rising up. Her rage was that believable.

Maybe all that guff she'd read in those acting books about mining her emotional memories had worked.

"I guarantee you, Mama's thinking of Husband No. 2 right there," Maddie said after one fiery take. "Did you see the murder in her eyes when she glared at the cowboy?"

Finally, the assistant director repeated *Cut* for the last time. Paul stepped out from the knot of people gathered with him around the monitor and strutted over to Mama.

"You were wonderful." He put an arm around her shoulder and drew her close, but not too close. His tone was friendly, but not too friendly. "You *were* Ruby. That was a fine piece of acting, Rosalee."

Jesse started the applause, and it spread through the dancehall set. Even Barbara clapped her hands together once or twice.

"That's my wife! Isn't she something?" Sal circled the crowd, slapping at backs. When he got to Paul, he shook the hand of the man he'd fought with just a day before. "You really know your stuff, man."

"Well, thank you, Sal. I had excellent raw material to work with."

Paul gave Mama a chaste kiss on the cheek. She fluttered her fake eyelashes.

Greg Tilton snapped off a sharp salute. "Welcome to the club," he said.

Sal slapped him on the back, too. "That's my wife! That's my movie star."

"Well, then you're a lucky man," Tilton said, returning Sal's back slap. Just a couple of normal guys, bonding.

Face lit with pleasure, Sal moved on to Maddie and Marty, draping a bear-like paw over each of their shoulders.

I leaned toward Tilton. "Thanks for being

so nice."

He bowed. "No problem, Mace. We're still on for our little chat later, right? Because you're going to see more nice. This is the new me."

I hoped that was true; but at the same time I wondered. How much changing was Greg Tilton prepared to do?

"Hey, need a hand?"

At my question, C'ndee looked up from behind a big aluminum pan of pasta she was setting out for the late afternoon supper.

"I wouldn't turn it down." She slid the serving pan onto a long folding table, which was draped with a white plastic cover. The spot was reserved with words written on the plastic in heavy black felt marker, *Baked Ziti.*

I had to hand it to C'ndee. She was the boss, but she wasn't afraid to pitch in right beside the people she'd hired to help cater the movie shoot. As I assisted, ferrying pans out from her mobile kitchen, I noticed a sheet cake waiting on the dessert table. It was shaped like an old-fashioned, clapper-style slate — not completely accurate, since modern devices for marking scenes now included digital readouts. But it looked good, in black-and-white frosting, with "That's a Wrap!" scrawled across the top in big cursive letters.

"Cake looks super," I said.

"Thanks. Barbara wouldn't pay for anything extra, so I donated the cake and thirty gallons of ice cream. These people worked hard on the movie. They should have some kind of celebration for the final day of Florida filming."

"Speaking of working, or at least working the crowd . . ."

I nodded toward the front of the tent, where Mama was making her entrance followed by her personal entourage: Sal, Marty and Maddie. She accepted congratulations as she went, like the silver screen star she now believed herself to be. I prayed her scene wouldn't get cut in the editing process. She'd never get over it.

"I hear she did great," C'ndee said.

I felt an involuntary surge of pride. "You know, she really did."

"You sound shocked."

"I shouldn't be, right? We've always known Mama was a drama queen."

"You said it; I didn't." C'ndee grinned.

"Said what?" Mama, still bursting from the bodice of her Ruby-the-Protestant gown, sidled up beside us. She swiped a finger through the frosting at the bottom of the cake, where she thought no one would notice.

C'ndee slapped her hand. Not so long ago, that would have been the start of the Second Civil War. But after what they'd survived at Mama's wedding to Sal, the Jersey Girl and the Southern Belle had become friends. Sort of.

"You should have seen me, C'ndee. I killed."

"Not literally, I hope."

Mama trilled, "Oh, honey, that's just a Hollywood saying we actors use."

C'ndee wriggled her brows. "So now you're an actor, after one line?"

"Two, honey." Mama held up her fingers. "I also got to slap somebody. Of course, we're taught to pull our punches, so I didn't actually hurt him. Film-making is all camera angles and sound effects, C'ndee. That and good acting, of course."

"Of course," C'ndee said.

An hour later, the hordes had come and gone. Tiny specks of food were all that remained in the silver serving pans. The cake table looked like a desert scene from Lawrence of Arabia: vast, swept-over, and empty. I'd even seen one crew member scraping with a plastic knife at the last dabs

385

of cake frosting on the cardboard sheeting.

C'ndee's shoes sat on the floor beside her. With her legs elevated, she'd propped up her aching feet on a chair across from her. Mama and I sipped at cups of hot herbal tea as we waited for my sisters to show up.

I glanced at the entrance, and checked my watch again. Five-fifty. Tilton was now almost an hour late. The horses were waiting at the corral.

"Are we keeping you from something, Mace?" Mama asked.

I decided not to tell her I'd been stood up. So much for the new Greg Tilton.

FORTY-FOUR

Mama looked at me like I'd asked her to crawl all the way to the Mason-Dixon line and take up residence on the wrong side.

All I'd done was ask her to change out of Ruby's dress, and give me a hand with the horses.

"Honey, I can't do that. I'm expected at the wrap party tonight. All the actors are going. As soon as Sal finishes up here with security and all, we'll go home and I'll start getting ready."

I shook my head, but managed to hold my tongue.

"Don't you roll your eyes at me, young lady. You are not too old to get the switch. Aren't your sisters coming back here to help you at the corral?"

"They're home, fixing dinners for their husbands."

"And they said they'd be back to help you feed and trailer the horses, right?"

I gave Mama a grudging nod.

"Well, then, you don't need me."

I hated to admit it, but she was right. Besides, escaping to the corral would mean I'd avoid the hundredth re-telling of her acting achievement. I'd miss the nonstop soliloquy on where in her house she should make room for her Supporting Actress Oscar.

Mace, how do you think my award would look on that shelf where I have all my ceramic cows right now? I could move the cows next to the gingham-collared ducks in the kitchen . . . but that would put the symmetry all off, wouldn't it? You know, since the cows are bigger than the ducks. So, maybe I'll move the ducks to that shelf with the bunny rabbits, since they're about the same size. Then again, ducks live in the water, and the rabbits don't even like to swim, so that doesn't seem to make sense . . .

When I saw a re-energized C'ndee, waving me over toward the exit of the tent, I made my getaway, mid-discourse. I don't even think Mama noticed. As I left, she was musing on the possibility of Sal building her Oscar statuette its very own shelf.

"I saved a piece of cake for Carlos," C'ndee said, as she wiped down a table. "Where is he, anyway? I haven't seen him all day."

I shrugged. "Probably at Kelly's trailer, 'interviewing' the movie star some more."

C'ndee gave me a sharp look. "Oh, no. Are the on-again-off-again lovers off again?"

I sighed.

"Why don't the two of you get married, so you can make each other miserable full-time?" she asked.

She picked up some stray plastic plates. I followed with a handful of dirty cups. "Spoken like a woman with two ex-husbands," I said.

"Still two shy of your mother's record."

"Yeah, but only if you count the one who died as an ex," I said.

We dumped the garbage, and I helped her heft the big trash bags onto a trailer that would transport them to the county dump.

"How about your rodeo cowboy? What happened to him?"

"He fell off the wagon big time last night. Plus, Jeb is not my cowboy."

"Whatever you say, Mace."

I gave one last glance around the tent. Still no Tilton. Mama had cornered one of the grips, and was yakking away, probably grilling him as to how to build a shelf that would support an eight-and-a-half-pound Academy Award.

"Well, I'm off to visit the horses," I said. "If that drunken, shiftless cowboy hasn't shown, I'm going to have to see to his cattle, too."

"If you spot Toby on your way, tell him I saved some cake for him."

"Toby hasn't been around?"

"Not many of the cast has. I think everybody's getting ready for that wrap party tonight."

"Want me to tell Jesse you've got a piece of cake for her, too?" I grinned at C'ndee.

"Ha!" The word shot from her mouth. "I wouldn't give that little witch a single crumb if she was starving. I bet we find out she's the one who killed Norman Sydney, and caused all the trouble on this movie set since then. Little Miss Jesse is definitely the murdering type."

Given C'ndee's family connections, she ought to know. Even so, I disagreed. Jesse's father dedicated himself to saving lives as a doctor. His daughter might be shallow and messed up, but I just couldn't picture her intentionally taking a life.

"I'm just glad we never had a second murder," I said. "It's almost over. Aside from Norman, it seems like the rest of us will get out of this okay."

C'ndee made the sign of the cross so fast,

her hand was a blur. "Don't say that, Mace. You'll jinx us. Whenever you let down your guard, that's when something bad happens."

A short time later, as I made my way along the wooded path to the corral, I thought about what C'ndee said. I vowed to keep up my guard until the last Hollywood star left Himmarshee.

I slipped a halter over Rebel's head, and ran a hand along his sturdy neck. "You've done a good job, boy. You know that?" He swished his tail. "I bet you'll be happy to get back to working cattle, instead of working for the cameras, won't you?"

I knew I'd be glad to close the book on this movie job. Soon, all the horses would be loaded onto two trailers for their ride home. They still had to be fed and groomed. They'd go back to Rocking Horse Ranch looking just as good as when I got them.

I tried to call my sisters to ask them when I could expect them, but I couldn't get a signal on my cell phone. Instead, I started on the chores that had to be finished.

Slipping an oversized metal comb out of my back pocket, I began loosening some knots in Rebel's mane. The late-day sun warmed my back. I heard the buzzy call of a grasshopper sparrow, feeding in the pasture. The bird's *chirp-chirp zzzzttt* kept time with the rhythm of grooming: *Comb, chirp-chirp, comb, zzzzttt. Comb, chirp-chirp, comb, zzzzttt.*

Suddenly, the sparrow's song ceased. The sound of pounding footsteps, human footsteps, broke through my trance. I looked over the back of the horse, and out into the open pasture.

Greg Tilton loped toward the corral, arm lifted high and waving hello. "I'm so sorry, Mace," he yelled. "I got to the food tent just after you left. Better late than never, right?"

I returned my attention to the horse, not bothering to acknowledge Tilton. He'd caught me on a bad day for being disappointed by men. He pulled up short, outside the fence of the corral. "Are you mad at me?"

"You were the one who begged to meet me. I waited around like a dummy. Let's just say standing me up is not very 'new Greg Tilton.' It's not nice."

He found the gate, opened it, and stepped through. "I'm sorry. I was on the phone with my agent. I couldn't break away. I still want to talk to you, though. I *need* to talk to you."

C'ndee's warning ran through my mind.

Tilton's clothes were too tight to be hiding a weapon. Even so, I planned to keep him in my full line of sight.

"If I hadn't hung around waiting, I'd be an hour into my work by now." I handed him a stiff-bristled Dandy brush I'd balanced on a fence post. "Make yourself useful while we talk."

I nodded at the Percheron tied on a lead rope to the fence. Tilton looked the huge horse up and down. "Are you sure the pony doesn't need brushing instead?"

"You want to talk, it's the plow horse or nothing."

He went to work with barely a smirk, surprising me with how well he knew his way around the animal. "How'd you learn so much about horses?" I asked.

"The same foster home where I learned to hunt. The family kept all kinds of animals on a little farm; nothing as big as this ranch, though."

The word "farm" triggered a thought. Tilton had spent time on a farm. Vermin were common on farms.

"You know we never really talked much about that sandwich the raccoon got into," I said. "Where'd it come from again?"

"Like I told the cops, it was left at my trailer, in the fridge in a basket with some sodas, snacks, and sweets. The cops took the whole thing. I just assumed somebody from the production company brought it around to the stars' trailers."

"Do you always eat food that shows up unexpectedly?"

The brush in Tilton's hand slowed, and then stopped. The Percheron stomped one huge hoof, splattering mud all over the movie star's expensive-looking jeans. He scowled at the mud, and then narrowed his eyes at me.

"What are you getting at?" he asked.

"Did you have chores on the foster family's farm?"

"Yeah, all the kids did."

"Like what?" I asked.

"I helped clean the barn, feed the animals, and stuff like that."

"Do you ever remember seeing rats around the feed?"

"Sure, but they put out bait to control them."

"Kill them, you mean. Was it strychnine?"

"Yeah, I think so. Why?"

Now, my hand went motionless, too. I willed my breathing to slow. I didn't want Tilton to guess at the thoughts flying through my mind.

"Why?" he repeated.

When I didn't answer, he laid the brush back on the fence post. Then he stepped toward me, closing the distance between us. The nearer he got, the harder it was for me to breathe. The air felt thick, laden with danger. When he spoke again, his voice was edged with threat.

"I asked you a question, Mace."

"The raccoon," I whispered, sidestepping my way along Rebel's body. Tilton moved with me, close enough now so I felt his hot breath on my cheek. It smelled rancid, like rotten onions mixed with stale whiskey.

"What about it?" he asked, pressing his body against my side.

I scanned the pasture. It was empty. We were alone. My eyes darted around for something to use as a weapon. The mane comb! My fingers tightened around one end. If I slammed it into his face hard enough, maybe the shock or the pain would give me the upper hand.

"What about the raccoon?" he asked again. "Is there something wrong with your hearing? Maybe I should stand a little closer."

I felt him push, his hip pressed against mine. He lifted a hand and cupped my left breast. That was the moment I needed. I spun, catching him across the bridge of the nose with the pointy teeth of the metal comb.

"Oh, my God! My face!" He reeled back, clutching at his nose with both hands. "What is wrong with you?"

"You killed the raccoon!" I yelled. "You killed Norman Sydney!"

He stopped howling. When he lowered his hands to look at me, his face registered pure puzzlement. That, and an imprint in the shape of a comb.

"What the hell?" he asked.

"Exactly right," I said. "What the hell were you thinking? Did you really imagine you could get away with it?"

"No, I meant what the hell kind of psycho bitch are you?"

"Me?" I said, insulted.

"Yeah, you. You smack me in the face for no reason . . ."

"No reason? You were about to try to rape me."

"You're insane. I was copping a feel. Big deal. I thought maybe you'd reconsidered about getting it on. I thought you were sending signals that you were interested." He pumped his lower region, back and forth, making combing motions at the same time. "That whole horse-grooming thing? Very sensual."

Now, I was certain my face looked as bewildered as his had. "You need to work on your signal-reading. Do you really think I'd be turned on by a murderer?"

"Murderer?" He barked out a laugh. "Jesus, you *are* a psycho. Where'd you come up with that?"

"The raccoon," I said, a bit hesitant now. "I thought you poisoned it to make it look like you were a target. If you were the target, you couldn't be the murderer."

"I'm *not* the murderer. The person who killed Norman tried to kill me, too."

I circled to the other side of the Percheron, putting the big horse between us. Tilton and I glared at each other over the creature's broad back.

"How do I know you're not the killer?" He pointed at me. "You made no secret of how much you hated all our 'Hollywood crap.' Maybe you wanted to sabotage the movie so we'd shut it down and just go away."

"Now you're the psycho," I said. "I don't do the murders, I find the murderers. I've gotten kind of famous for it, actually."

"Really? Then how come you haven't found this one?"

I didn't want to say, "Because my boyfriend dumped me, and I've been feeling really bad," so I just kept my mouth shut.

Tilton rested a hand on the big horse's withers. "Well, we'll all be out of your hair after today. You can have your heat and humidity, your mosquitoes and pounding rainstorms all to yourself again. God, I can't wait to get back to LA."

Like a curtain descending, an awkward silence fell over us.

"I'm . . ." I finally blurted out.

". . . Sorry," he said at the same time, averting his eyes from mine. "I misread you again, and I'm sorry. I really do want to change, Mace. I just can't seem to do it."

Studying his face, I saw some tiny dots of blood at the bridge of his nose where the comb broke the skin.

"I think you can change, if you want it bad enough. Get yourself some help," I said. "Listen, I apologize for smacking you. The murder and all on this movie set has me as skittish as a weanling filly."

"Forget it. I was out of line. Again." He gently touched his nose and winced. "I better get some ice on this."

I reached across the Percheron. Tilton jumped back. "Jeez, I wasn't going to hit you," I said. "I just wanted to shake hands and tell you goodbye."

"You mean good riddance, don't you?"

He offered his hand and a tiny smirk. We shook.

"See you in the movies," I said.

FORTY-FIVE

Thunder growled, an angry rumble in the distance. The sky to the south was a sheet of black, a sure sign a storm was brewing over Lake Okeechobee. I climbed to the top rail of the horse corral, rotated my phone, and checked the signal. I wanted to call my tardy sisters, but I still couldn't get anything. The movie carpenters had built the corrals at the lowest point in the pasture. If these had been real Florida cowmen, instead of a cast of Hollywood actors, they would have had to wade through standing water three months of the year to get to their stock.

There was still work to do with the horses. After my encounter with Tilton, though, I was too wound up, not to mention embarrassed, to enjoy the easy rhythm I had before. All I wanted now was to finish up, see my sisters arrive, and get the animals loaded and on their way. If the storm broke first, the movie company would just have to pay the rental fee to keep the horses another night. I wasn't about to try to get storm-spooked creatures onto metal trailers as lightning flashed across a wide-open field.

Florida is the most dangerous spot in the country for lightning strikes. I didn't feel like tempting fate; not with the way my luck had been running. I was about to review in my mind all the things I felt bad about — Carlos being at the top of that list — when the slam of a car door put a stop to my self-pity parade.

That had to be my sisters. Finally! A cheerful whistle pierced the muggy air. Neither of my sisters is a whistler.

Squinting across the pasture, I saw Savannah lean in to retrieve something from the back seat of a small SUV. That door slammed, too. She strolled the short distance toward me, holding a beribboned gift bag in one hand. Her bobbed hair swung with each step. A straw sunhat was pushed off her head, no longer needed in the fading afternoon light. It bounced against her back as she closed in on the corral.

There was one more reason I liked Savannah: Instead of mincing her way around cow chips and horse patties in girly-girl footwear, she strode confidently over the rough ground. Her feet were clad in well worn, ranch-style work boots.

"Hey you!" she shouted. "Need some help?"

"Do I ever!" I called back. "C'mon in and grab a horse."

I quickly outlined for Savannah what needed to be done. We immediately set to work in the dwindling daylight. She didn't waste a motion. When she went to the trailer to get horse feed, she came back with halters slung over one shoulder, lead ropes coiled in the crook of an arm.

"I can tell you've done this kind of work a time or two," I said.

She began filling twenty-quart buckets with feed, big enough for the horses to poke in their heads and eat when the buckets are hung on the fence. "Yep, we've got a dozen horses on the Jackson ranch," she said. "I love to ride, and I've never been afraid of hard work."

Within fifteen minutes, we were in pretty good shape. The small herd was groomed, tied at the corral, and munching away happily at a late afternoon supper. Savannah had been a godsend.

"Hey, would you mind if we saddle up one of the horses for me to get in a quick ride before the light goes? I've got a long drive ahead of me, and I could really use some exercise first."

I glanced at the sky. "Looks like it's going to storm."

She looked up, too. "Nah, it should hold off long enough for a quick ride. Besides, these are Florida horses, right? I know they're used to the rain!"

What could I say? I didn't really want to drag the saddle and tack out of the trailer again. But the woman had helped me out. Not to mention, her director husband was the "king" on the movie set, and I was still looking for a paycheck.

"Sure thing," I said, and went to get the gear for the even-tempered Appaloosa.

In no time, the horse was ready. More relaxed now, I leaned against the fence and took a look around. Across the way, Jeb's cattle were herded together in a corner of their pen. No sign of him, and still no sign of my sisters. I was sure Maddie and Marty had tried to call, but couldn't get through. I scanned the sky. Savannah may have been right. The clouds seemed to be stalled over the lake. I noticed the colorful gift bag she'd brought, sitting on a fender of one of the horse trailers.

"What's in the sack?" I asked.

She grinned. "Just a few little things for you and your mama; sweets, mainly. I've really enjoyed getting to know you. You're good people, Mace."

"The feeling's mutual," I said.

"We're going to have so much fun when you come out to Jackson to visit. You have to bring your mama, too. She is something!"

"Yeah, something or other," I said dryly.

"Speaking of somebody who's a something or other . . . I saw Greg hightailing it away from here as I was driving in. Was he giving you trouble again?"

I thought about telling Savannah what happened, how I'd accused Greg Tilton of being the murderer. The story made me look like an idiot, though, so I decided against it.

"Nah," I said. "Tilton was fine. I think he just wanted to come say goodbye to the horses. I'm glad I got the chance to say goodbye to you, though. Weren't you all packed up and supposed to leave this morning?"

"I had to stick around and help Paul with some business problems." She hesitated for a moment, seemed to be weighing whether to tell me more. "Anyway," she said, "I'll be on the road real soon."

"Back to Jacksonville?"

"Jacksonville?" She cocked her head, puzzled. "There's nothing for me in Jacksonville. I've got a flight from Orlando tonight, connecting through Denver to Wyoming."

"Who looks after your cattle for you?"

A strange look played across Savannah's face. Then she slapped a hand against her forehead, as dramatic as an actress in community theater. "Cattle!" She glanced toward Jeb's herd, penned across the pasture. "Is that cowboy of yours around?"

"Haven't seen him all day. And he's not my cowboy."

"Whatever. I came over here earlier, looking for you. I noticed one of his heifers has a bad open sore on a hind leg. It looks like she might have gotten tangled up in some fencing. I wanted to make sure Jed knew about it, before an infection sets in."

"Jeb," I corrected her.

"Right," Savannah nodded. "Want to take a look-see, make sure the poor gal hasn't gotten any worse?"

At the cow pen, coiled ropes still hung from several of the cypress-wood fence posts, along with an old-fashioned leather cow whip. A replica of a McClellan saddle straddled the fence's top rail. At least the moviemakers got that detail right: The military saddle was popular with Florida cowmen after the Civil War. A shiny new shovel, which Jeb's ranch hand probably used to dig a trench to drain off rain water, was a jarring modern touch next to the old-timey whip and saddle.

I clambered onto the fence and peered over the top at the cows. They moved, of course, trotting away from us to the far side of the enclosure. "Which one is it now?" I asked Savannah.

She peered between the lower railings, trying to get a look at their legs.

"I'm not sure," she said. "The light's really getting dim. And they're mostly black, so the blood doesn't show up well. I need to get a little closer."

I climbed off the fence and unwound the rusty gate chain the movie people had insisted upon. I opened just one side, in case any of the cows had a mind to make a break for freedom. I motioned to Savannah to step through. She did, and then pointed across the pen. "I think it's that one. I remember her ears were kind of droopy."

I closed the gate. Even though I moved slowly, calmly, toward the cattle, they still scattered this way and that. Luckily, Droopy Ears headed in my direction. I leaned down low to try to get a glimpse of her hindquarters as she darted past. I didn't see anything. I wanted to check her out on the opposite side, though. I walked toward her, trying to shift my position to be in the right spot when she ran past me again.

We repeated our dance a couple more times. I'd advance; she'd retreat.

I finally stood still and watched her, waiting to see which route she'd pick. The heifer stared me down, taking her time. While I waited, I happened to glance out across the pasture. Still looking for my sisters, I guess. The wind had picked up a bit, blowing from the south. Now, it seemed likely those storm clouds would be on their way.

Low in the sky, the sun spread out last rays like feeble fingers. They reflected off the windshield of Savannah's vehicle. Her white vehicle. Suddenly, an image popped into my head of Savannah coming across the pasture, her oversized straw hat bouncing against her back. Almost instantaneously, I recalled Toby's voice, as clear as if he were sitting right in front of me again, describing his near-miss with the car in the parking lot:

Big hat. Sun glinting off the windshield. I couldn't tell who was behind the wheel . . .

That thought was the last one I had before something hard and solid smacked me in the back of the head. Then the whole world went dark.

Forty-Six

My legs wouldn't move. As I returned to consciousness, fear registered. What was wrong with my legs?

Other impressions came to me in disjointed pieces. Something tight cut into the flesh near my feet and hands. I smelled hay and manure and imminent rain. Gritty sand lodged in the crevices of my teeth. A calf bleated.

Slowly, I realized I was lying on my side, hogtied; wrists to ankles. I tried to lift my head, and felt a searing pain arrow up from where I'd been hit. My cheek in the dirt, I looked out over the ground. I could see the shovel twenty feet away, blade side up. Ranch boots moved toward me, splashing through mud and manure. Savannah's boots. They stopped, right next to my nose. They smelled of wet leather and cow dung.

"You awake?"

I closed my eyes and lay there, holding

my breath. I tried not to move a muscle, even as my mind raced to figure out how I'd gotten in this jam.

Savannah prodded me with the toe of her boot, jabbing it into my shoulder.

"Your head's probably hurting pretty bad right now." She stooped down, put her face close to mine. I could smell her breath, disconcertingly sweet, like milk chocolate and pralines. "The first hit stunned you, but I had to whack you a couple more times with the shovel before you went down. Won't matter. Those bruises will just blend into all the others after the cattle stampede."

I squeezed my eyes shut. If this was a nightmare, I really, really wished I would wake up. Maybe I'd find myself in my bed beside Carlos. Maybe the last week — the movie shoot, our breakup, all of it — would turn out to be a dream. Slowly, I opened my eyes. I saw the curve of Savannah's cheek; the swing of her chestnut-colored hair. She gave me a friendly smile. Her eyes looked crazy.

Crap.

I looked across the ground. The tip of that leather cow whip that had been on the fence now trailed in the dirt by Savannah's boot. I could see the legs and hooves of the cows, all gathered together in a corner of the corral. I scooted backwards, trying to get away from Savannah. The ropes restricted my movement, but I could go no farther anyway. The rough wood of the fence came up hard and unyielding behind me. Scrabbling my fingers out over the dirt, I felt the tail end of the rusty chain that secured the gate.

Double crap. I was on the ground, outside the gate — right between the penned-up cattle and greener pastures.

I strained against the ropes, even while knowing they'd just pull tighter if I struggled. They did. I lay still again.

"Why?" The word came out in a hoarse whisper. I wasn't even sure she heard me.

She sat down in the dirt, the whip curling across her lap. "Because you wouldn't leave it alone, Mace. You would have kept wondering and asking questions. Sooner or later, the answers would have led you to me."

I remembered the flash of images that played in my mind right before she hit me. Savannah's hat. The slant of sunlight. Her white SUV.

"So the murder . . . and everything else. That was you?"

"And Paul. He did what I told him to, used the skills he had, to throw the production into chaos. Like sabotaging that light. We wanted it to blow up. It was a stroke of luck it happened right over your head." She shook a finger in front of my face. "You should have quit right then; taken it as a sign."

She leaned down and looked me in the eye. "You know, like in the cartoons? How a light bulb always goes off over the character's head?"

She chuckled, like we were having a friendly chat. "Funny, right?"

"Sorry, I don't really get the joke," I said. "I think lying, hogtied, in a pile of cow shit might be affecting my sense of humor."

I could hear the wind beginning to gust, rattling the fronds on the cabbage palms. The smell of approaching rain was stronger now. The cattle surged nervously around the enclosure. A horse nickered from the corral across the pasture. Was it Rebel, I wondered? Did he somehow sense I was in danger? Of course, even if he did, it wasn't like Rebel could run and get help like the collie always used to do in those old episodes of *Lassie*.

The daylight was almost gone. An owl hooted — ominous, considering my circumstances. Didn't an owl's call always portend death in those old movie Westerns?

I wanted to keep Savannah talking. Maybe Jeb would finally come to take care of his cattle, or my sisters would show up. They'd arrive in the nick of time to save me, just like in the movies.

"I meant why to all of it, Savannah. Why murder Norman? Why stage all the other 'accidents' and near-misses?"

"So is this that scene in a movie where the villain spills all her secrets?"

"Indulge me," I said. "It's the least you can do since you so enjoyed getting to know me. I'm 'good people.' Isn't that what you told me?"

"Honey, I'm a murderer. Do you really think it bothers me that I'm a liar, too?"

Suddenly, I thought about lies. Something Savannah said about Jacksonville ran through my brain. "You weren't in your car on your way to Jacksonville the morning Norman was murdered, were you?"

She lowered her face next to mine and grinned. Before, that grin had seemed friendly and full of fun. Now, it just looked cruel.

"No, duh, Mace. 'There's nothing for me in Jacksonville.' As soon as that phrase was out of my mouth, I knew I'd made a mistake. I forgot I'd made Jacksonville my alibi, and then lied about growing up there. You didn't catch my screw-up then."

"I didn't," I said.

"Yeah, some detective. Your sorry love life was too distracting. I knew you would catch it, though; and you did."

Too late, I thought.

She lifted the whip, waved it to the corners of the cow pen. "I had to think on my feet, come up with a plan. I saw the shovel. The ropes. The cattle. Everything fell into place, really fast."

Her face glowed with pride. Did she want me to compliment her on her clever plan to kill me?

I closed my eyes and thought about Carlos. An image of his face replaced Savannah's, in front of me. Would I ever see him again? Would I see my family? Maybe the cattle wouldn't kill me. But if those pounding hooves struck over and over at my head, my brain would be so scrambled I probably wouldn't recognize those I loved. With that kind of head trauma, I may as well be dead.

I strained against the ropes. They seemed to pull tighter. Hair fell into my face, brushing my nose and making me want to sneeze. I wriggled my nose, but the hair didn't move.

"Don't struggle, honey. It'll just make it worse. There is one little bone I can throw you. A parting gift, as it were." She reached down, and almost tenderly pushed away the hair from my itchy nose. "That cop is crazy about you. I could see it in his eyes the other night at the bar. While you were moping over your beer, he was watching you, even when he was dancing with Kelly. Whenever you *weren't* looking at him, he was looking at you."

I wouldn't think my heart, already racing with adrenaline, could feel a flutter, but it did. If I ever got out of this, I was going to throw myself into Carlos's arms and never leave.

"Thanks for that," I said. "I wish I hadn't been such a fool."

She sighed. "You said it at the bar. Love makes us do strange things."

"Is that why you killed Norman?" I asked. "To avenge Jesse?"

"What?" She leaned close to my face; scrunched up her forehead. "Hell, no. What Norman did to Jesse had nothing to do with it. This film was Paul's absolute last chance to save his reputation as a director. Norman was going to fire him. I couldn't let him do that. What would I do without Paul's income?"

Get a job? I thought it, but I didn't say it.

"I was poor once, Mace. I don't intend to ever be poor again."

Savannah glanced at her wedding ring,

the big diamond winking in the diminishing daylight. She seemed lost in thought. Almost to herself, she said, "All the other stuff was to cause confusion on the set, to divert attention from Paul and me."

"What did you mean when you said Paul did what you told him to do?"

"My husband was definitely on board for Norman, but he was reluctant about the rest of it. He didn't want anyone else murdered. Well, maybe except for Greg Tilton."

"Yeah, that poisoned sandwich could have killed him."

She laughed. "That's funny, because we had nothing to do with that sandwich. Toby? Yes, that was me; and Paul skinned that cable for Jesse's close call, too. Johnny Jaybird was in the wrong place at the wrong time, though."

"What do you mean?"

"When Paul planted the loaded gun, we thought Toby would use it to rehearse with Greg, not the A.D. Johnny's talent was useful to us; Greg, we didn't need."

Thunder clapped, loud enough to split the sky in half. Savannah looked up to roiling black clouds. She stood, dusting her hands against her knees. "I'm sorry it's come to this, Mace. It's time for the climactic scene. It's always been the same, way back to the days of silent film. Ever hear of *The Perils of Pauline?* That poor gal got into some crazy jams. There she'd be, tied to a train track just as a locomotive was bearing down."

Sensing the storm, the cows jostled and shifted together at the pen's far side. Whip in hand, Savannah gestured toward the animals.

"Right there is your locomotive, Mace."

I knew it wasn't possible, but the eyes of the cattle seemed to gleam with menace.

FORTY-SEVEN

I watched Savannah's boots as she strode away, continuing across the pasture in the direction of the horse corral. What was she up to now?

I did remember seeing those ancient film clips from *The Perils of Pauline*. Someone always rescued the silent movie heroine at the last possible moment. Unfortunately, my horizon looked pretty scarce on the cavalry.

I started flexing and contracting the muscles in my wrists, trying to work on loosening the ropes. The pressure eased a bit, but there was no way I'd get the knots untied by the time Savannah returned to carry out the rest of her plan.

I started to pray. I might be rusty, but I still knew enough to ask for God's hand to guide me.

I hoped the big man was listening. Within moments, hoof beats pounded the ground outside the pen. Galloping up, Savannah stopped the Appaloosa just short of the gate. The mare shook, and snorted though her nose, close enough for me to feel a fine mist spray down onto my face. Savannah's boots hit the ground. The chain jangled as she unwound it from the gatepost.

The cattle paced on the far side of the pen, their big heads swaying. The Appaloosa stepped through and stood inside the gate, waiting patiently for her rider to remount. Savannah pulled the gate closed, but didn't chain it.

The cows, wary, regarded the horse and rider. Thunder crashed like a bomb exploding. A fat raindrop splattered in the dirt beside my head. Savannah began uncoiling the whip from the saddle.

A huge streak of lightning turned the dark clouds silvery white. In the burst of light, I saw red in the distance. Mama, still wearing Ruby's red dress and shoes, picked her way across the pasture toward the pen. She'd probably spotted Savannah on the horse, and mistaken her for me. Head down, concentrating on avoiding manure stains on her Ruby shoes, Mama was silent.

I prayed she'd stay that way. No such luck. Closer now, she called out: "Yoo-hoo! Mace! Honey, you better get in before it really starts to rain . . ."

As soon as Mama's voice rang over the pasture, Savannah whirled in the saddle in her direction. A moment later, Mama, who had quit watching the ground, stepped on the shovel blade. The handle shot up and hit her in the forehead. She staggered backward. Fingers pressed to her forehead, she fought to keep her balance.

"I'm over here! Help, Mama!"

Maybe it was the desperation in my voice, but she caught on quickly for somebody just smacked in the face with a shovel. Of course, it was just the narrow wooden handle, not like the full force of the blade that had hit me.

Mama's head swiveled, like a camera panning the three points of a triangle: Savannah in the saddle, unwinding the whip. Me on the ground, in front of the gate. The cows in the corner, awaiting their cue.

Savannah cracked the whip. The cows scattered, starting into a trot. As the rain fell harder, she edged the horse into the herd, driving the animals into a line that hugged the curve of the fence. One followed another, picking up the pace. I could guess what she was up to. She wanted them to circle the pen a few times, gathering speed, before she funneled them out the gate, and over me.

Crack. Crack. Crack.

As Savannah snapped the whip, Mama grabbed the shovel. She raced toward the gate. "Get back, cows! Go on, now! Get back!"

With Savannah in pursuit on horseback, wielding that whip, the animals paid little heed to Mama.

Dropping the shovel, she fell to her knees beside me. The hem on Ruby's dress dragged through a puddle of rain and cow manure. Her small, nimble fingers worked at the ropes that bound me. They were the same fingers that had treated my tomboy injuries; patched the childhood clothes I ripped by playing too rough.

Hooves thundered on the other side of the fence. Mama picked and pulled at the knots. Her breath came in short, frantic gasps. Rain streaked down her face. But when I looked into her eyes, I didn't see a trace of fear. There was nothing there but steely determination and a mother's devoted love.

I saw Savannah, starting to shift the horse's position. We had only seconds before she'd move the cattle, pushing them through the gate and out the enclosure. Mama gave a final tug, and I was free. I enfolded her into a protective embrace, wrapping my arms and legs around her.

"Roll!" I shouted, taking us both to the sodden ground.

Entwined like two TV wrestlers, we tumbled over and over, trying to get away, as the animals thundered past. Their huffing breath filled my ears. My arms stung from bits of rock kicked up by their flying hooves. I tucked my head tight over Mama's and held on, feeling her racing heartbeat clear through her back.

I wasn't even certain we were in a safe place, until, suddenly, the cows were gone. Knowing I had to move fast, I let go of Mama. By the time Savannah got herself clear of the stampede and turned to see the results of her deadly plan, I was off the ground and onto the fence. Snatching one of the coiled ropes from a post, I climbed up to straddle the top rail.

She was in range. I'd get only one chance. Would my muscles remember those endless hours of roping practice, all through my childhood and the years of high school rodeo?

Coils in one hand, loop in the other, I flipped the rope over my wrist and swung it in circles over my head. Then I let the loop end fly. It floated toward Savannah, seeming to hang forever right above her head.

Then the loop dropped, just where I intended it to.

I jumped from the fence and pulled the rope taut. Savannah was so surprised at being lassoed like a Corriente steer, that she dropped the horse's reins. With both hands, she tried to free herself from the rope, now tightening against her midsection. Still holding on, I moved hand-over-hand along the rope as I closed the distance between us.

Meanwhile, Mama grabbed the shovel and used it to goose the horse's sensitive flank. The Appaloosa bucked, and started to bolt. Savannah's boots flew from the stirrups.

That was the moment I needed. I yanked on the rope with all my strength. She tumbled from the saddle and hit the ground.

Standing over her, I jerked tight as she strained against the loop. "Don't struggle, honey." I repeated the words she'd used on me. "It'll just make it worse."

Mama came up beside me. Jamming the shovel's blade into the muddy ground just inches from our captive's face, she said, "Looks like this was your last roundup, Savannah."

FORTY-EIGHT

"I tell you girls, when that shovel smacked me, I saw stars!"

At the horse corral, Mama brought my sisters up to speed on what happened. My fingers explored what felt like a small mountain range of bumps on the back of my head.

"It was only the handle that hit you, Mama."

"Still . . ." she cut her eyes at me, and continued her story, "I didn't know if I'd be able to stand up, until I heard Mace calling out for me to rescue her."

Not surprisingly, in Mama's tale she had the lead, not the supporting, role. I didn't care. Fact is, if she hadn't stumbled onto the scene, I might not be here. I'd be torn and trampled; maybe even dead.

My sisters had been stuck in a backup on State Road 98, after a tractor-trailer jack-knifed across both lanes of the highway.

Mama and I were drying out, after the storm's fierce winds blew the weather system north. The rain clouds were probably pouring misery over Disney World right now, derailing the vacation dreams of legions of tourists.

The security guard we'd met on the first day of filming had accompanied Maddie and Marty to the corral. "You can't be too careful," he'd said, with a smitten glance at my little sister. "It's getting dark, and I didn't think these ladies should be out here alone. Not with a murderer on the loose."

That's when Mama and I pointed across the pasture to the cow pen. Savannah was trussed up and tied to the fence. Once the guard picked his eyeballs off his chest, he radioed base camp to call the cops. Then he went to stand watch over Savannah, who made it pretty clear her confessional mood was over.

"That woman is crazy," she shouted, gesturing toward me with her chin. "I want her arrested! She tried to kill me."

Since I was the one with the goose eggs on the back of my head, and the welts where I'd been hogtied, the guard looked doubtful about Savannah's claims. The fact that Marty vouched for my non-homicidal character only confirmed his initial decision.

Now, word seemed to be spreading. One of the Teamsters was easing a big generator truck into the pasture, as crew members hurriedly laid cable and set up movie lights. Soon, dusk would seem as bright as noon.

Tilton loped toward the corral. Toby was right on his heels, followed by a loose knot of cast, crew and production types. There was Jesse, and Johnny Jaybird; Kelly, and her love-struck shadow, Sam. I didn't see Barbara or Paul. I wondered if Norman's ex-wife was even now turning over the director to the law? Or, was she so obsessed with the man she was helping him escape?

I ran my thoughts past my sisters and Mama. "Savannah said Paul did what she told him to do. He helped kill Norman, and stage the other threats and 'accidents.' "

"Maybe so," Maddie said, "but he probably didn't agree to share a murder rap."

"I don't know, girls." Mama, watching the stars approach, patted her hip through the fabric of Ruby's gown. Had she hurt herself rolling on the ground? "Paul didn't seem like a bad sort to me. He wore a cross in his ear."

Catching my eye, Marty shook her head and grinned.

As Tilton drew near, I could see him waving something over his head. "Mace!" he yelled.

My sisters whirled at the sound of his famous voice. Mama's fingers scrabbled at her hip through the voluminous folds of the dress.

"Put out your hand," Tilton said, as he reached my side.

Considering the red outline revealing how hard I'd whacked him with the mane comb, I expected a handshake shock, or maybe a poisonous spider. There were plenty of witnesses, though, so I flipped my wrist and opened my palm.

In the center, he laid a chocolate and pecan treat, still in its plastic package. *Savannah City Confections,* the wrapping said.

"This was in the food basket with the sandwiches I gave to the cops. I forgot I'd taken it out, and put it away for a late-night snack."

"Maddie, run get that gift bag off the horse trailer." I pointed to Savannah's beribboned present, now sodden and bedraggled.

She gave me a look.

"I could have a concussion, sister!"

Marty nudged her, and she hurried to get the bag. When she brought it back, I shook

426

out a collection of treats with the same label I'd seen before. Pralines, pecan clusters, and chocolate chunks with veins of marshmallow.

"It was Savannah," Tilton said. "She tried to poison me."

I narrowed my eyes at him. I knew what Savannah had said about the tainted sandwich. Why would she cop to all the other crimes, and deny that one? Then again, she'd been eager all along to cast suspicion on Tilton, to try to ruin his image. He stared into my face, his eyes shining with honesty.

I still hadn't made up my mind whether it was truth or acting, when Mama sidled up to the movie star. Her hand darted to her full skirt like a sparrow after a crumb. She pulled out a little autograph book and miniature pen.

"Now that our shoot — and the shooting — is over, would you do me the honor?" She jabbed the pen at his hand like a student nurse trying her first IV.

His eyes flashed irritation for a second, then the corners crinkled into a good-natured smile.

"Why not?" He shrugged. "You sure worked for it."

Sirens wailed in the distance. "Carlos!" I wasn't even aware I'd said his name aloud until Marty clutched my hand and squeezed. Maddie patted my back.

Tilton signed with a flourish and handed Mama back her pen and book. Tucking away the set in the gown's cavernous pocket, she brought out a tiny mirror and her tube of Apricot Ice.

"Here you go, honey." She offered both to me. "It was a miracle these didn't break or get lost the way we tumbled across that ground. I'd say that's a sign our Lord wants you to spruce up a bit before Carlos gets here."

Mama's 'miracle' seemed kind of paltry, compared with Jesus raising Lazarus from the dead or feeding a multitude with just two fish and a few loaves of bread. Still, I had walked away from what seemed certain death, or at least grave danger. I wasn't about to argue with a sign.

"Hand it over," I said to Mama. "Anybody have a hairbrush? Maybe a breath mint?"

FORTY-NINE

D'Vora slapped a rolled-up magazine against the counter at Hair Today, Dyed Tomorrow. Her glittery purple nail polish sparkled in the sunshine pouring in through the salon's front window.

"Y'all are NOT going to believe this!"

She displayed the front cover of *People*. A headline screamed, *Murderous Movie: What Really Happened in Florida?*

"Does it say if Paul, the director, has turned up yet?" I asked D'Vora.

Betty looked at her over the poodle perm of the bank president's wife. "How about the shop? Does it talk about Hair Today?"

Mama grabbed for the magazine. "Let me see. Does it mention I'm in the movie?"

"Well, I didn't have time to read it." D'Vora ducked out of Mama's reach, hugging the magazine to her ample breast. "I ran right over as soon as I saw the magazine in my mailbox."

It'd been fifteen days since the movie people packed their gear and exited Himmarshee; two weeks since Savannah was arrested on murder charges. We all gathered around the counter as D'Vora flipped open the magazine and leafed through the pages. The banker's wife got up, too, her protective cape billowing around her like a lavender sail.

The first page of the article showed a big picture of Savannah, sitting in leg shackles in a hallway of the courthouse before her first appearance. Shackles. You've got to love our criminal justice system in Florida.

She'd entered a plea of not guilty, of course, and everybody expected her high-powered attorney to try to cast suspicion anywhere but on Savannah. The photographer had caught the same crooked smile Mama and I had seen when we first met her; the same mad gleam in her eye I originally took for playfulness. Her attorney was right beside her, whispering in her ear. He looked a lot less playful than she did.

Photos of the stars of the movie ran along the right-hand side of the page.

"Ooooh, there's that Greg Tilton. He's gorgeous." Mrs. Bank President clutched a hand over her heart.

Tilton would no doubt be pleased his

picture was first: top billing. "I could have been killed!" The caption underneath was a quote from the action hero.

Jesse looked horrible in her photo, not to mention high. "Oh, my! I didn't know they were allowed to use a picture of her shooting somebody the bird." Mama tsked. "That poor gal still hasn't learned that the media can be an actress's friend."

Betty raised her painted-on brows.

"Mama is referring to the article about her role in the movie that Buck Aubrey put in the feed store newsletter," I explained.

Mama patted her hair. "Publicity is publicity, Mace."

"Listen to this, y'all. It's about Toby." D'Vora began to read.

"The young star surprised Hollywood insiders when he agreed to appear as grand marshal in next year's Gay Pride parade in Long Beach, Calif. Wyle said, 'I look forward to a day when all people will be treated equally and accepted for who they are, whether they're straight or gay; black or white; Christian or not . . .' "

"That doesn't sound like too much to ask, does it, Mama?"

"Hmm," she said, but didn't rise to my bait.

"The next bit is about the assistant director," D'Vora said. "Did y'all know him?"

"Awful man. He screamed at me the first day on the set," Mama said.

"Jonathan J. Burt," I said. "And I'd hardly call it screaming. He only threatened to kick her out because Mama ruined a scene when she ran in front of the cameras, waving her arms and carrying on. Then the poor guy got shot. What's it say about him, D'Vora?"

"He's taking a position to monitor Hollywood movies for the Gay and Lesbian Alliance Against Def . . . Defam . . ."

" 'Defamation,' " Mrs. Banker helped out. "Our oldest son is gay."

If Mama had intended to do a biblical discourse on homosexuality, the revelation by the wife of a community pillar cut her short.

"Still no sight of the director," Betty said, reading over D'Vora's shoulder.

"Well, Paul won't get away with it," Mama said. "If Carlos has to hunt him down personally, he'll catch him. Carlos Martinez always gets his man."

At the mention of Carlos's name, Mama gave me a quick, guilty glance. An uncomfortable silence descended. Only Mrs. Bank President was unaware of the history, hard feelings, and pain attached to that name.

Betty changed the subject. "How do you

suppose they'll finish the movie without a director?"

"I'm sure Barbara already has a list of names to bring in somebody else," I said. "Norman Sydney was about to fire Paul, which is why Paul had such a powerful motive to get rid of him."

A pout parked itself on Mama's face.

"What?" I asked.

"I just hope the new director recognizes the star quality Paul saw in me."

"Well, Paul saw something in you, all right."

When Betty and D'Vora snickered, I felt bad. "I'm just kidding, y'all. Mama did a fantastic job with her scene. She *killed.* Right, Mama?"

She fluttered her lashes modestly. "All I did was employ the methods of the great acting coach, Lee Strasberg. I tapped into my 'affective memory.' "

"Say what?" D'Vora scrunched up her face like she was doing calculus.

"Don't ask," I said.

"What happened to Paul's girlfriend, Barbara?" Mama asked. "Did she help him get away?"

"She says no," I said. "She was busy making arrangements to get her ex-husband's body back to Hollywood. They had the funeral two days after Savannah was arrested."

D'Vora's periwinkle-shadowed eyelids suddenly went wide. She pointed out the front window. "Don't look now, Mace, but there's your gorgeous ex."

Carlos stood on the sunny sidewalk, squinting into the beauty parlor. Worried frowns passed between the four other women in the shop.

Betty aimed her comb toward the alley behind the shop. "Go on and run out the back door, honey."

I thought of how I'd lain in the dirt by the cow pen, praying I'd survive. I remembered the image I'd conjured of Carlos's face, and what I promised myself if I escaped.

"No need, Betty. I think I'll go out the front."

As I passed, Mama's mouth dropped open so wide you could have run a John Deere tractor inside. Carlos smiled as I stepped out the door. I ran to him, eager to fulfill my vow to throw myself into his arms and never leave. Ever since the movie people departed, I'd been fulfilling it every chance I could.

I saw the astonishment on Mama's face, now pressed against the window. She hadn't suspected a thing about Carlos and I getting back together. As we stood in front of the shop, kissing in full view of Himmarshee's biggest gossips, I heard a horn blow on Main Street.

A battered white pickup rattled past. Jeb Ennis leaned out the window, waving his cowboy hat. A silly grin split his face. He shouted, "Hey! Why don't you two lovebirds go get a room?"

We pulled apart. Carlos's eyes gleamed with amusement. "That sounds like a pretty good idea, *niña*. We can go to my apartment. I rented us a movie."

I gave him a long look.

"I've had enough of Hollywood," I said. "How about we skip the movie, and go straight to the matinee?"

Carlos and I snuggled together on his couch. To build back the energy we spent on our movie-free matinee, Carlos made us a snack of buttered popcorn. It filled a bowl on my lap.

Smoothing a strand of my mussed-up hair, he smiled at me. I grinned back, hoping there were no stray kernels caught in my teeth.

"How come you keep staring at me?" I asked.

"Just happy to have you here, *niña*."

435

I kissed him. "The feeling is mutual."

I dug to the bottom of the popcorn bowl, searching out my favorite half-burned, half-popped kernels. My fingers found a foreign object that didn't feel at all like popcorn. It was circular and hard, with something pointy on top. Fishing it out, I placed it in the palm of my hand. Surrounded by a few stray kernels, a diamond winked at me from a golden band.

I looked up at Carlos. His dark eyes met mine. I saw love, and strength, and maybe a bit of nervousness there.

"Is this what I think it is?"

He nodded. "Even with all our ups and downs, we belong together, Mace. I love you; and I think you love me, too."

It was my turn to nod. "I realized just how much in that cow pen, when I thought I'd never see you again."

He lowered himself from the couch to the floor, where he got onto one knee. "I want us to be together." He gently took the ring from my hand, and then held it up to me. "Will you marry me?"

I swallowed and took a deep breath. Then I said yes.

When he slipped the ring on my finger, I wasn't surprised at all to see it was a perfect fit.

ABOUT THE AUTHOR

Like Mace Bauer's, **Deborah Sharp**'s family roots were set in Florida long before Disney and *Miami Vice* came to define the state. She does some writing at a getaway overlooking the Kissimmee River in the wilds north of Okeechobee, and some at Starbucks in Fort Lauderdale. As a Florida native and a longtime reporter for *USA Today,* she knows every burg and back road, including some not found on maps. Here's what she has to say about Himmarshee:

Home to cowboys and church suppers, Himmarshee is hot and swarming with mosquitoes. A throwback to the ways of long-ago southern Florida, it bears some resemblance to the present-day ranching town of Okeechobee. The best thing about Mace and Mama's hometown: it will always be threatened, but never spoiled, by suburban sprawl.